The Man Diet

Zoe Strimpel's first writing job was on the *Times Money* section, where she confirmed that she has no interest in the finer points of pensions, annuities and insurance. She thus threw herself into writing about books, food and life, hitting a popular nerve with a piece for *The Times*'s *Times2* about how talkative women put men off. There's something in this man–woman thing, she thought, and soon landed a long-running, popular column about the single life in the ex-newspaper, *thelondonpaper*. In 2008 she began writing a book about what men really think, conducting interviews with hundreds of them on the topic of their romantic leanings. In 2010, *What the Hell is He Thinking: All the Questions You've Ever Asked About Men Answered*, was published. *The Man Diet* is her second book.

She grew up near Boston, USA. She studied English at Cambridge and is the Lifestyle Editor of business newspaper *City A.M.* She blogs at zoestrimpel.com and tweets at @zstrimpel.

ZOE STRIMPEL

The Man Diet

AVON

AVON

A division of HarperCollins*Publishers*
77–85 Fulham Palace Road,
Hammersmith, London W6 8JB

www.harpercollins.co.uk

A Paperback Original 2011

1

© Zoe Strimpel 2011

Zoe Strimpel asserts the moral right to
be identified as the author of this work

A catalogue record for this book is
available from the British Library

ISBN 978-1-84756-305-7

Set in ITC Century Light

Printed and bound in Great Britain by
Clays Ltd, St Ives plc

MIX
Paper from
responsible sources

FSC
www.fsc.org
FSC™ C007454

Thanks to my agent Bill Hamilton, for helping me shape the initial idea, and for spurring me on to get on with it. Also to Charlie Brotherstone for getting it a home. Thanks of course to the ladies at Avon – particularly Claire Bord and Helen Bolton – who stayed calm and encouraging through-out the relatively short but intense creation of this book, and with whom it has been a pleasure working.

Thanks to my two favourite grownups in London: Diana and Mike Preston, who have always showed such support, and to whom I owe much gratitude (and delicious dinner).

Thanks to the delightful Janet Kwok, who provided invaluable help.

Thanks to Tom Stammers: you know how invaluable you are.

Thanks to all the wonderful, intelligent and passionate women willing to share their most personal experiences and views on trust, and huge thanks to the experts who gave their time to help illuminate my points. Val Sampson, Ricky Emanuel, Susan Quilliam, Janet Reibstein. You all provided invaluable insight and I couldn't have written this book without you. Cecilia d'Felice: a massive thank you for being fundamental in your inspiration for this book.

Thanks to Allister Heath and the folks at *City A.M.* for granting me leave to write the book – it was a great show of faith and meant a lot.

Lexie, Diane, Lucie, Terri, Danya, Ruth and the rest of the lovely ladies: you know who you are. And thanks to Jonathan Silberstein Loeb, who has brought countless interesting articles and ideas to my attention.

And a huge thank you to my grandpa, who at 91 still enthralled me with his time-honed insights on women, men, life, love and the universe.

Thanks to Lisa Bud for her amazingly acute guidance. And to my brother Daniel for providing an illuminating contrast to my way of life and raising questions I'd never consider otherwise.

Finally, my parents as always deserve thanks for being my longest-standing supporters.

To my old, dear friend Eleanor Halgren.
And, of course, to *all the single ladies*.

Contents

How I Came to Write this Book

Here's a little story ...

I'm with this gorgeous guy, we're two-thirds of the way through a free bottle of champagne that I'd arranged through PR contacts and I'm calculating the likelihood of a kiss or maybe more when we're finished. Just as I'm picturing his bedroom, and what a triumph it would be to see it, his iPhone rings. It appears that another girl needs him – an on-off friend 'with issues' – and so off he goes. Not, however, before I wrest a smooch off him as he unlocks his motorbike.

But when I get home, instead of feeling jubilant about kissing a text-book hottie that had entered my life as a very professional masseur at a spa in central London, I lie on the bed and feel ... down. Rejected. Crap. Tired. Like I've sold myself short, but I'm not quite sure why. What had I been hoping to gain? A romp with a man – albeit a muscular one – who I'd had to lure out on a date with the promise of free alcohol?

Here's another story: *My friends Kim and Kate are watching Uruguay play Holland in the World Cup semi-final and end up snogging a couple of happy Dutch fans. However, expecting their snogees to be eagerly in touch afterwards, both Kim and Kate are dismayed when they hear nothing. Kim follows up with an email only to receive a downright rude reply. It would have been comical – if it hadn't made her feel crap and empty and induce a week-long funk of low self-esteem in which she threw the baby out with the bathwater (job bad; career trajectory stalled; life going nowhere). And for what? A randomer! Meanwhile, Kate's lad does respond and agrees to meet her for a drink. He isn't free for a week, during which time Kate gets moderately excited. When they meet, it's at a grotty pub of his choosing, and afterwards he seems to expect her to accompany him home. She allows him a snog and then – three days later when she still hasn't heard from him – she sends him a drunken text. He doesn't reply and she too enters a few days of self-loathing and anger.*

We're meant to be having the times of our lives but, as the above stories suggest, being single and content in the 21st century is far from straightforward. Ruth, 29, puts it well: 'Being single is a job. But it's a secret job.' We're constantly juggling our private anxiety about being single with a free 'n' easy public persona. So while being single sounds like a barrel of laughs for the well-waxed, sexually liberated, financially solvent young woman, it is far from being a walk in the park.

What made me want to write this book is the fact that the Western single woman has never had it so good. She's got more opportunity than ever before – professionally, socially and sexually. She puts up with less harassment and fewer superiority complexes from men than ever before. She earns more, shags more and drinks more than ever. She can do what she wants. But somehow – when it comes to society's ultimate flash point, sex and love – she can't get no satisfaction. Or not enough.

The Man Diet expresses my belief that it doesn't need to be that way. I want to help the single woman cut through the biggest obstacle to her happiness today: junk-food love. I want to help lift the sense of doom and even worthlessness many of us feel if we are

> *'Being single is a job. But it's a secret job.'*

sporting neither a rock nor a man on our arm so that we can get on with the business of being – and feeling – awesome.

Easy highs, easy lows: welcome to a world of junk-food love

Badoo is a mobile hook-up site for the straight market with 120 million users and 300,000 more added per day at the time of writing. Floxx, which originated as FitFinder, is a microblogging site where users describe hot people nearby in salacious terms (a perving portal, in other words), while tube.net allows users (female only, interestingly) to post pictures of hotties photographed surreptitiously on the Underground. Flirtomatic allows users to send electronic flirts – the homepage is a surge of photos that come forward then recede ever so slightly sickeningly. There are dozens more like this being conceived every day. I'm going to sound hideously prim here, but I see these sites as a natural by-product of a dating environment that's becoming increasingly high in poorly made fast food and low in slow-cooked, well-sourced nourishment. There, I've said it.

Back at the beginning of 2010, when I became single again, I was all about the fast-food style of love, and warmly embraced the 'many fish in the sea' idea. I was a bit manic, going after men and saying yes to them as if it was my job to do so now that I was single, and – as I said above – supposedly 'loving it'.

It was psychologist and relationships expert Dr Cecilia d'Felice who first recommended that I go on a 'Man Diet' after I told her about my experience of being single.

> 'With each failed encounter – a man that doesn't ask for a follow-up date, a guy that is rude, or a date you didn't enjoy – there is the potential to lose self-esteem. Too many negative experiences will chip away at your self-worth leaving you feeling low and anxious about your date-ability.'
> Dr Cecilia d'Felice, clinical psychologist and relationships expert, author of Dare to Be You

So, I hear you all ask, what is a Man Diet? Well, pure and simple, it's a diet, in which you take a break from chowing down on men – literally and otherwise. You let them go. Forget about them. Instead, you focus on building up your sense of self-worth, your interests, your personhood. Your 'you'. You relax, and give yourself a time out on dating, romantic timelines and so on.

I thought more about this brave idea. Could I do it? And ultimately, did I want to do it? I had to admit it sounded tempting and challenging in equal measure. I wasn't sure I could do it, but equally, I sensed I'd benefit massively if I did. The Man Diet smacked of a path to somewhere good, not without its tiring uphills but generally pleasant and with interesting scenery along the way. It seemed like the kind of ride whose uphills would leave you with excellent, enviable glutes and thighs at the end of it.

I started not only to pay close attention to where I was going wrong, but to quietly observe my single friends' behaviour, rather than just urging them to keep going in order to erase the bad taste of one unsatisfying encounter with another one. Of course we were all roughly going wrong in the same ways: giving ourselves away too much and to too many people, for no particularly good reason. Great men – potential life partners – don't grow on trees these days (did they ever?) and you know them when you see them. We weren't seeing them, so instead we channelled a Samantha from *Sex and the City*-style quantity-over-quality approach, and guess what: it wasn't making us happy. Nor did it appear to be increasing the chances of meeting someone worthwhile – the types of guys we were attracting never really improved or changed.

And if we weren't getting action – if we were in a 'drought' – we talked about that, using up our emotional energy. Follow-up dates with guys we didn't particularly like spending time with – whether we met them online or elsewhere – bruised and eroded our self-esteem, too. With men or without them, we seemed to be defining ourselves in relation to men.

Who fancies you, how many hook-ups, shags, suggestive texts, Facebook come-ons or intrigues you can run up seem to be the single girl's bread and butter (or rather, her high-carb fix). I began to see that, in reality, they're our poison. Not because they are bad in themselves, but because they so easily become like drugs: without them, we feel crap, and when we have them we can only think of our next fix. Are we ever left feeling satisfied? Of course not.

Identity and the single woman: am I hot enough?

Hotness, like gold (only not nearly as solid), has become society's most sought-after social and sexual currency.

In *Female Chauvinist Pigs*, a brilliant book, Ariel Levy states in no uncertain terms that the image-generated, 'overheated thumping of sexuality' in the West is far more about consumption than real human connection. Indeed, people spend a large amount of cash acquiring this glossy form of hotness.

As Maria, 31, puts it: 'Everything comes down to: "Do you think I'm good looking or not?"'

Somewhere, nestled deep inside our brains, is the childhood idea that good things come to pretty girls. Namely: knights in shining armour; doting attention; popularity. So, lacking her knight as well as a range of good options, the single woman feels she has to prove to herself and others that she's not single because she isn't attractive. While being considered hot is a huge motivator for women of every romantic status, I think it's an even more emotional concern for the single woman. We feel a bit like this: 'Show me I am pretty enough so that I know I really am. Otherwise I'm afraid that people – myself included – will see my singleness as a function of subpar hotness. And that will crush me.'

The false promise of shagging like a man

We want to show we're hot, and sex is one way we do it. But it has to be easy, breezy casual sex because we're independent women and are led to believe that a good way to show independence is to shag a lot or outrageously.

Getting notches on the bedpost has become a widespread symbol of empowerment, but in my view a false one, because the quantity over quality equation doesn't add up to happiness for most women. This conviction is based partly on my experience as a single person – numerous generous offerings of my body with little repayment of the friendly, caring or (God forbid) emotional variety. (Random Italian men with sub-zero IQs in hasty encounters in borrowed flats and drunken German cheaters in broom closets at parties may sound like rollicking fun but they lose their appeal very quickly.) It is also based on a whole host of research, some convincing, some not. After all, the last thing you need is male researchers saying that science shows women should be chaste while men should continue to enjoy rampaging the field because it's in their DNA. And authors such as Natasha Walter in *Living Dolls: The Return of Sexism* and Cordelia Fine in *Delusions of Gender* are excellently enraged on the topic of biological determinism and will convince any thinking woman to take prescriptive biological arguments with a rigorous pinch of salt. But there are grains of useful, fair evidence about women and sexual profligacy that can help substantiate what I have learned from experience and observation, of which more later.

The idea of 'throttling up on power ... and having sex like a man' seduced a whole generation of young women through the delicious portal of *Sex and the City*. We thirsted to see Carrie, Miranda, Charlotte and, of course, Samantha, the show's proudest sexual figurehead, hilariously and frankly discussing, then actually *having* 'sex like a man' (their stated goal in the first episode). There was a kind of competitiveness to it, and many of us watching this and numerous other episodes in which the girls indulge in purely utilitarian sex (the norm for Samantha) felt an urge to chant 'yeah!' and fist pump the air. After all, it looked an awful lot like feminism – indeed, the casual and experimental sexual ideal presented in *SATC* helped define the kind of feminism known as 'third wave'. US magazine *Bust* co-founder Debbie Stoller has said that in their quest for sexual fulfillment , the 'lusty feminists of the third wave' are leaving no stone unturned. Toys, techniques: we're trying them *all*.

However, I think a friend of mine called Kristen, 32, presents a picture that's closer to reality than the powerful one of clacking Manolos and perfectly coiffed just-had-sex hair in *SATC*:

> 'There's this expectation that we're supposed to be having casual sex, that it doesn't touch us – but it does. We see casual sex as empowerment. But when I was having "casual" sex with my flatmate, I would lie there sobbing in my room while he had sex next door with someone else. It didn't feel all that empowered.'

Several of the young women interviewed in Levy's *Female Chauvinist Pigs* explain frighteningly well how they and their friends are using a gung-ho, blokeish approach to sex to show they're not 'girly'.

Boatloads of casual sex does not signify actual empowerment (though it's not *necessarily* contrary to it). Empowerment isn't feeling like shit when a guy has used you as a masturbatory aid, or pretending you don't care. Empowerment isn't insisting: 'I can do what I want and if I want to get hurt and misused and undervalued and feel corroded and lower my self-esteem, I can!' And it's not about *performing* empowerment through sex. You are empowered if you pay close attention to what really builds your sense of wellbeing, and to knowing and understanding the difference between fun and crap treatment masquerading as fun.

Social discomfort and the single woman

As if the cake needed any more topping – single women today still feel an anxiety about their non-manned status that ranges from the manageable to the debilitating. Women are no longer defined by their childbearing and house-cleaning skills. But that doesn't seem to diminish society's obsession with female romantic and sexual status. In the US, successful professional women are known to take two years (TWO YEARS) off work to plan weddings.

> 'There is this societal pressure whereby if you're a single woman in your 30s, you're seen as mad, desperate or somehow lacking. It's like Stanford in Sex and the City says: "you're nobody until someone loves you". But I don't want to reach 50 and be really successful and live in a nice flat and all anyone can see is I'm single. I don't like being reduced to that – a failure because you haven't got someone to shag you long term.'
>
> Ronnie Blue, 30, journalist

Reality shows about weddings and man-finding are cultishly popular and spawning like rabbits: *Bridezillas*, *The Bachelorette*, *My Big Fat Gypsy Wedding* and dozens of others. In the UK, the hen party has become a kind of adulation akin to goddess worship and money is not meant to be an object to the full homage the bride-to-be deserves. 'Marriage has become a cult,' says Ronnie. 'The hen-dos have become insane as if getting married is the biggest achievement a woman can have. If you're single, it makes you feel like you're a total failure. But if there wasn't that pressure, that view, you wouldn't become so anxious about finding someone, and that anxiety affects the way you are with men. It makes you less attractive.'

The waning glory of the single woman: from Cleopatra to Elizabeth I to Bridget Jones

It's worth remembering our proud origins. The most terrible epithets were thrown at non-widowed single women – they were, at the bare minimum, assumed to be either shameless whores or hideous spinster frigid virgins. But many of our predecessors, from Joan of Arc to Florence Nightingale, saw their singleness as essential to the pursuit of the kind of work they wanted to achieve. Cleopatra spoke nine languages fluently as ruler of Egypt and could barely tolerate lover (not husband) Antony's idiocy. Elizabeth I remained a virgin, 'wedded to her people'. Catherine the Great of Russia had numerous lovers who she paid off generously when they no longer satisfied her – meanwhile changing the course of European history.

Such stateswomen were, of course, rare among rare exceptions to the rule of 'to be a single woman is to be pitied and kept down', and the obstacles facing them were enormous (men mainly, and the laws written by men). Now that we're free to get on with doing whatever we want with or without a man, with as kinky or polygamous a sex life as we want, we should be racing ahead, full of the joys of freedom.

Yet instead of seeking to emulate Catherine the Great's astonishing approach to lovers and imperial policy, it's Helen Fielding's hilarious but terrifying model of early-mid-life singleness, *Bridget Jones*, that exerts real influence. We adore that chaotic jumble of career ineptitude, vulnerability, embarrassment and frustration in part because it seems to say, 'this is you, too'.

On the page, in that nice font, it's all charming and fine and ends in a fairy tale marriage. Reality is different, though, and we can do better. The more I observed and considered, the more it became blazingly clear that Dr d'Felice was onto something – we're filling our lives with too much junk-food love and instead of making us stronger, it just bloats us with dead emotional weight. So I decided to give the Man Diet a go.

The Man Diet explained: what's it for?

The Man Diet explains and explores ten rules designed to wean you off junk-food love, namely:

- negative man-related experiences
- corrosive man-obsessing thoughts
- damaging man-related actions

It is designed to tweak your behaviour – mental and social – in such a way as to strengthen your core sense of self. In doing so, it should make your singledom healthy, creative and, yes, happy. Many books either add to the stigma of being unattached, by trying to show you how to snare a man, or aggressively trumpet the message that you can be happy *even though* you're single. This one shows you how to treat yourself well – emotionally and intellectually – *while* you're single.

Diets are hard. Is this one?

Not hugely, but it's not a breeze either. Though definitely less painful than following a food diet (though not necessarily less challenging), the Man Diet does require significant effort. It does involve a cutting down of widely available, habitually consumed junk-food love. JFL is everywhere – it's in our Facebook newsfeeds, our availability online, our multiple inboxes, our short attention spans. It's in the belief that emotional attachment is bad and that it certainly doesn't go with sex; that some guy is better than no guy; that the easiest and best way to pass the time is to think and talk about men. It's in the guys themselves: men fed on a culture of porn and anything goes, in which chivalry is dead and – miraculously – sex grows on trees.

Remember, good love is around, too. That's why this diet is ultimately positive. In cutting down on bad love, it opens up space for good love. Good love can involve good men, or good things with men you like, or it can mean you feeling good without a man. The Man Diet is a method of discerning the wheat from the chaff: emotionally, sexually and romantically. Whether you're enjoying dating and having fun, you're long-term single and feeling desperate for a shag, or serious about finding a life partner, cutting down the junk-food love is a major bonus.

Can I date when I'm reading this book?

Yes! But in the healthy, Man Diet/No Junk-Food Love way. You can snog men and even shag them on the 'diet' – but only if you're doing it in the right way, from the right place and, to put it bluntly, with a nice man. It's about cutting down on junk. In other words, the Man Diet is about setting emotional, not physical, boundaries.

Who is the diet for?

The diet is not just for people that are having their doors banged down by voracious men: man droughts are just as common for the attractive single lady as unhealthy man binges. No, it's for anyone that thinks too much and unconstructively about men, or whose lives are being adversely affected by their presence – or absence.

Your goal is to feel whole, and enjoy your wholeness, entirely separately from men and the validation their attention gives us. The purpose of this book is to inspire you to embrace self-respect and to pursue your interests singlemindedly. As you. Not as a person who desperately wants to be chosen, and who thrives only on male attention and the validation it brings.

The key to satisfaction, as the Man Diet will show, is not sleeping with another fittie or having a little affair with the married guy at work, or trying to lure that beautiful man from the gym on a date. Rather, it is entering a robust and respectful relationship with yourself. Yes, I know, 'love yourself' is the oldest and least well-explained piece of advice in the book. But if you're a single woman or a woman with a dodgy relationship with menkind, the Man Diet will show you how to do it. Or, for those with a slight issue with the word 'love' in relation to themselves (my hand's up), it'll put you on a track to happiness as you, your own woman. The rest – finding Mr Right and all that – should follow naturally, though being your own woman is the primary goal here, and a brilliant end in itself. The Man Diet is for anyone who wants to feel her best – particularly if she's finding it hard as a single woman.

The 'Mix and Match' Diet Plan

If you're a perfectionist and someone who likes drastic measures, you can do all of the rules at once, cold-turkey style, but you're likely to get frustrated or feel bored – much as with a food diet.

I prefer a more flexible approach – one of the reasons I like the Man Diet is that it's perfect for mixing and matching rules, as well as the intensity with which you do them. I recommend picking anywhere from three to seven to do simultaneously at any given time.

How do I follow the rules?

The first part of each chapter explains the social context of the rule and why women may need it. At the end of each chapter there is a 'how to' that ranges from the general to the very specific.

How do I know which ones to pick?

At the beginning of each chapter is a guide to who will benefit most from the rule, along with which other rules they complement/work well with. When I started, Do Not Pursue (rule seven) was the one that felt most urgent. You will have a gut feeling about *your* biggest problem area, too. Some of the rules have to be done in their entirety right away – and Do Not Pursue is one of them. Others can be done to greater or lesser degrees, like No Talking About Men.

Once I began relaxing my constant lookout for potentials, sending follow-up texts and so on, I followed my nose about the next rules to follow. I was doing well not pursuing men most of the time, but at night, after a few glasses, I'd feel my fingers twitch towards the phone. Equally, when I got home I'd head straight for Facebook. So next up: curb your drinking (rule two – and something I'd long wanted to do anyway) and No Facebook Stalking (rule three).

The rest followed soon after, but you can't expect to do them all hard-core at once. Start with your most pressing rule and roll them out. Do Not Pursue and No Facebook Stalking go together, for example, and Do Something Lofty with No Talking About Men.

How long will it take to work?

You can go on the Man Diet for two weeks, a month or a year (or forever). Its benefits kick in anywhere from within a day to a month of starting – long enough for lifestyle tweaks to really have an impact. And once you've felt its benefits, going back to the old attitudes and ways will probably be a bit less appealing.

Doing something asexual/lofty (from reading a good book to doing a good deed) makes me feel like a stronger, more complete woman immediately. That's because it's an active rule. By contrast, something like cutting down on talking about men (rule four) can take a little longer because there's more of a weaning period involved, for both you and your friends. But after a week or two – depending on how much you get to practise – you should notice a genuine rewiring of your brain and emotions for the better. For best results, employ as many rules as possible at once (though not all – as I said, you don't want to get frustrated) and keep them going for a month to start with. The benefits will go deeper than that surface pleasure at having, say, picked up a difficult book or fought an impulse to stalk a guy on Facebook.

Followed with some degree of discipline and passion (but also patience with yourself), you should manage to enhance your self-esteem in the long term, as well as sharpen up your act – as a woman and a person – overall. Other benefits of the Man Diet include flourishing at work, finding new outlets for creativity, and exploring new territory with friends.

Do I have to do it forever?

Not in the strict sense. You can do it for a week, or month or two months and feel the benefits. When you return to your pre-Man Diet ways, you'll be more aware of what you're doing, and how it affects you.

Ideally, the Man Diet will give you a useful outlook, of which a part may become second nature after a while. You may choose to stick to certain rules as a matter of course

– having tasted the freedom afforded by No Facebook Stalking, you may never open Facebook again. Other rules you may let slide. But the thoughts, feelings and ideas you'll have while doing the Man Diet for however long will stand you in good stead.

Will it drive me crazy?

No. Quite the opposite – it'll make you happier. Plus, the rules are a fun, not a gruelling challenge. I promise.

I've been single for ages! The last thing I need is a Man Diet!

Ask yourself the following questions and be really honest with yourself: Does the absence of men in your life get you down? Have you been rejected – perhaps more than once – in ways that make you sad or that lower your self-esteem? Are you spending a lot of energy plotting new ways to meet a decent guy to go out with? Does it annoy you that your friends constantly feel the need to discuss your romantic prospects with you? If you answered yes to any of these then you can benefit from the Man Diet. Because it is about emotional, not physical boundaries.

What are the first signs I'm benefiting from the diet?

Well, within a few weeks of Man Dieting, I lost a whole load of *empty* emotional weight. It was like an end to water retention and wheat-related bloating. I felt better psychologically and focused better on real things like work and books and good conversations, as opposed to the ever-changing shape of romantic possibility. The same will happen to you.

The other thing that you will notice with wonderment is that with the men you do meet you will have better conversations because they won't be so loaded with expectation. Whether they get in touch or not will cause you little wasted mental energy. For me, simply not conniving to get in touch (rule one) freed up a good bit. The saying tends to be: 'No pain, no gain.' Well, I found that on the Man Diet, it was more 'Less pain, more gain'.

Which would have been immoral, really, to have kept to myself.

What if I fall off the wagon?

You're human. Get back on – and read the SOS sections at the end of each chapter. Honestly, this diet is not about deprivation and self-punishment – it's about happiness and self-worth. I invite you to follow the diet as closely as possible, but when life takes you in a different direction, ask yourself why. Don't beat yourself up about it! Sucky diets never work, anyway. Just ask the folks at Weight Watchers.

Rule Number 1

Refuse to Have No Strings Attached Sex

You need this rule if you ...

- Have lots of No Strings Attached (NSA) sex but it doesn't make you particularly happy.
- Feel crap when a guy completely loses interest after sex.
- Always say yes because you:
  - don't want to let them down
  - think they might like you more if you do
  - think it's your 'job', as a single woman, to do it
  - figure 'better something than nothing'
- Are afraid of appearing demanding if you get attached.
- Want to show you're a tough cookie and a modern woman and you are sure this is the way.
- Have a number in your head you'd like to get to.
- Want a relationship but have got into the habit of 'shag first, think later'.

Goes well with ...

- Dwell on Your Sense of Self
- Do Something Lofty
- Do Not Pursue

Lucy, 33, was out on the town with her friend Karen, 29. They met two guys, and it wasn't clear at first who fancied who. Soon it became clear that both the guys fancied Karen. But Karen wasn't up for it with either of them – one was downright unattractive, let's call him Bill, and the hotter one, let's call him Bob, didn't do it for her either. When Lucy, who had been single for two years and felt insecure about her attractiveness, asked Karen if she'd mind if she took Bob home with her, Karen gave her the thumbs up. 'But don't expect anything,' she called after Lucy as she got into Bob's BMW. Karen worried about Lucy when she did this kind of thing, since she always wound up hurt or with a sense of self-loathing.

What happened next …

Lo and behold, the next day Lucy rang Karen to talk about Bob, who had not made much effort to show he liked Lucy either in the bar or after sex. Lucy knew he wasn't a candidate – he was good looking but a typical sports-car-owning chump and none too bright. She knew she wasn't supposed to have had any expectations, or to have developed any.

And, like a 'good' girl, she'd made it clear to him the night before that it was a one-off. All the same, like a 'bad' girl, she'd developed expectations since they'd shagged. And now she felt rejected, angry with herself for doing this again, used and a tiny bit abused. What for? Because she was horny and it would be fun, she'd thought, but since he hadn't been that into her, the sex hadn't been warm or nice or horn-satisfying; it had been alienating and detached instead. She'd felt compelled to do it even though she knew it would be like that, she confessed to Karen.

What does 'no strings' sex really mean?

Technically, it means both parties walk away from the sack unfettered by commitment and, supposedly, any *desire* to commit. It means that you can sleep with lots of people at once. It means you don't have to be burdened. In reality, it means that guys don't have to do anything boring like call the girl or seem interested in dating her (or date her) after sex. As a woman, it means that you'd better not show attachment, need or expectation after sex – if you do, you've broken the rules and you have to go to your room for punishment. Bad girl. Above all, it's a term that goes hand in hand with 'fuck-buddy' and 'friends with benefits', and that often doesn't bear much relationship to reality – at least, reality as it is for women. Who are, of course, half the heterosexual sexual equation.

Why it's a hoax

The drive to undersell our needs in love and in bed is amazingly strong. Recently a friendship of mine with a suddenly single man turned flirty. I suggested, as did he, that some sex could be fun, but refused to guarantee I would do it without feelings. 'If we do it, it'll have to be on my terms,' he said. 'What are they?' I asked hopefully – rather relishing the prospect of something as-yet unnamed with him. 'No strings,' he replied curtly, accessing with instinctive ease that cold, sibilant rule that enables men (and women) to forbid the natural by-product of sex and one of its great joys – actual intimacy – to come anywhere near the act. Great for men, perhaps, to whom ridiculous amounts of research has attributed a desire for quantity over quality in sex, as well as a lower amount of oxytocin, the post-sex attachment hormone. But not great for me; or for most women. Post-Man Diet, I refused to recant this rule, and we didn't end up doing anything. But there have been many times when my mind has returned to his offer. Even though I know I'd have hated it when, after we'd slept together, he'd inevitably have boasted about other conquests in front of me, and that I'd have to present this chipper, tough facade so that he didn't think, God forbid, I'd felt a string of attachment.

The audacious Mary Wollstonecraft, mother of Mary Shelley (author of *Frankenstein*), rages wonderfully against the injustice of a slightly different type of sexual servitude in 1792. Lambasting her infuriating contemporary, she writes:

> 'Rousseau declares that a woman should [...] be governed by fear to exercise her natural cunning, and made a coquettish slave in order to render her a more alluring object of desire, a sweeter companion to man, whenever he chooses to relax himself.'

She's right: being ready to indulge male predilections for NSA sex, for fear of not being wanted at all, makes willing slaves of us. The Man Diet should ignite a resistance to being available for whenever a man 'chooses to relax himself' (for all intents and purposes).

Put those feelings away: why NSA is worse for women

The 'no strings' proclamation before sex is far more evil than it might sound. It slams the door not just on the here and now – as in, this sex will be about bodies only, so don't you even think about enjoying it too much in your head or heart – but on the whole question of possibility and potential. It says: 'You will only ever be about sex, because I don't fancy you enough to think about anything else, and I will never fancy you enough to think about anything else.' This is an immensely bitter pill to swallow for women (and perhaps some men), and yet so many of us – myself included – have swallowed it numerous times.

That a lot of no-strings sex is bad for women is widely acknowledged by the psychological community. Dr Cecilia d'Felice, clinical psychologist, says: 'In studies we have found what you might expect: that if you offer men opportunistic sex, most of the time they'll take it. If you offer women opportunistic sex, most of the time they won't. There's a huge difference in the programming of risk-taking between men and women. Women are biologically more risk averse for obvious reasons.'

Relationships therapist Val Sampson says women are hardwired to be quite choosy about who we have sex with. 'So even if women say they're fine with no-strings sex, it's not necessarily the case. If you become just a vessel a lot of men have sex in, you're going against the grain. Whereas men can compartmentalise sex more easily, women feel a sense of being let down. All that potential they could use in a sexual act isn't being used – it's actually being rejected and this triggers a feeling of "What am I worth?" She may end up feeling like a hooker but get no money at the end of it.'

No-strings sex and its spirit of female denial and stagnation is lambasted deliciously by Germaine Greer in *The Female Eunuch* in 1970. In her forward to the Paladin 21st Anniversary Edition, she lists all the sexual freedoms women can now enjoy since the book was first published. 'What else could women want?' she asks dangerously. 'Freedom, that's what … Freedom from self-consciousness. Freedom from the duty of sexual stimulation of jaded male appetite, for which no breast ever bulges hard enough and no leg is ever long enough … The argument in *The Female Eunuch* is still valid, for it holds that a woman has the right to express her own sexuality, which is not at all the same thing as the right to capitulate to male advances.'

Just say no … but why is it so hard?

For one, agreeing to no-strings sex is easy. All the terminology is laid out and ready to go: 'fuck-buddy', 'friends with benefits' and so on. And, as I said in the introduction, it masquerades as empowerment for women, whereby shagging like a man is what we do now because we can and, as 'feminists', we should.

But on a personal level, a deep fear of seeming needy has taken hold of women – the stereotype of the woman who encumbers her man and everyone around her with a bottomless pit of wanting and needing and insecurity has reached epic proportions, and floats tyrannously through our minds as we conduct ourselves sexually and romantically. Dr Janet Reibstein, Visiting Professor in Psychology at the University of Exeter and the author of a book reporting on what makes couples happy, observes: 'It's seen as somewhat shameful to say "I want to settle down." The shame comes from admitting prioritising relationship over independence. If a woman says, "I don't want to have sex with you because I want a relationship," a man may respond with alarm: "uh-oh, she's trying to capture me!".' Reibstein also thinks there's a political accent to the NSA idea: 'Settling down is not part of the feminist heritage. It was a mistake of the feminists of the 1970s, of which I was one, not to stress how important relationships are.'

After the escapade with Bob, I asked Lucy what motivates her to offer herself no-strings, when inevitably she'll want strings. 'Feelings are NOT ALLOWED,' she told me over sushi. 'Even though we wish they were. But since they're not allowed, we don't go with them. But we have them. And so we're confused. And fragmented.'

Of Bob, she explained: 'That was casual sex but it was fine because I didn't have any expectations. The worst is when you take a guy home and have expectations. With this guy I didn't cry. So that was a win. So I say empowered, but what I mean is that it just wasn't a disaster.'

The rise of the NSA creed has its roots in a culture that has turned sex into an anecdotal accessory, a must-have store of experience, and a branded display of power, as determined by the status of the person you've shagged or the quantity of 'shagees'. Sex is the social currency (it's what people talk about most), sexualisation is the social and entertainment aesthetic (advertising, magazines, posters, cereal boxes, newspapers are a jamboree of limbs and post-baby, pre-summer, post-break-up bikini bodies), porn is the private backdrop ('A Billion Wicked Thoughts', as per the name of the recent massive study of internet porn by Ogi Ogas and Sai Gaddam), and choice of prospective sexual partners is almost infinite, thanks to the internet. As usual, women's bodies, preferably naked or near enough, are at the centre of this highly visual culture of hypersexuality.

Women and the rise of the one-night stand

Modern female one-night-standers are riding the wave started by the feminists of the 1970s, who wanted us to have sexual freedom and a chance to explore our sexual natures beyond the strictures and servitude of mid-century wifehood. But those feminists split into warring factions: crudely divided into the 'sex-positive' (those in favour of porn as a slice of the sexual freedom cake) and the 'sex-negative' (those who saw porn as degrading to women). For various reasons, such as having the extremely rich Hugh Hefner on side, the sex-positive, pro-porn group won out, and their influence evolved into what many girls and women today call feminism – i.e., stripping, shagging, 'choosing' to use their own bodies for public or pornographic enjoyment. This is a deeply simplistic account, but I think it's essential to note that the NSA norm originated – however perversely or ironically – from the brains and hearts of some of the 20th century's noblest feminists.

Unsurprisingly, one-night stands have risen sharply. According to the National Survey of Sexual Attitudes and

Lifestyles, in 1990, 53 per cent of men and 79 per cent of women considered one-night stands to be wrong. Ten years later only a third of men and half of women held that view.

Teenagers – tomorrow's adults – are leading the charge. Teen specialist Raychelle Lohmann notes in *Psychology Today* that high school relationships are being replaced by a hook-up culture, where no-strings pulling rules. They are to become the women for whom Natasha Walter says, 'having many sexual partners without much emotional commitment is often seen as the most authentic way to behave'.

It's not that this kind of sex has been digested wholly by society – Hollywood, for one, is not comfortable with it. That doesn't mean it's not obsessed with it. Consider three recent films whose protagonists begin with a seeming paradise of strings-free sex but end up choosing monogamy: *No Strings Attached* has Natalie Portman's character coming round from a booty call mentality to a relationship; *Hall Pass* has Owen Wilson's totty-ogling husband given free rein by his wife to go off with other women for a week, and *Friends with Benefits* stars Mila Kunis and Justin Timberlake using each other for sex.

All these films want to show us that no-strings sex is not a good idea – unless it's leading to love. It's a nice sentiment, but by showing repeatedly that shagging for shagging's sake is one way into a happy, romantic ending (after all, who wouldn't want to steal the heart of Ashton Kutcher?), Hollywood is, as it's always done, giving us a fairy tale that has very, very little to do with reality. (Unless, of course, you look like Mila Kunis or Natalie Portman.)

NSA sex: the reality

Inevitably, raunch culture has taken a toll on the way women see themselves in relation to sex. We are voracious seekers of answers to the question 'Am I hot?', and tend to seek validation externally rather than internally. I know that when I go out hunting down a man, or hoping to be hunted, I'm looking for the thrill of a compliment – not of my brains, but of my beauty, or more specifically, my sexual allure, as much as for intimacy.

So for many women (although certainly not all), that quaint old duo of sex and love has been decoupled, leaving us performing sex for sex's sake in a mechanical vacuum with our inner sexual impressions, feelings and needs somewhere tucked under the carpet, away from the public and the male eye. Putting the two back on the same track, if not the same train, feels much better when your self-esteem has been worn down by a single spell. It also helps with raising the quality (i.e., human element), rather than the quantity of sexual contact.

The sense of numbness and dissatisfaction that women experience in casual encounters is palpable and ruinous. Lillian, 28, told me she actually weeps during casual sex, such is her feeling of disconnect.

'The amount of times I've had sex and cried and the person hasn't noticed … I'm so detached it's bananas. I'll cry, waiting for him to notice. The callousness and detachment you feel is astounding. Sometimes I feel that I have no other option to express myself.'

What NSA sex does is just that: clamps down on your options to express yourself. Things got so bad that Lillian had started on a sort of Man Diet of her own. When I had a coffee with her a few weeks after the crying confession, she said she was now asking herself, 'Why should I sleep with someone?' rather than 'Why shouldn't I?' I shared the Man Diet's 'say no to NSA sex' rule, suggesting that she should not be embarrassed to send NSA wannabes packing. And that if she chose only to have sex with men that were offering her what she clearly needed emotionally (i.e., some degree of familiarity and affection), she'd feel infinitely better overall. Nor would she be missing out on anything apart from the odd bout of cystitis. Whereas previously she'd been having sad sex to prove something – that she is desirable – she found that not having sex (for the moment) was the thing that actually made her feel desirable. After giving the Man Diet a go (she did 'Refuse to Have NSA Sex' alongside 'Do Something Lofty' and 'Dwell on Your Sense of Self'), I'm proud to report that her days of sobbing mid-sex are over. She still hooks up with men she's not attached to and vice-versa, but having recognised that for her there is something uniquely alienating in intercourse, she stops at your trusty old foreplay. She now seems so much more relaxed and happy. Go Man Diet!

Just as Lillian did, many women feel numb or detached during non-intimate sex. But luckily, her story shows that you can work on it and improve your emotional experience of sexual contact pretty quickly.

Like Lillian, Lisa, 31, is in dire need of the Man Diet. I include her story because it so perfectly – and woefully – captures that detachment the modern sexual woman needs to combat. Lisa told me that she has sex with her eyes closed because not being face to face with an actual person helps her remain thoroughly detached and tough through-out. The one time she did open her eyes – with a boyfriend – she saw him looking everywhere but at her, and promptly closed them again.

Wham bam

Lisa's a lovely girl, very warm, clearly sensitive, and open. And yet, she says defiantly, as though having subcon-sciously taken on the male preference for 'wham bam' sex: 'I'm not a big cuddler – especially if I don't like the guy.' Also she says she 'loves' rough sex. 'Doggy style is my favourite position,' she says, obedient again to male preferences. Why does she close her eyes, why doesn't she like to cuddle? 'Because it's all about me. It's my moment.' If that was the case, you'd think she'd at least be getting some serious 'me-time' pleasure out of it, but Lisa has never orgasmed with a man. 'The truth is, we're playing the men's game,' she says. 'They've got all the rules set up to suit them. We can fight it or match it – so I match it. I'm a post-modern feminist – I don't think we need to be like men, we're good as we are etc etc, but … with sex it's different.' And clearly, as women like Lisa and Lillian make abundantly clear, the man's game of strings-free sex isn't exactly a non-stop jig of healthy fun.

What they show, too, is how far women have internalised masculine sexual stereotypes, making them their own with a flick of the pseudo-feminist whip (and then, in the case of the more emotionally tuned-in, feeling lousy about it). As Germaine Greer puts it so well in *The Female Eunuch*:

'Love-making has become another male skill, of which women are the judges.'

Natasha Walter's excellent survey of contemporary female sexual culture, *Living Dolls: The Return of Sexism*, takes a searing look at women's sexual mores and their context. One group of well-off, late-teen female students she interviewed spoke in hostile, competitive, mercenary and utterly soulless ways about sex:

'I'm much more attracted to the guys who don't give a shit,'

'We were saying that one week we should go out and try to notch up as many lovers as we can, with the most variety possible – age, gender, jobs, backgrounds …'

They go on to cite their feeling of solidarity with Miranda in *Sex and the City* when she has to call her long list of past lovers after contracting an STD; they also admire Belle de Jour, the call girl, and other sex diarists as glamorous examples of non-committal, pornographically adventurous sex. Walter concludes: 'Because they had so successfully subtracted emotion from their sex lives, these young women were perfectly in tune with the culture around them.'

These girls are probably a good deal younger than you and me – after all, they're not even 20 yet. Perhaps their aggressive 'I'm a shagger' standpoint stems from the fact they're not yet worried about settling down. But equally, I think it's even more poignant that while they could be starry eyed and dreaming of 'the one', they're setting themselves up as sexually liberated toughs for whom 'no strings' sex is the only sex. They're the women of tomorrow.

The wrong kind of fun

The sex-mad, attachment-loathing students in Walter's book seem more directly influenced by sexual imagery and sexual pressure than most of the professional women between 23 and 35 that I know (including myself). All the same, I have felt very driven by a particular notion of 'fun' attributed to and expected of the single woman. In fact, the word fun crops up a hell of a lot in relation to the no-strings sex single women are meant to be having lots and lots of. I remember in the early days of my current single spell somewhat shakily telling my friend Carol about an alcohol-drenched encounter with someone wholly inappropriate, and her replying: 'Ah well, it's just fun.' Says Wendy, 31: 'All my friends are pairing up so I do want to meet someone special. In the meantime … why not have fun?' Or, as Ruth says: 'People will constantly ask: "Why are you single?" You're supposed to say: "I enjoy being single. I enjoy having unencumbered sex with strangers."'

But all that pressure to have fun stops being fun and becomes more like an exhausting task. '[Sexual encounters with men] feel very achievement based,' says my friend Molly, 27. Almost every woman I interviewed for this book used the words 'tiring' or 'exhausting' in relation to fun – whether it was in dating to the max, going out non-stop, or making the effort to appear fancy-free. 'It's exhausting being empowered,' as my friend Michelle, 27, put it.

Bringing home the bacon

That mercenary, bedpost notch approach to men isn't healthy and it doesn't make most women particularly happy. But neither do a lot of things that seem (or are) fun at the time. Which is why, despite its seemingly obvious badness, I can relate perfectly well to the urge to 'get the numbers up'. There's something that seems empowering about it, like you've gone out hunting and have brought in several good pheasants that you can cook and share with your friends (what else is the post-shag narrative breakdown with your mates if not a triumphal communal meal, hosted by you?). There's also the vague sense that you're delivering one in the eye to those guys that think women always get all attached, needy and psychotic after sex. Needless to say, that's a terrible reason to do something, not least because the only eye that's getting something in it is yours, when you've slept with someone rubbish and he doesn't even call. Delving deeper, I think some of us think that the more men you sleep with, the more attractive you must be. Enjoying the intense but often false intimacy that a sexual encounter provides is also a reason for accepting loads of NSA sex.

Note the bragging, bravado twang to the way I used to refer to hook-ups, before the Man Diet put me off that notchy approach: 'bringing home the bacon'. It was tongue-in-cheek, but telling. With or without pork metaphors, friends often congratulate each other on numbers of men shagged or bagged. The presence of an alien pair of male shoes outside a flatmate's bedroom door elicits back slapping the next day. A good friend of mine used to check in with me: 'What's your number [of sexual partners to date]?'

Still another would say: 'I want to get to 35 before Christmas.'

I'm not just moaning here, or being holier than thou. This attitude towards sex was making me feel fragmented, anxious and doubtful about my worth. I've seen it have the same effect on other women. And because something as simple as swearing off no-strings sex made me feel about a thousand times better – even though I've slipped once or twice – I'm hoping it'll do the same for you, via the Man Diet.

Sex and the single girl

The neon pink link between fun and the single woman was drawn with powerful clarity by Helen Gurley Brown, former editor of *Cosmo*, in her 1962 classic: *Sex and the Single Girl*. No social theory here – oh no. Just jaunty tips and the dos and don'ts of having affairs with married men; decorating your apartment in a man-friendly way; and workplaces where you're more likely to meet men. Reprinted in 2003, Gurley Brown jauntily speaks of not needing a husband in your prime years (read: prettiest). Indeed, she says that men are more fun taken in large quantities than on their own.

To be fair, it's a hilarious book, and very frank. It's just not particularly helpful to imagine us all as this 'glamour girl' troupe of burnished affair-havers with cute apartments in Greenwich Village.

Today's single woman and *Sex and the City*

Have single ladies changed much since the 1960s? Of course – back then, Germaine Greer and the other feminists of the 1970s hadn't made their mark yet. Crucially, we are also more economically successful. And with more cash comes more consumption, and with more consumption, more devouring. Not just of shoes and houses, but of sex, too.

Thirty-plus years after Gurley Brown showed us how a single girl can live – in a little apartment in the Village, having the odd affair, going out to dances with her girlfriends and working as a secretary at a man-tastic barge company – *Sex and the City* came along. It far more powerfully stamped an idea on our brains and an image on our retinas of how the single life should look – it should revolve around sex and men, a powerful, glamorous professional life, and lots of fun like shopping and drinking. New York writer Ariel Levy, a lover of the show

'I'll have an order of sex with that cocktail, please.'

just like I am, calls it a consumerist vision of 'vertiginous gobbling' that shows sex as something to be eaten up just like Manolos, cocktails and handbags. So seductive is its twinkling montage of intelligent girl chat, cosmopolitans, sanitised sex, wonderful clothes, great bodies, clinking glasses, hot restaurants and – most importantly – happy endings, that it was hard not to desperately want all that.

'Gobbling' is indeed a good word for the *SATC* vision of sex. Meg Daly, a so-called 'third wave' feminist and author, has talked about Samantha-style sex in terms of the 'swaggering pleasure' that comes from counting the bed-post notches, and the joy of boasting about sexual techniques. Daly seems just as drawn to sex for the bragging rights as the pleasure of the act itself.

Recall the back slaps, bedpost notching and 'bringing home the bacon' attitude among my friends – are we merely gobbling men and sex, too? Sometimes it feels like it. Which is why, before I started the Man Diet, I felt like I was carrying around so much extra empty emotional weight. Gobbling will do that to a girl.

Mr Big: the ultimate NSA male

It's also worth mentioning how the concept of closure is vilified in *SATC* – turning all sex, ultimately, into the strings-free variety. Yes, the Mr Right idea is the forceful, steady line drawn through the entire series – dangled, played with, and ultimately accepted. But as Joanna Di Mattia put it in her essay, 'What's the Harm in Believing?': 'It is a deconstruction of the Mr Right myth that enables romance to continue without closure.' Ultimately, Carrie can't deal with the closure Aidan offers – before she breaks away entirely, she tries to rebel, albeit feebly, by wearing the engagement ring around her neck. And, of course, she breaks into hives when trying on a white, frilly wedding dress. Mr Big, on the other hand, is constantly and obviously Mr Right waiting to happen. His defining characteristic, of course, is that he never offers real commitment. He's so evasive, so no-strings that he doesn't even have a name. Of course, Carrie's resistance to romantic closure serves an important structural purpose: it makes way for years of single gal fun that we get to ogle. The impression is that closure and commitment get in the way of having fun and being wild.

And his female equivalent: the impossible Samantha

Carrie was never my favourite. Samantha was (and is). For years I cited her as the torch-holding feminist on TV. She was the only woman on TV who didn't fall for slushy romance, ever reveal a true needy nature, nor desire the typical fairy tale marriage story. All this while exhibiting gobsmacking sexual appetite, without ever feeling low, used or at sea. In more recent times, I still adore Samantha, but I don't try to emulate her now, because I realise she's too good to be true. Or rather, she's just not true and trying to be her was really not good for me.

'Some have explained Samantha as basically a gay man in women's Versace.'

Almost unsurprisingly, there is an academic course offered as a tie-in to the show, called '*Sex and the City* and the Contemporary Woman'. In the Samantha section of the syllabus, billed as 'the sexual woman', the first question posed is: 'Is Samantha a liberated woman or a slut?' What a wrong-headed binary to strap her into. The implication of this question is that, indeed, sexual profligacy alone will make you either a slut (I had hoped this old woman-hating notion was dying out) or 'liberated' (the point is that nowadays, liberation shouldn't really have to do with how many penises enter your vagina – but, as per Walter and Levy, it has become an essential part of the definition). It gives a hell of a lot of credence – moral, social and political judgements are squeezed in between 'slut' and 'liberated' – to the act of sex. And to pop good old Sam in either category with any degree of earnestness is silly, once again betraying confusion about how to interpret the reality peddled by the show. Some have explained Samantha as the product of gay scriptwriters and producers on *Sex and the City* – that she is basically a gay man in woman's Versace. Whatever – there are women writers too on the show, and she's a fabulous character. It's just that to see hers as an achievable type of lifestyle, parcelled in a box of imperturbable self-sufficiency, is to be deluded.

SATC: influential, or what?

Many of the women I spoke to said *Sex and the City* hadn't influenced their actual way of behaving – and if they did identify with a character, few admitted it was Samantha (although one said ruefully she wanted to see herself as Carrie, but in reality she was probably more Samantha). But without doubt, *SATC* infiltrated female culture and its ideas of sex, fashion and urban lifestyle since it hit the air in 1998. One strong bit of research that explains why a mere TV show like *SATC* could actually impact the decisions women make – whether they admit it or not – was done by Albert Bandura, in 1977. He proposed Social Learning Theory, the idea that if you watch someone else do something, you can learn what rewards/consequences are attached to that behaviour (and thus if you should do it, how to do it). This research was innovative because Bandura found that watching a real person or a person on TV (as a character) doing something could be *equally* effective in observational learning. The different components of this 'watch-and-learn' model are Attention, Retention, Reproduction, Motivation. Your motivation reaches you through the rewards presented when you watched someone else do whatever behaviour.

According to Janet Kwok, who studies human development and education at Harvard, 'Watching the ladies on *Sex and the City* find their happy endings despite participating in problematic behaviours was a large-scale social learning theory crisis, if we want to be dramatic. Their behaviour was easy to remember (Retention) and there were attractive rewards depicted (Motivation) without the potential consequences that might have been more representative of the viewers' experiences.'

I'd add to Bandura's theory and say that the fun of watching *Sex and the City* can be confused with the fun of actually doing what they do – i.e., have lots of no-strings, fun (if problematic, but ultimately brunch-analysed) sex. The problem is, while the *SATC* ladies proved to some extent that sex could result in the outcome most women desire (husband, kids, riches, happiness, success), we cannot always be assured of the same outcome. And our path to getting there will be all the rockier until we realise it's not possible to be Samantha, either in numbers or approach. Or, for that matter, while we deny ourselves the right to bear strings.

The sex diarist: seductive mistresses of the strings-free shagathon

There's another thing confusing our notion of 'fun' that is closer to home, perhaps, than the bars and bedrooms of Upper Manhattan. And that is the sex diarist, who romps the streets and clubs of London, and inhabits the pages of UK newspapers and the shelves of UK bookstores. I knew this culture of do-and-share a bit from the inside, since for one and a half years I was the Girl About Town dating columnist for *thelondonpaper*, a now-defunct but wildly popular evening freesheet. I was a novice, and at first I shared too much. People loved it when I did; all the same, I pulled back, feeling deeply awkward at the idea that everyone, from the Islamic extremist who threatened to kill me to my 12-year-old cousin, was reading about my exploits.

When I wasn't enthralling the world with my numerous dates and hook-ups (of which a good few were, ahem, embellished), it was my job to depict a sort of glamorous lifestyle, a bit like Carrie. I was encouraged to namedrop cool bars and locations around town that made it sound like I had a big night out every night, never got tired, and was always getting into exciting scrapes. I created a world in which sexual adventure, romantic mishap and great night-life flowed seamlessly together. I assume it was seductive – I stuck to it for a year and a half, after all, and people still fondly remember the column today.

But I was only a dating columnist. I was completely vanilla – even alongside the others on the same paper. My rivals were a different story. They were properly telling all – Catherine Townsend of the *Independent* was spilling the beans about the length and strength of her orgasms; Belle de Jour (real name: Brooke Magnanti, scientist) was setting the world alight with her stories of sex as a call girl.

Zoe Margolis's book *Girl with a One Track Mind*, published under the pseudonym Abby Lee, set out to address the problem of prudishness. 'My own friends appear quite happy to sit in a pub, swapping *Sex and the City* anecdotes and joking about rabbit vibrators. But, the thing is, if I want to get into more detail and mention something like, say, wanting to try out a cock ring on a guy, whole fingering his arse, they all suddenly become rather quiet … And I'd be left sitting there staring at the bartender's trouser bulge …' And in case you were unclear about the kind of sex she likes to have, and its exact definition, she's included a handy list: The Girl's Guide to Fuck-Buddies: Definitions. 'A fuck-buddy is someone with whom you are sexually involved, but with no romantic or emotional strings attached. They are NOT a friend that you fuck … the fuck-buddy relationship is purely sexual.' Or, lest you foolishly still thought that you might be allowed to squeeze a bit of humanity into the transaction: 'With a fuck-buddy, there is no real intimacy beyond nudity and mutual hotness … It's not like meeting up with a mate to watch a movie and talking about the plot afterwards over dinner. By definition a fuck-buddy relationship happens on a physical level only.'

A far cry from the words of early 20th-century anarchist Emma Goldman in *Living My Life*, who was put in prison for her defence of women's rights to contraception: 'I have propagated freedom in sex. I have had many men myself. But I have loved them; I have never been able to go indiscriminately with men.'

Ricky Emanuel, the psychotherapist, is despairing at the One Track Mind culture. He told me in the canteen of the Royal Free Hospital: "This is the commodification of sex and it's extremely damaging to girls. I have some patients having sex with five people at the same time, described as "friends that I do stuff with". This is infantile sexuality; it's about excitement, fizziness, completely devoid of emotional depth or benefit. Young women feel they have to do it – but the lack of meaning makes them depressed. I have to ask: what's happened to courting? Getting to know someone? It's not by chance that biblically they used "know" as a meaning for deep and emotional sexual contact. These days much casual sex has nothing to do with knowing.'

Catherine Townsend's well-written book, *Sleeping Around: Secrets of a Sexual Adventuress*, is about: 'Threesomes, sorbet sex, drunk dialling, multiple orgasms, girly gossip-swaps, buying silk underwear – welcome to dating the modern girl's way.' Wait, so if I have sex with (or is it while eating?) sorbet and buy silk underwear and cosmos, I'll have multiple orgasms? This is similar to the picture presented in *Sex and the City*, the seductive mixture of lifestyle and sex – but even in *SATC* you're not guaranteed a multiple orgasm. That's because even having one orgasm during sex isn't easy for a lot of women – it's thought that 20 to 30 per cent of women can do it through vaginal penetration; the rest require a degree of confidence to ask for other stimulation in a particular fashion, which takes time and a bit of trust.

The sex itself

Have you noticed that the sex you have when you don't know or like the person you're sleeping with is sort of actually not that great, when you think about it? What happens is that you do it, you get excited by this fact, tell all your friends, then forget the actual moments of alienation in the sex itself.

We saw earlier how Lisa and Lucy talked about their casual sex experiences – one cries during sex, hoping to be noticed, the other keeps her eyes closed. A friend of mine,

Melissa, was devastated by a one-night stand she had with a much older man she met in a bar; weeks later, the lack of intimacy and the repulsion she realised she'd felt for him when she sobered up still made her depressed. She mainly remembered just praying he'd hurry up and come – an experience common to many a casual sex encounter, when you're just guessing what's going to work. I am not writing off all casual sex for women in a Protestant fury, but this rule stems from the observation that while we think it's great and fun at the time, it's often damaging later.

'You have to act ridiculously into it'

Junk-food sex ranges from the dangerous – unprotected – to the callous and insultingly selfish, to the pseudo-intimate, whereby it's good and you wish strings were allowed. More and more, though, you're expected to do whatever it takes to be sexy. Ruth, 31, says:

> *'I told a guy I wasn't going to sleep with him, and he said,
> "At least, let me put it in your ass."'*

Indeed, a desirable male acquaintance told me that women compete to sleep with him, offering him anal sex immediately 'to distinguish themselves from the other girls.' Holly, 32, a successful fashion journalist says:

> *'There's massive pressure to be good in bed – having to act
> ridiculously into it and up for everything; giving the
> "knowing" blow job etc – it's not enough to just do your
> basic missionary. Which is ironic, because mostly boys are
> shit in bed.'*

Another lethal junk-food sex trend is men saying they can't possibly perform while wearing a condom, thus making the woman feel guilty if she insists on safe sex. Ruth says: 'I can't believe that would influence me – but it does. All you're supposed to be is sexy and make them come, that is the most important thing. I never think about my own pleasure – the only time I will ever orgasm is in a serious relationship.' Statistics about women and anal sex are telling – anal sex, for most women, is not a pleasant experience (anal beads can apparently help) and is not usually one that women will proffer. It's more something they do because men want it. In a 1992 study that surveyed sexual behaviours, published by the University of Chicago, 20 per cent of women aged 25 to 29 reported having anal sex. In a study published in October 2010 by the Center for Sexual Health Promotion at Indiana University, the instances of anal sex reported by women in the same age group had more than doubled, to 46 per cent.

Self-consciousness

Even loving, relationship sex often has a whiff of the casual encounter's anxiety about it – one friend of mine said she's so paranoid about her boyfriend of four years seeing her in an unbecoming position that she never had sex without a camisole covering her torso (she lets the straps down). Indeed, *Company* magazine commissioned me to write an article for them revealing seven sex positions that not only achieved G-spot access (which is still not properly understood) but were *flattering*, too. For example, anything where your stomach is stretched out and your head thrown back. Try fitting that in with remembering your G-spot, and then the fact that there is another real live person partici-pating, too.

That self-consciousness – whereby a woman is fully occupied in trying to make her body appealing – is nothing new. Naomi Wolf, author of the essential feminist manifesto *The Beauty Myth*, explains with typical ingenuity the way in which the female experience of her own body is frag-mented. She notes that since the 14th century, masculine culture has revelled in deconstructing women's bodies. Troubadors specialised in listing the feminine 'catalogue of features', while poet Edward Spencer took this catalogue to a new level in his hymn *Epithalamion*. This fragmented approach to female features, says Wolf, continues today in 'list-your-good-points' features in women's magazines, and in collective fantasies about female perfection fuelled by heavy marketing. She's right: whether you are selling watches or yoghurt, it seems that images evoking the perfect, milky-skinned package is essential.

Porn-consciousness

'I trotted out every parlour trick and sexual persona I knew.'

Commercial culture's jamboree of female torsos, lips and legs aside, I believe that much of the self-doubt in the sex experience for women is the awareness and ubiquity of the porn standard. I don't watch porn, it feels like a pollutant to me, but many people do, women included (about a third of porn is viewed by women). I've seen it, though, and I know how extreme (to me) even its most savoury acts seem. I also know that most men, including those I'm likely to end up in the sack with, will be porn consumers. They may not require the porn standard – I interviewed dozens of men for my last book and most of them were far more generous about our bodies than we believe. But we know porn's there, a click away, which is almost as bad.

Natasha Vargas-Cooper, a prominent American writer, has captured very well the jig the single woman plays in bed, as well as the discomfort she'll happily accept to make the man come – that is, to get past Go and collect $100. She talks about a one-night stand with a well-heeled, polite old acquaintance of hers in which the sex failed miserably. He couldn't stay aroused, despite her trying every trick she knew, from playing the coquette to acting submissively; from yelling with (fake) excitement to going silent. In the end, he requested anal sex. Vargas-Cooper asked why that – of all things – would arouse him. The reason he gave was that it was the only thing that would make her uncomfortable. Instead of walking out, Vargas-Cooper instantly complied. Looking back, she notes how this encounter does not exactly fit the feminist template of sexuality. The reality is that pleasure and displeasure are two sides of the same sexual coin, a contradiction 'neatly' resolved through porn, and thus, she notes, very much in favour of men.

Clearly, the issue of porn is an absolutely huge one, and not what this book is about. But I think it's helpful to acknowledge that its presence, all those ubiquitous, easily-activated pixels behind a billion clicks, only adds to the complexity of sex for women today. In a non-supportive, no-strings shagathon, that complexity is simply too jagged and unwieldy to be processed; and, like a piece of silk shoved in the washing machine, it turns out very badly.

Orgasm machines: women and a brave new (hypersexual) world

'We have this thing that's been superimposed on female sexuality, basically this orgasm-hunting tiger.'

What makes Lucy cry and Lisa close her eyes during sex is alienating detachment – the loneliness of an exposed female body being pounded by a male one. But this purely anatomic, male-orgasm-driving experience of sex sits very neatly with contemporary depictions of the act. Take *London Amora*, the European touring show that parked for a year in Piccadilly Circus, excitedly billed as 'the world's first attraction about relationships, seduction and wellness'. Its goal: 'to make your world a sexier place'. This means more orgasms for women as well as men, of course. To look at the *Amora* website was to be confronted with numbers, exclamation marks, commands and bright colours. 'Ten secrets women wished you knew'; 'The silent clue men give off when they're in love'; '250 tips and hints for a healthy sex life and wellbeing', PLUS aphrodisiac lounge, Amora boutique, How-To workshops and – wait for it! – 'Over 80 interactive and engaging experiences to enhance relationships and spice up your love life'. Yet there was something bordering on the depressing about the erogenous zones finder; the squeezing of various-sized dildos and designing your perfect partner on an interactive screen. Katherine Angel, a historian of sexual science at Exeter University observed in *Prospect* magazine that Amora was governed by the porn aesthetic; proof of how far pornography and everyday ideas of the erotic now overlap. Noting the predictable presence of numerous 'ecstatic' female bodies (far more than male), Angel concluded that the exhibit was 'yet another' place that invited women to self-scrutinise their bodies and sexual performance according to an ideal.

Along with linking images of hot female bodies with sexual ecstasy, *Amora* drives home the point that one orgasm isn't enough to satisfy your average lusty woman. This is the general message on the airwaves. For example, CAKE (cakenyc), an 'internationally recognised brand promoting female sexual pleasure', is all about the new hypersexual woman. Reads the website: 'In September of 2000, CAKE hosted the first of what would become the infamous CAKE parties at club FUN, under the Manhattan Bridge. Billed as a Porn Party, the hosts showed clips of explicit videos edited together and displayed on floor to ceiling screens.'

Yet the pressure to be an orgasm machine has reached what Melissa Goldman, the maker of a documentary called *Subjectified: Nine Young Women Talk About Sex*, calls 'hysteria'. In the US, she says, 'it's got so bad that women think they have a pathology if they can't orgasm through penetration. We have this thing – this Samantha from *SATC* thing – that's been superimposed on female sexuality, basically this orgasm-hunting tiger.' Indeed: the pressure exerted by contemporary ideas of sexiness, sex, and sexual pleasure as a measure of personal success exerts a hard, cold pressure on women. And nobody feels it more than the single woman, who is most open to accusations of not being sexy or attractive enough – if she was, wouldn't she have a partner?

By refusing no-strings sex for a while, we might avoid Greer's proclamation that 'Sex for many has become a sorry business, a mechanical release involving neither discovery nor triumph, stressing human isolation more dishearteningly than ever before.' We might also avoid the following image of the man who 'politely lets himself into the vagina … laborious and inhumanly computerized'. Indeed, Greer speaks to the daters of 2012 with important prescience: 'The implication that there is a statistically ideal fuck which will always result in satisfaction if the right procedures are followed is depressing and misleading. There is no substitute for excitement: not all the massage in the world will ensure satisfaction, for it is a matter of psychosexual release. Real gratification is not enshrined in a tiny cluster of nerves but in the sexual involvement of the whole person.' Amen.

Giving up NSA sex: actually doing it (well, not doing it …)

A lot has been covered in this chapter. Hopefully you found some of it useful/interesting for adding context to the way you (or your friends) operate. I for one find it very helpful to see where I got some of my strongest and least helpful notions about sex. Having some idea of where I fit into the sexual culture around me enables me to challenge these notions more directly.

I am aware that some of you reading this chapter will be saying to yourselves: all this NSA sex sounds great – at least it's sex! For those of you in, or familiar with, an interminable drought, I feel your pain. I've been there many times, and have ridden out barren stretches with a mixture of anger, frustration, acceptance and 'get-it-where-you-can' promiscuity, followed by remorse.

To the drought lady: putting this rule into play will improve your state of mind too. I promise. Here are some pointers to get you going, as it were.

1. Recognise your state of mind

Are you feeling like you'll never meet someone, that nobody ever fancies you, and that you may well be re-virginising? If so, be extra careful because right now you're most prone to self-destructive sexual behaviour. It's been at my most 'dry' that I've been taken in by the false promise of sexual servitude, thinking 'at least it's sex'. But that idea proves misleading when you feel not only left by the wayside afterwards, but tarnished by having sex with someone ranging from the unavailable to the disinterested to the downright awful. That's if you do have sex with them. You can equally get drunk and try – and fail, even when you've relaxed your standards, which is awful too.

2. Challenge the belief 'At least it's sex'

Thinking that you better take it because, like money, you should grab as much of it as possible, is a surprisingly common belief. When I went on the Man Diet, I was fully on board with it – that is, taking far too seriously my 'job' as a single woman to be wild, crazy and report lots of great stories. Dry patches tortured me.

I was genuinely happy to be uncommitted – I'd recently come out of a relationship, and my personality had gone a bit wonky under the strain of being a 'cool' (i.e., permissive, generous, not-needy, relaxed) girlfriend. But I assumed that the alternative to 'I'm not ready for a relationship' was 'I am going to get out there and bed as many people as possible' and 'if I'm not seeing someone or some people, I'm wasting valuable time as a young, single woman, panic, panic, what is wrong with me'. Stopping, staying still, and allowing the borders of myself to extend to other spheres than my sexuality was balm to my soul.

3. Gotta be cruel to be kind: go cold turkey

If there's a lot of NSA on offer, just stop it abruptly. Turn them down, defriend them on Facebook, block their number. (I did a lot of the Facebook defriending to prevent sudden chat popping up, taking me where I didn't want to go.) After that cruelty, kindness dawns fast: as soon as I brutally sloughed the NSA types out, I felt clean, clear and energised, and acutely aware that I'd been dragging myself down before. Relationship counsellor Val Sampson says:

> 'It's not that being Victorian prim gives you high self-esteem. But sleeping with the guy that doesn't want to go on a date, or who doesn't find you particularly interesting as a person, is bad for self-esteem.'

4. Extract yourself from a friend

This is a different story from getting rid of the one-, two- or five-night-stand guy. Certainly you two will have a deeper or different intimacy than with someone you don't know. You may well be in love with him. It's the hardest thing in the world to pull away because so much is mixed up in it. But the bottom line still applies: he's getting the milk without the cow and sees no need to change that fact. So, if you can summon all your strength, you just need to come clean. It shouldn't be hard. He'll run a mile – thereby making the job easy for you – if you say: 'Next time you initiate something, I'll assume it's because you want to date.' Or if it's you who booty calls him, make it plain you're going to want more – and he'll probably stop encouraging or even allowing your late-night visits.

5. Think about what you want

Women seeking a serious relationship need the sex (or sex-on-mind) hiatus time for gathering thoughts about the correct approach going forward. Janet Reibstein believes one of the biggest issues facing women who self-define as being non-committal, or who proceed by default with no-strings sex, is habit that will stitch them up later. 'If you want children, we don't have the freedom to put things off the way men do,' she says. 'Women have to be more honest with themselves about what kind of relationships they're getting themselves into – if you're saying "this is NSA" and you're 28, and you're still doing it at 30, and that's the modal way you're doing your relationships, you're dwindling your chances of meeting someone to reproduce within a committed relationship.'

I'm not sure about children yet. But I take to heart something else Reibstein says: 'Until you figure out your own terms, you are likely to be pleasing the man on his own terms.' This part of the Man Diet is there to help us figure out those terms, which is no easy task in a (still predominantly) male value society. But giving yourself time off the biting, stinging sex jungle is the best way to start.

How I followed this rule:

Pre-Man Diet

I had no 'say no to NSA' policy in place at all. I knew it didn't make me particularly happy, but I thought it was an essential part of my single-woman persona – that of the liberal, adventurous, sexual singleton. My romps made for great stories but too often they smacked of adventure for adventure's sake. This, I think, is because my view on sex was: 'Why not?' rather than 'Why?'

How I did it

All I did was think about it more. I reflected on the simple idea that going through the motions – albeit often pleasurably, or at least excitingly – wasn't really how sex was meant to be. That disconnecting real intimacy from physical intimacy probably wasn't the best I could do. It's amazing how much just thinking can achieve – in merely reflecting on this topic I began to be far more choosy. Not because I was depriving myself of anything – just because I stopped feeling like having such a simplistic approach to sex, since I am not a simple person. Nor are you.

The other thing that kept and still keeps me in check is this question: 'Do I want to be exhausted tomorrow?' Let's be honest – NSA sex often involves unplanned sleepovers with next to no sleep involved. On weeknights they're lethal. On weekends, pretty sad if you had any plans to do things the next day.

Specifically, if a guy came along and it was on the cards, I would …

🧍 Just leave. If he wanted my number, great. If not – had I lost anything? Probably not, apart from a notch.

🧍 If something was happening, like a smooch, I'd just extricate myself. 'It's getting late' or 'I need to take the Tube'.

🧍 I considered very carefully how I wanted to feel the next day. Usually, the desire to be alert and well rather than wrecked and pointlessly buzzed triumphed.

How it felt

Good. Very good in fact. I felt in control, and very clearly that I was respecting myself. And, banal as it sounds, I also felt smug at saving myself a lot of trouble (attachment to guys who were far from appropriate; potential worries over STDs and so on). Did I feel deprived of lots of wild no-strings sex? Not for a good while. Which brings me to …

What I let through the cracks

I find going for very long periods without any physical intimacy rather tricky – many women do. And so, every now and then, I let situations take their course – or even, in (usually intoxicated) extremis create the situations. I'm not sure I feel better after, but I feel different. It shifts my energy. But allowing for NSA is a last resort.

And now?

I try not to partake in NSA sex. It seems unsatisfying. And upsetting in subtle ways if it goes nowhere or is with someone below par. I used to call this kind of thing 'fun' – now I'm more careful with my definition of fun. When desire for something to happen takes over, I go into it with eyes wide open, but even being realistic doesn't necessarily help – a little part of you always either wants sex to be meaningful or thinks it will go somewhere.

SOS!

If you've had one NSA sex experience after an empowered run of dieting, you're either feeling a) sated or b) remarkably shitty. Well, take hope from the fact that if it's the first, you were able to enjoy it exactly because of a period of declining it (the Man Diet) and your strength and self-esteem has risen. If b) you now know you're not missing anything even remotely great by saying no to NSA sex and you're very much on the right track with this rule. Here's what else:

- Don't beat yourself up about it. You haven't done anything wrong – you've just given yourself a bit of short shrift. You will either be feeling a naturally negative reaction, which is punishment enough – or you'll be moving on with your life. Do the latter, but don't think, 'That didn't fuck me up, I'm going to do it all the time!' Because that would be a pointless back step. And a sure-fire way to feel fucked up (possibly again, depending on your past).
- If you feel post-sex strings, acknowledge them to your heart's content but there's no point making the whole thing worse by prostrating yourself at the man's feet. If it was NSA going into it, it was almost certainly NSA to him and will remain so.

♟ If, by chance, the no-strings part of the sex came with heavy boozing and lax protection, don't brush it under the carpet. Go along to the clinic in three months (the HIV incubation period – yes, sex can have a long afterlife), and make sure you're good to go.

Rule Number  2

Cut Down on the Booze

You need this rule if …

- Once you start, you can't stop.
- The bulk of your sexual encounters as a single woman follow excessive drinking.
- You can't imagine not drinking on a date.
- You worry about being boring when sober.
- You think you only come alive sexually after a bottle.
- You frequently do things with men when inebriated that you later regret.
- Your big nights out involve necessary consumption of ten times the government's recommended weekly number of units.
- Your hangovers trouble you far more than 'my head hurts'.
- You worry that your boozing is affecting your overall health and mental alertness.

Goes well with …

- Refuse to Have NSA Sex
- Dwell on Your Sense of Self
- Do Something Lofty
- Do Not Pursue
- Know Your Obstacles

S arah's alarm went off. She couldn't bear the task in hand: getting up and going to work. She prolonged the agony of getting out of bed by trying to decide what was most horrible about her current situation. Was it her physical state – pounding heart, vile aftertaste of red wine sharpened with gin from the G&Ts she'd thought were a good nightcap, inflamed eye sockets and sharp head pain? Or was it the inevitable mental distress that would descend when events from the night before came creeping back?

Her eyes are still closed, her alarm still beeping. Sarah's normally a cheerful, emotionally stable woman. But when she wakes up like this, which she does no more than any of her friends or the other millions of women in the UK who occasionally binge drink, she's not cheerful, or even okay. She feels an intense horror at herself; dread at what she might have done. Or has done. She pictures a massive black well out of which she must pull herself in order to regain her hold on life.

What happened the night before ...

In this case, what Sarah had done wasn't particularly bad, but it was the fact that she'd been making a habit of it. The night before had started out as work drinks; some lawyer contacts had hired a space at a bar for a group of her colleagues. A bottle of wine per person was already waiting for them on the table, along with some nibbles. It went fairly rapidly; and suddenly it was closing time. Feeling a naughty pulse rise in her – the desire to make some kind of trouble for herself involving men – she decided to see what she could rustle up. She wanted sex; she felt reckless, wild, her romantic dissatisfaction and fragile ego about to be pummelled under a wave of alcoholic courage.

It was a multi-pronged attack: first, she dispatched a few texts to men she'd either had something with before, or thought she could have something with now. She didn't like any of them enough to see them when sober. Then, she started homing in on the seemingly interesting candidates that were out with her. Keeping up this dual-pronged attack, she eventually made headway. None of her textees replied – something that bothered her but that she could deal with in the morning. But thank God, one of the guys that turned up at the after-hours place they went on to seemed up for it. As soon as he showed unmistakeable interest, she suggested they go back to hers.

What happened when they got back hadn't been all that great; it was certainly not the intoxicating orgasm fest suggested in some representations of unfettered, big-city casual sex. Rather, it had been made plain how little regard they had for each other, and while Sarah enjoyed faking intimacy, the guy didn't have the slightest inclination to do so. He banged her (two seconds before condom; 20 minutes post-condom), he came, he suggested anal, she said no, they napped for an hour, and then he said, 'Shit, I have to go', got his stuff and left, only just remembering on his way out to ask for her number. It was just a vague politeness reflex; anyone could see that.

Now she felt horror – why did she always have that impulse to take someone home with her when drunk, even though she was too old for these completely unrewarding encounters? Why did she give herself to some random who couldn't even pretend to be polite in bed? And, worst of all, what of those seconds of sex before the condom went on? Was she willing to even risk her health when drunk? And for what? Through the cloudy pain of these reflections, she haltingly pulled on her clothes and made it to the Tube without being sick. The day was not pretty.

The regret had largely faded by night, though, and the next day she was ready to go again, the dark hole of the previous morning forgotten, and the sex of the night before already related to her friends as a highly amusing story.

It was Saturday night, and Sarah and her flatmate Lynn had a birthday party to attend. They got ready to the sound of their favourite tune, also Lynn's BlackBerry ring tone: Jamie Foxx featuring T-Pain's 'Blame It [on the Alcohol]'.

Flash forward to midnight. Lynn's snogging a good-looking guy. Sarah has drunk more than she should have, though less than the other night, and is now in guy-searching mode. Nobody bites, though, and she's starting to feel like she has no vibe. When a cutie hoves into view and offers to get her another drink, she gratefully accepts, even though she doesn't really feel like it. But in the presence of her potential ticket out of here tonight, she sucks the double Absolut through a straw and makes flirtatious conversation. She excuses herself to go to the bathroom, and when she comes back, the guy's gone. She looks for him everywhere, but can't find him. Now her buzz is gone, she's drunk, and she's got nobody. She starts talking to other guys, but it's a no-go. Eventually she gets a cab home – it's 3.30am and Lynn has gone off with that guy she's been wrapped around for the last three hours.

The next day's hangover is both better and worse than the one before. It's worse in that, when the pain of it dries up, she's got nothing concrete to show for it. No hook-ups. She feels like a failure of a single girl; she's meant to be able to hook up whenever she wants when out on the razz, and last night was a reminder that she clearly can't. But the hangover's better in that she's woken up guilt- and loathing-free, hasn't put herself at risk in the sack or given her body to someone undeserving. Oh, and crucially, she doesn't have to go to work. Still, her body is in a bad way and the calories she consumed last night were ungodly. She'll have to write off the day.

So I say ...

Take a break from the booze. Giving your body a rest – and showing it some love – will give you a fresh perspective.

The single woman and her tumultuous love affair with booze

This is not an unusual or crazy snapshot in the life of a single, fun-loving woman. It's not typical, perhaps, but it's a scenario that most British women aged 18–35 will relate to.

When researching this book, I asked women in their twenties and thirties if they drink more when single. Here's what they said:

> *'Defo, drank a hell of a lot more when I was single.'*
> **Naihala, 34**

> *'Yes, definitely – I got wasted all the time, it was the only way to get over my shyness with men. I lacked confidence and was massively body shy. So needed to be pretty out of it to disrobe.'* **Laura, 35**

> *'Definitely. And there's a lot of alcohol consumption when you've just started seeing someone – you know, lots of going out, getting pissed, eating crap, staying out late.'*
> **Laura, 32**

Another woman, a good friend of mine called Mary, frequently blacks out when drunk. 'I have missed lots from blacking out – I don't remember meeting half the people I've dated; and sometimes I'll wake up next to someone and not remember how we ended up in bed.' She's no basket case; Mary is a successful, grounded person who does not have an alcohol problem – it's just that a few drinks, even as few as three, can make her forget what happens to her. But instead of being terrified by the experience and its implications, she just accepts that it happens on big nights out. Such is the single woman's cross to bear.

Rising alcohol consumption among women is a horn that is tooted with great insistence by the media, and rightly so: the numbers suggest that we're the fastest growing demographic of boozers in the UK, with the image of the hard-partying single gal right up there. After all, women aged between 18 and 24 in the UK drink more than in any European country (Datamonitor, 2005). Across the pond, CBS news in the US did a shock-horror '*Sex and the City* syndrome' story, inspired by a rise in DUI (driving under the influence) accidents among young women. They worried about the 'girls' nights out and those pink drinks' *SATC* popularised. And well they should.

Reality check: do we really need to give up the booze?

This Man Diet rule is not about lecturing and tut-tutting; it's about giving you a respite from habits that might be dragging you down. Alcohol is not a simple topic – i.e., 'bad for you' – and it plays an enormous, complex role in most of our lives. Kate Spicer, a journalist, wrote a courageous 'life's too short not to drink up' piece for *The Sunday Times*. In it, she confessed to ticking a good handful of what the government might call 'alcoholic' boxes, but argued that when used appropriately, excess alcohol can be a source of pleasure and relaxation without necessary punishment. It's not alcohol that creates a mess, she concludes; it's people.

Spicer's view is appealing, and there's no chance I'll be giving up social drinking and occasional drunkenness for government-guideline-style imbibing any time soon. But when the single woman – under pressure to have more fun than everyone else (see NSA and No Talking chapters) – ends up in a run of alcohol-fuelled promiscuity followed by self-loathing hangovers, it's time to take a breather. In the same *Sunday Times* feature, I felt that student Ruth

Gilligan more accurately captured the mania of acquiring the experience, stories and gossip that alcohol often facilitates. She describes the experience of sitting in her college room, whilst next door, thumping music starts up, heralding the arrival of the girls invited over by the lads in the house. She listens as the word 'stawpedo' is bellowed en masse, then sighs with relief when the music stops – the group have headed out into the night. It's only Part One of the evening, though: she's certain at least three of the girls will be back later and that a sizzling stew of gossip will be ripe for the stirring in the morning.

Every woman has a pronounced relationship with alcohol. Some get trashed on weekends; others like a glass or a bottle of wine of an evening. Some use it as a massive social crutch, and morph from shy wallflowers into sexual predators on a few wines. Some women use it to show they're as hard/good/fun/wild as their male peers. Others don't get what the fuss is about – and get snippy when asked questions like, 'Do you binge drink?' Still others don't drink at all and face relentless social pressure to do so. Many of us worry a huge deal that we drink too much but make little attempt to cut down.

Clearly, women's relationship with alcohol is more complex than the oft-alarm-bell-ringing *Daily Mail* would have it – yes we drink too much but we're not all bingeing terrors of the night, constantly in hospital having our stomachs pumped. This complexity also applies to the connection between boozing and unwise sexual behaviour. As a Man Dieter, the concern is to minimise the psychological effects of uncomfortable run-ins with men – which chip away at self-esteem, as per Sarah's really rough mornings described above. So when I advise laying off the booze for a bit, I'm hoping for a double-pronged attack on:

a) low-quality sex with a low-quality person in a low-quality environment
b) the vile, self-attacking hangover, which is bad enough once in a while, but over time makes you feel really out of control and thus rotten overall

I maintain, once more, that the single woman is more prone to the stabbings of regret and self-loathing than the one who wakes up hungover next to her boyfriend, regardless of what she's done the night before.

'Does getting drunk actually make us prostrate ourselves unwisely on the loins of any available man?'

So what exactly is the link between drinking and the ensuing horror at what seemed perfectly reasonable the night before? Does getting drunk actually make us prostrate ourselves unwisely on the loins of any available man? Possibly. One study found alcohol use to be a stronger predictor of 'engaging in hooking up' for women than men, possibly because women feel pressure *not* to hook up due to societal constraints, so alcohol makes it easier to lower the barrier (Owen, Fincham & Moore, 2011). But the connection between booze and sex is, predictably, a more complex one for women than men.

Does booze turn you on?

In one study, published in the academic journal *Archives of Sexual Behavior*, it appeared that booze does not in itself make women more horny or aroused. It's just that we *think* it does. A 2011 survey got 44 men and women to watch erotic/neutral films while consuming either alcohol or juice. After drinking alcohol, more sexual arousal was reported even when watching neutral films than with no alcohol. However, women's genital response didn't increase with greater amounts of alcohol consumed. So, it looks like *perceived* sexual arousal increases even if actual arousal (that is, genital sexual arousal that was measured by a device) doesn't change. The researchers found that the best predictor of post-drinking sex was the intention to have sex before you went out.

Another theory of sex and booze linkage sounds more familiar. This is that it's the effects of booze that *causes* us to take sexual risks we wouldn't otherwise take – be it unprotected sex or sex with someone dodgy, or sex that is likely to have a negative emotional impact. This one is about the cues you respond to or ignore when pissed: according to the pleasingly named cognitive theory 'alcohol myopia', alcohol has a disinhibiting effect because it makes you less able to process information. Cues that instigate sexual behaviour continue to get processed, while more complex ones that would normally cause you to think twice get side-lined. The drunk brain can't deal with both and chooses the simpler path.

Here's a typical drunken 'horror' story from a friend of mine that illustrates this point:

Chloe, 28, had been sleeping with a man every weekend while single and had been using a dating website too. One night we were at a friend's house party together and she was getting nice and pissed. There were no good male options there, so she started rifling through the guys on the dating website on her phone, finding one, Mark, who happened to be online at 11.30pm on a Saturday night. She summoned him to the party – he clearly worked out but also pulled his trousers up way too far and fastened them with a pernickety little belt. He was balding. He was loud. He was ... not ideal. By now reeling from her numerous vodkas, Chloe and Mark headed out into the back garden where they appeared to be doing a mixture of feeling each other up and arguing. Suddenly they were gone.

Chloe told me the next day that she'd taken him home with her only to find out, just as she was sobering up, that he was a complete sex fiend (not in a good way) who wanted to re-enact degradation porn scenes and began addressing her as 'bitch' as soon as they got near her bedroom. After he pushed her head down for a blow job, she ordered him out. At first he refused – then she got violent with him and he left. She didn't tell me all those details that day – she was so horrified by the experience that it wasn't for another two or three weeks that she actually came clean about it. That was the last time she went online drunk – and the last time she went out of her way for sex.

From sober to sex kitten: drinking till we're drunk

'On a big night out I always end up going for it in some way or another, even if I secretly want a quiet one. It's just the format.' **Jane, 31**

We act crazier and more sexually regrettably when we're drunk because that's the expectation – that's the image. A classic study found that post-drinking behaviour is driven by pre-drinking beliefs 'in the manner of a self-fulfilling prophecy' (*Journal of Drug Issues*). The idea of the self-fulfilling prophecy hits home. After all, how many times have you headed out on a 'big night out' and not at least made a good attempt at acting like someone on a 'big night out'? When you're 'larging' it, you can't very well 'small it' at the last minute without being a party pooper.

The expectation to act like you're drunk is a double-edged sword. Not only do women expect themselves to be more sexually up-for-it, but men expect us to be so when we've been drinking. 'Drinking women are perceived by men as being more sexually available, and coerced sex with a drinking woman is less likely to be viewed as rape,' said Maria Testa and R. Lorraine Collins in a 1997 survey. These perceptions, say the authors, lead to women being fed more booze by sexually hopeful men. But they also make us feel like we have less of a right to say no to sex because we're aware of the impression we've given by drinking heavily. In short, we're afraid of appearing to be teases.

More evidence suggests that boozing makes us *seem* like wanton sex machines even if, as per the study carried out by Prause, Staley & Finn, we're not actually more aroused. Other studies have found that when we drink more we're significantly more aggressive and ready to engage in foreplay. It's also interesting – though hardly surprising – that perceptions of female sexual disinhibition were significantly enhanced if the man bought her the drinks. *Working with Substance Misusers: a guide to theory and practice*, a compilation of essays from experts, argues that 'alcohol does not "make" you behave in a way that is alien. However, it is certainly the case that alcohol is often used as an excuse for inappropriate behaviour.' In other words, the blame – contrary to what Jamie Foxx and T-Pain say in their anthem 'Blame It' – is on us, not the alcohol.

Beer goggles: fact or fiction?

Fact. One thing that studies show for certain is that the more you drink, the better looking people of the opposite gender appear, but you don't need me to tell you that. What is interesting is that despite being studied, 'the mechanism [that makes us find people more attractive when drunk] remains unclear'. One possibility suggested by other experts is that being trashed makes it hard to assess facial symmetry and other attractiveness cues. Other studies suggest that as the night wears on, people look more frantically to find someone to go home with, thus lowering their standards. The role of 'beer goggles' is obvious in the regret-causing antics we get up to when drunk, but whether we fall under their sway because we literally can't see properly, or because of a more complex cocktail of factors involving suppressed needs and desires for intimacy (my money's on this), has not been determined yet by our friends in social science.

Not everyone, of course, puts on beer goggles or, once bespectacled, heeds their blurry commands. I've often wondered at how some people are no more sexually assertive when drunk than when sober (sometimes less), while others go absolutely ballistic and throw themselves at anything that moves after a few. Sensation-seekers are more likely to engage in 'risky sexual behaviour' when drunk, a finding that sheds welcome light on the way in which we morph from one person to another when intoxicated. Those with sensation-seeking traits prefer to lose 'all inhibition' when drunk, rather than have 'good conversation' in 'quiet groups'. According to *The Indian Journal of Medical Research*, they tend to fall into the categories of 'thrill and adventure seeking', 'experience seeking', 'disinhibition' and 'boredom susceptibility'. So if you're bored easily and love the thrill of new intense experiences, or even obliteration, you might be more prone to shagging the wrong man when drunk.

Regret and the morning after blues

Women are universally acknowledged to be physically harder hit than men by alcohol consumption. But guess what? Booze makes us more depressed than men, too – or at least, studies have found that there is a stronger link between binge drinking and depression in women than in men.

If it's more likely to be a downer for us on the night, it's almost certainly more painful the day after. First of all, women are more prone to regret than men – as psychotherapist Ricky Emanuel says (see the NSA rule), we engage in masochistic behaviour, such as looking at pictures of ex-boyfriends on Facebook, more often because of the way we internalise our anxiety. As for regrets, women are more than twice as likely as men to have regrets about their romantic life, according to researchers at Northwestern University.

But no amount of research can capture – or indeed is needed to capture – that uniquely self-loathing pit that women fall into the morning after a heavy boozathon, particularly when something sexually unwise has happened. Men tend to be more jovial or better at denial. A paper called '"Every time I do it I absolutely annihilate myself": Loss of (self-)consciousness and loss of memory in young people's drinking narratives' studied the ways in which young men and women tell stories of their blackouts and other drunken antics. The women were reluctant to discuss them and seemed to have more anxiety related to the memories ('Young women struggled to manage the spectre of sexual assault, shame and the loss of respectable femininity associated with getting very drunk and passing out'); whereas the men's stories 'were more straightforward tales of ritualised "determined drunkenness"'.

Martha, 26, knows all too well that stomach-churning feeling of self-loathing after a heavy binge drinking session ...

She had headed out into the night with a huge crush on a French guy she'd met at a wedding recently. She was off to meet her girlfriends from work at a City bar. Four glasses of wine later, she saw a guy across the bar that she swore was her hot French crush. She swayed over to him with a big 'Hiiii!' It wasn't him, but there was something about his mouth that reminded her of him, and she stuck around, coming on strong. Maybe this guy was a long lost brother. Meanwhile, her friends kept coming over and saying something to her, annoyingly interrupting every five seconds. She kept ignoring them. Another glass, and she invited him back to her house. She doesn't remember much else. She woke up the next day, looked next to her and saw that she'd bedded her best work friend's ex-boyfriend. It was the worst move of her professional and social life, ever.

Boozing and shame

Female reticence about their drunken behaviour – which often has a sexual element lurking – is reflected in literature, too. There are countless brilliant passages of male hangovers, described (of course) by men: Kingsley and Martin Amis excel in this area (Kingsley's *Lucky Jim* and Amis's *Money* in particular); Patrick Hamilton's noirish *Hangover Square* is oozing alcoholic fumes (alcohol, sex and manipulation are stitched together), Malcolm Lowry's *Under the Volcano* is an iconic depiction of an alcoholic British Consul in Mexico. But apart from *Bridget Jones's Diary*, when it comes to women – and we've been liberal and open in our alcohol consumption since the 1970s – it's hard to find anything published at all. Or perhaps we're not so open: it's still the case that female alcoholics tend to be closeted, whereas the image of the male drunk is a totally banal, public one. Clearly, despite our hurtling into formerly male domains, there is still a tension between what women are 'doing like men' and how they are allowed to do it. Booze is a prime example.

(Drunk) woman seeking man: the badness of the drunken pursuit

I do find it odd that there isn't a classic tome about the trials of the female drinker in the modern urban setting – after all, as the media makes it abundantly clear, women's relationship to alcohol is one of the big stories of our time. And heavy drinking is great fodder not just because of the damage it does, but because of its psychological potency. For the truth is, there's more we can do when drunk that either puts us in danger or in a more disadvantageous position than men.

The drunken text

Pursuing or making clear your sexual intentions is not the 'fair play' behaviour it is for men. For my last book, *What the Hell Is He Thinking?*, I interviewed lots of men about what puts them on or off women. The main turn-off for men was a woman who seemed too keen – i.e., who pursued him or made herself clearly available. One guy gave the example of a woman he'd been out with a few times. Between dates two and three, she'd drunkenly texted him, saying she would come find him as she was horny and wanted a piece – not quite in those words, but not far off. Not only was he not available, he was utterly put off.

The agony of it is that it shouldn't be like that, but it is, and we know it. We know that if we've drunk texted, we've transgressed one of the biggest social rules governing gender relations. Proclaims The Frisky, a blog: 'Once Again Ladies, Drunk Dialling Is Strictly Forbidden' versus 'A Man's Guide to Drunk Texting' on www.sloshspot.com, which provides dudes with gems such as 'Text an ex when you find out she has recently become single' and 'Text with persistence'. We sort of know at the time that drunk texting can't end well – either it'll be a booty call of which we weren't in full control (and that the guy only accepted because we were totally available), or it'll come back as a rejection.

> 'I can't help it. When I get drunk I just have to find a man to hook up with; I feel like I'll do absolutely anything, it's my top priority and I block out the consequences. If nobody around me looks likely, I start on my phone book, usually with the last guy I hooked up with, whether we've been in touch since or not. I don't mind having a laugh with him the next morning if I've stayed over, but if you get ignored, it leaves you feeling like a complete loser.' **Mary, 32**

Even if you do hook up, if it's a drink-fuelled booty call don't start expecting anything more than a no-strings romp. Boozing and strings-free sex have merged and to expect more is simply not realistic – as Kathleen A. Bogle, a sociology and criminal justice professor at La Salle University says, 'Alcohol culture and dating culture have collided to form a hook-up culture.'

There's something much more dangerous about being the drunken sexual aggressor if you're a woman: the rejections still hurt like hell and leave a nasty imprint of humiliation the next day. If you're not rejected, you stand a bigger chance of having unsafe sex – when you're pursuing any Tom, Dick or Harry in your intoxicated late-night search, you could very well end up with a real prick. The debate about whether or not women should pursue men (obviously, we *should* be able to) rages on between the social theorists, biologists and psychologists. (For more on this, see Chapter Seven, *Do Not Pursue.*) Is it sexist society, cowardly men, or the risk aversion hardwiring in female brains that determines the norm? Probably a bit of all three – but the fact is, if you're going to admirably break the rules about pursuit, do it when you're sober and thoughtfully aware of the risk of rejection. Drunken pursuit of men, with the attendant ignominious rejection, just spells horror. In Kanye West's 'Drunk and Hot Girls', Mr West describes the tiresome antics of the drunk (but hot) girl in a club, then says he ends up with her. He doesn't sound overly thrilled about her continued presence in his life. Let his weird but quite catchy song serve as a reminder that dodgy things can come of being drunk and hot, or even just drunk and horny.

Booze and dating

The single woman often has a more involved relationship with alcohol than her relationship-bound peer, and it's not just because she wants to be wild and fun, or because she has more energy to spend on going out and getting twatted. Much of it, of course, is to do with dating.

I had coffee with the folks from Match.com recently, and asked them what the biggest difference is between American dating and British dating; and the answer was, in a word: booze. Americans can handle a coffee date; our top choice of venue for a date is the pub.

'It is all too easy to rely on alcohol to buoy you through the first date,' writes dating blogger Abi Millar. 'Nerves beforehand? Quell them with a quick tipple. Conversationally inhibited? Oil yourself up with a bevy. Date turns out to look like David Gest as imagined by Picasso after a particularly rough weekend? Buy yourself a double – and get her one too, the poor lady. Booze razes a potential social minefield into a lovely, hazy butterfly field of woozy, lurching delusion. And of course, it's pretty much obligatory if you're thinking of pouncing on your date.'

I can't remember one date in the history of my single life that hasn't involved a couple of drinks; nor can I recall one instance of having a 'crazy' story to tell that didn't arise from boozing too much. Funnily enough, the only date that didn't involve booze was the first one I had with my ex-boyfriend. Following our sober stroll around Hampstead Heath (at my request; imagine how delicate I was feeling to have requested a walk), we went out for a year and a half.*

It doesn't take rocket (or even social) science to explain why we drink more when we go on dates. Meeting someone new – particularly someone who you may snog or more at the end of the night – is socially stressful. Not knowing someone can make relaxed conversation a challenge, so awkwardness is always around the corner. When we feel awkward, we act weirdly. Weird behaviour kills chemistry. I used to keep a little airplane-sized bottle of vodka in my handbag to swig on the Tube en route to a particularly menacing date (i.e., with someone suspiciously good looking but potentially dim) – and it usually softened the initial blow (as well as making me feel like a proper drunk).

But dating in the UK is so shrouded in booze that making the choice not to drink when you're out meeting people

* We met, however, at a house party via a lot of alcohol.

becomes a massive act of will. Most speed-dating events revolve around alcohol. Sue Ostler, a relationships guru and author of *Relationships that Rock!*, runs her Flirt Diva seminars (including Bag a Boyfriend) via a website called vodkaandchocolate.com. Wine-tasting is a popular format; I went to an event by a company called Grapevine Social which offered singles five cocktails over the course of the evening, with the goal of getting people sufficiently wasted to bump and grind on the dance floor. Lovestruck, an urban dating service, sends out weekly emails about singles' evenings. Rejoicing in the fun-potential of one of its favoured event venues, the email says: 'Even better news is that their Happy Hour runs from 5–7pm – 30 per cent off all drinks!'

Boozing and mating are completely inextricable in the UK. But it's worth detaching them so you can see what lurks there. Whether it's fear of boredom; the desire to perform a mental light-dimming to make hooking up less intense, or the inability to relax and feel sexy sans booze, that relationship deserves some exploration. After all, at this stage in the game of life, you definitely want to build up the confidence to know you can dazzle unassisted by three vodka tonics. But can you? Take a social risk and treat yourself to the answer. If you and a guy like each other even with you on the San Pellegrino, the second date looks very promising. As a good friend put it to me when we both decided to try a night out without drinking (and did so successfully): 'If you can pull on water, that's the real compliment.'

Cutting down on booze: actually doing it

Swearing off the booze entirely is probably too much to ask. This isn't a physical weight-loss book, after all, nor a crash course in martyrdom – I once went for three weeks sans a single drop because I was doing Phase One of the Atkins diet. And another week I didn't drink because I was on antibiotics. Those weeks had their upsides, but they were hard.

The week off because of antibiotics (prior to the Atkins period) struck me as so outlandish that I pitched it as a diary feature to *The Times* and it ran in *Times2* with a billing on the front page. It was basically: 'Young woman goes a week without alcohol.' During the week, I'd noticed myself being more anxious about pleasing my social partners; I knew I was letting them down by not ordering a wine, so I'd work overtime to be witty on the Diet Cokes. That I felt such pressure is clearly not to be applauded; but it's a feeling many will relate to.

And the options for drinking seem only to expand – Mondays are the new Thursdays (there has been a massive upswing in the amount of corporate parties being held on Mondays; perhaps because venues are cheaper and people think a Tuesday hangover is a good way to start the week). Thursdays have been the new Fridays for quite some time, but the thing is, Fridays are still the old Fridays and Saturdays still Saturdays. Saying no to some of this is possible – you can make rules fairly easily about Monday and Tuesday – but saying no to all of it is a major undertaking and abstinence is not the point of the Man Diet.

Personally, I had to think hard about this rule, deciding where to draw the line between being realistic and being soft on myself. Even though I really enjoyed waking up clear headed every morning, the antibiotics and Atkins weeks were a strain, and not realistic.

I'm out most nights with friends. I can say no to work-related bashes easy peasy, and the mountain of untouched drink in my flat is impressive. But when I meet my friends – whether for a play, meal, or night out – alcohol will generally be ordered and enjoyed. Swearing off booze entirely would be to feel like I was missing something fundamental in my nightly social gatherings. So I earmarked Sunday–Tuesday as mostly booze free, and let myself have what I wanted on other nights, within reason. Of course, it was the nights out on weekends that were hardest and most important for the Man Diet – but I found that if I really listened to myself, I reached a natural limit *before* being too horribly drunk, and breaking Man Diet rules. Of course I sometimes forgot to listen to myself, and instead listened to everyone saying: 'Another round! What do you want?' Balancing social life, genuine enjoyment of many alcoholic beverages and living in booze-addled culture with healthy restraint is an ongoing battle for me. Thus I offer you these three guidelines:

1. Unless it comes naturally, don't swear off all booze. But take a serious, serious look at how much you drink and when. If it's been months since you've had a night off, do two nights of complete abstinence. You'll feel brilliant – and it'll give you a refresher course in declining booze, which is a handy skill (most of us have done it at some point; from the January abstinence crowd to the antibiotics-takers; but one forgets so easily …).

2. Set personal challenges – if you think you or other people are only interesting when you've had a few, see if you can try it without. Arrange to meet the girls for a night out and see what happens when you just order water. What are their reactions? Do you get bored sooner? Practise booze-free dating – yes, it can be hard to say 'Mine's a water' when it tends to be the norm to drink in these situations. But I guarantee the results will be interesting and not as bad as you think. And when you wake up completely clear-headed the next day, you might get a taste for it.

3. Learn to say no to people. It may feel like a major social manoeuvre to decline offers for drinks or to say: 'actually, can I pay less since I didn't drink?' at dinner, but it's not. It's easier than you think – and it feels good to put yourself first like that. Worst comes to worst, and you're out with loads of lads who are constantly overriding your 'no thanks' and plopping tequila shots in front of you, covertly dump the shots into empties lying about. Or leave before anyone can stop you.

I've always learned a lot about myself when I've sworn off booze. Ignoring the din of 'Drink me!' from the wine bottles nearby, as well as the 'I want more, and more' from yourself once you've got stuck in, gives you a chance to actually commune with your body at baseline. That is, you can hear your body putting out its 'more, less, yes, no' signals because it's not clouded or falsely influenced. When you return to drinking, you're much more aware of the way it makes you feel – fuzzy, headachy, impetuous, high. It's those first few days back on it when you question more

closely the relationship between what your body wants
(water) and what you're giving it (a bottle of wine). This is
a useful thing to notice and store up for future reckonings.

If you want to have a night in with your flatmate and
drink a few bottles of wine – fine, but I don't recommend it
while you're on the Man Diet. Not just because you'll be
breaking this rule, but because that old 'Hey, maybe he …'
or 'What if I texted …' is more likely to happen. Your intentions may be stellar at the outset, but they can very well be
corrupted by a half bottle of Malbec. Even if you don't end
up sending a text of doom – you're more likely to break
some other cardinal Man Diet rules by either plunging into
counterproductive rumination about a guy or the whole
'man sitch', or by diving into a massive Facebook stalking
session.

So as someone who feels eternally tempted by the prospect of a drink, I've listed below a few situations that come
up for many women, and how I cope with them while Man
Dieting.

How to handle …

1. **Nights in with a mate or flatmate:** Have a night in
   with your flatmate, by all means. But make it a different
   kind of night in – not a boozy one. Girls are lucky; we
   have many formats for cosy bonding. Why not have a
   delicious health night in, where you make a yummy
   spread of food that allows you to revel smugly in your
   'virtue'. Get out the herbal teas; make your own chai
   lattes with soya milk and chai tea bags. Choose some
   top-notch televisual diversion: I am always a fan of the

period drama; *Downton Abbey* seems never to hit a
bum note; Dickens and George Eliot adaptations are
good (I am partial to *Daniel Deronda* – Hugh Dancy as
Daniel reminds us what kind of man is truly worth
getting worked up over, as does Colin Firth as Mr Darcy
in *Pride and Prejudice* – there is literally no limit to
that BBC drama's watchability, in my view). *Mad Men*
is always good but might give you pangs about the
unattainable beauty of the actresses (though you'll be
glad you're not under Don Draper's sway); or opt out of
the world of figure-hugging dresses and dashing dudes
and head for a violent, suspenseful movie. A girls night
in with some couscous salad, herbal tea and a viewing
of *The Usual Suspects* is hard to beat.

2. **Night out with girls:** If you're at risk to your Man Diet
   when drunk, you'll need to watch these nights out –
   which tend to be the booziest – like a hawk. It's the first
   cocktail; so sweet and delicious, that makes you want
   more. If the thought of ordering a lemonade while
   everyone is going all out on the margaritas makes you
   unbearably depressed, have a drink. But don't get a
   sweet and delicious cocktail. Get a really disgusting,
   super-strong martini that is not a pleasure to drink,
   gives you a vague headache after a few sips and sort of
   makes you wish you could flee to the safety of a Diet
   Coke or cranberry juice. Best for this is the Manhattan
   – whiskey, vermouth and bitters. (Nobody ever acted
   coquettishly on a Manhattan.) Vodka and gin martinis
   are also unbearably strong and you won't want more
   than one. And in the time it takes you to have one, your

mates will have had four mojitos. If everyone's having wine, you're better off. Wine is less sneaky in its effects than cocktails. If it's horrid wine, think about how bad it tastes. If it's good wine, see how long you can make a glass last (it's all about the personal challenge). The best trick is that if you're out for dinner with a couple of friends, let them split a bottle. You can just go by the glass. If they're going for red, be in the mood for white, and vice versa. If you're interested in testing yourself, just don't drink at all. You can still have lots of fun – I had my best dancing club night ever in Dublin, of all places, in trainers and on water. I burned lots of calories and woke up fresh as a daisy.

3. **Work drinks:** These are dangerous as the booze tends to be either subsidised or free. They're extra dangerous as you have more of a chance of breaking the Man Diet by offering yourself, drunkenly, to a married or otherwise below-par man. I'd actually recommend skipping them if you're not sure you can stick to a glass or two. If the 'free' aspect is too enticing to resist, keep ordering the most expensive non-alcoholic beverages you can think of. Or ones that taste boozy – like tonic water with lemon. Beer is also good – I don't know many women who can get drunk on beer. It's too filling.

4. **Dinner parties:** You're at low risk because you're stuck with the people there – and at this stage in our lives many of them will be coupled up. Plus, you'll be distracted by them; you'll be too busy chatting to think about who you can get up to mischief with. Also, the

setting tends to be more wine-and-cheese than happy hour, and I find that even when I drink too much in such settings, there's something about them (an air of civility?) that keeps you from getting too drunk. But equally, what do you stand to gain by overdoing it on the vino at such an affair? Not much – keep up a leisurely sipping throughout the night, listen to your body carefully so that when it says 'I've had enough', you hear it, and look forward to feeling good the next day.

5. **Dates one to three:** Just swallow your fear and resist the urge to grab a quick pre-date drink with a supportive friend. (This applies mainly to first date.) Once there, just take the plunge when he asks what you want: 'Actually, I'll have a tonic water.' Feel free to go overboard with the self-justifying if it makes you feel better. 'I just had the heaviest weekend and I've got to give myself a break', or 'It's my new thing, to see if I can drink less, even on dates [with a big grin]'. It can turn into a good topic of chat and paint you as someone with a hard-partying past. On dates two and three, if you've really gone heavy on the self-justification about no boozing, just say, 'Don't worry, I'm not going to become a teetotaller, but I am quite getting into this drinking less thing.' If you give in and have a glass, imagine the excitement.

How I followed this rule:

Pre-Man Diet

The Big Night Out was a massively important part of my
life. I'd mindlessly tear through drinks whether I felt like it
or not, and – like clockwork – I'd start going after (or
attracting) trouble. At the beginning of my slightly manic
'single and loving it' period, midweek hangovers weren't
uncommon (nor were midweek romps). I was feeling run
down far too much of the time and that feeling of sickly
regret was far too common; a weekend staple.

How I did it

Well, I wasn't pleased with a) the physical harm I was doing
myself; b) the hangovers; or c) the situations I'd wind up in.
Plus, I felt that there was an overall downgrade in my
mental state since I'd become single and was drinking more
– I was more anxious. At the same time, I found it very
hard, come 7pm, to put myself in a 'restraint' frame of
mind. The a, b and c of my discontent seemed far away
when the vodka tonics came out and the music went on.
But when I decided to do the Man Diet, I just asked myself
more strenuously as I called for another glass of wine, 'Do I
want/need to feel like shit tomorrow? What's the point?
Who is it for?' I found simply asking myself those questions
instantly put the brakes on. As I thought more about my
drinking, I also started asking myself if it was strictly

necessary to sacrifice my actual bodily wellbeing for this particular idea of fun. I felt bad for my poor old body. What had it done to me to deserve this beating? Nothing. I resolved to give it less of a hard time.

Practically, this all meant that I ...

- Had a few pre-party drinks, then only one or two at the venue.
- Developed a firm but relaxed 'I'm fine, thanks' to offers of one too many.
- Cultivated a taste for a late-night San Pellegrino with ice and lemon.
- Learned to listen to myself, so if I felt tired, I'd go home rather than keep going.
- Communed with my inner (and outer) snob, and tried to stick to high-quality drinks – Burgundy rather than tequila shots, for example. These are more expensive and less toxic, so you have less and feel better.

I felt ...

- Relieved that I had less to regret, particularly in those awful, befuddled moments when you go to the toilet, parched as hell, at 4am.
- Happier overall due to fewer hangovers.
- Richer.
- Better slept and clearer-headed.

The physical upsides to cutting down on the boozing are well known, but I cannot tell you how good it was to take drunken hook-ups, or attempted hook-ups, out of the equation for a while. It was like removing an edifice of yuck.

What I let slip through the cracks

The odd night of excess. Sometimes you just have to. The fact is that I love the social aspect of boozing, I like being a bit drunk. I like men and the excitement and ease with which hook-ups happen when you're intoxicated. But this group of preferences adds up to a slippery slope – so on the rare occasion I let myself go down it a bit, I scamper back up to the top as fast as I can the next day, and stay there.

And now?

I'm constantly working on my relationship with alcohol – both in general and in relation to 'good times' and meeting men. I get drunk a lot less than I did pre-Man Diet. Occasionally I end up in an excessively boozy phase, particularly if I'm feeling edgy or insecure and/or horny (read: in need of action), but I catch myself quickly, see what I'm doing, and have a firm word with myself along the lines of 'getting drunk in the hopes of a gratifying hook-up isn't going to make you happy.'

SOS!

OK – we all slip up. Boozing is such a major part of our culture and most of our lives that it would be ridiculously draconian to beat yourself up for a night off the rails (and a possible junk-food love binge). As long as you end up safe and sound, put it down to the stresses and strains of modern existence and keep looking forward.

However, one big night out often leads to more … and more and more, once the hangover from hell clears. To pull yourself back onto the diet:

- Don't let yourself get into a pattern. When your friends are talking about the following Friday night and you can tell it's going to be a big one, don't be afraid to take yourself out of harm's way. Make this the weekend you visit the parents, or arrange to have a quiet one with someone who is off the booze, or not a big drinker. You won't miss anything apart from a few laughs and a(nother) hangover from hell.

- Remember discipline. Removing yourself from the problem is a good way to get back on board. But you need to remind yourself how to have a relatively sober good time when the drinks are flowing – i.e., you need to be able to enjoy and handle reality. We all have a point when we tip into drunken 'whatever' mode and discipline goes out the window – force yourself to stop right before that point. Be honest about when it is, and if you don't know or can't tell, have two drinks, then stop – at least for a few hours.

♂ Assign a friend to stop you after two or three drinks – choose someone who doesn't get wasted even if they do drink a lot. One of those protective – sometimes overprotective – friends would be perfect.

♂ Remember – and repeat to yourself four million times or until it sticks – you don't need to be wasted to hook up with a guy. For many reasons, it's good to believe this. One of them is that it's true – a man that doesn't find you attractive sober, and vice versa, is probably not one whose seminal fluids you should be sharing.

♂ Be positive. You're great! You can do this! It's just habit: knocking back fourteen glasses of wine isn't all that. In fact, your body would be really thrilled if you stopped at two. Or zero.

Rule Number 3

No Facebook Stalking

You need this rule if you ...

🧍 Are bad at setting time limits on internet time-wasting.

🧍 Are prone to procrastination

🧍 Have an ex with a juicy profile .(that you can't stop looking at).

🧍 Feel crappy after Facebook stalking sessions.

🧍 Can't meet a guy for a date without having thoroughly checked his whole internet presence.

🧍 Don't believe what he says or what he's like until you've seen it confirmed on Facebook – i.e., that he has friends and interests.

🧍 Know 100 per cent more than what he's told you, thanks to Facebook snooping.

🧍 Know what your ex is doing day-by-day.

🧍 Know the name and weight of each female friend he adds.

🧍 After telling yourself to get off Facebook, end up checking out someone else or re-checking the object of your interest.

🧍 Have stayed up past your bedtime more than six times to keep snooping and browsing men.

♂ Have felt weird about seeing a guy again after having looked him up.

Goes well with …
♂ Do Not Pursue
♂ Cut Down on the Booze
♂ Do Something Lofty

L auren has lustrous brown hair, juicy lips and a predilection for 1970s garb. She favours bright red lipstick, has very brown shoulders, loves Florence and the Machine, has just finished a PhD at Berkeley and has a brother called David. Her favourite author is Jonathan Safran Foer and she loves the book Catch 22.

She's also in a relationship that's been going on for 22 months with a guy I used to be completely obsessed with. She has no clue who I am, as I haven't been in touch with the guy for years, which makes my knowledge of these facts somewhat pointless. Not just pointless: unhealthy. I feel something in relation to her, envy tinged with sadness, even though we have absolutely no relationship whatsoever. That is, my knowledge and feelings towards her are not only one-sided; they're not based on reality.

What happened next …

I had a moment of 'what am I doing?' and realised that I felt worse, not better, the more I learned about her this way. The moment I began looking at her friends' friends' pictures at 11pm one night was actually the moment that I realised my Facebook usage for this kind of voyeurism had gone too far, and that there was definitely a chapter of a book to be written about it. I vowed to stop checking up on people I'd never met and, having succeeded in not looking up Lauren for a week or two, soon forgot about him and her.

So I say …

Let the Facebook stalking go. It's zapping your energy, it's creepy and it's not going to enlighten you in any positive way.

THE MAN DIET QUIZ

THE EX

1. **How often do you check your ex-boyfriend's Facebook page?**
   A. Every day.
   B. Twice a day.
   C. Every time you go on Facebook.
   D. Only when he or a friend comes up on your newsfeed.
   E. Never.

2. **How much do you know about his current girlfriend?**
   A. Her name.
   B. Her date of birth, favourite music and mother's name.
   C. The names and occupations of all her ex-boyfriends.

D. Absolutely everything.

E. Nothing. You don't want to know.

3. How well acquainted are you with his FB friends?

A. You know he has a lot.

B. You know how many girls there are.

C. You have identified all the possible ones he's slept with.

D. You know each and every name and last five holiday destinations of the ten prettiest ones.

E. Not well acquainted – don't care.

4. How many times has looking at his profile resulted in feelings of anger, frustration or sadness?

A. Once or twice, when it's changed from 'single' to 'in a relationship with Joanna Bloggs'.

B. Every few days or so while getting over him.

C. Every day.

D. All day, every day – i.e. you can't stop looking, even though it makes you cry.

E. Never, because you defriended him as soon as you broke up.

THE CURRENT SQUEEZE

1. How many pictures of him have you looked at?

A. Just his profile snaps.

B. All of them.

C. All of them, as well as those of all the pretty girls he's friends with.

D. All of them, as well as all of his friends.

E. None. Why would you?

2. **How many times have you looked at his Facebook profile and felt shut out, jealous or uneasy?**

A. Once, and decided not to do it again.

B. Several times, after each date.

C. After and between each date.

D. Every day you've known him.

E. Never.

3. **How often do you show his FB pictures to your mates so they can admire them?**

A. Only when they demand it.

B. After the third date.

C. After the first date and then whenever he posts anything new.

D. Before the first date, then at least three times during each girls night out, while they secretly yawn.

E. Never; they can wait till it's time to meet him.

4. **How much do you know about his life that he hasn't told you?**

A. Only what a quick Facebook profile sweep reveals.

B. That he has a best friend called Annie with an awesome bikini bod.

C. What he wore to the beach on his recent Spanish holiday and what his best friends are called (and look like), along with the senses of humour of all his female friends.

D. Pretty much everything (you think).

E. Nothing – why jump the gun?

HOW DID YOU DO?

Mostly As: Pretty healthy where Facebook use is concerned, with only the tiniest tweaks necessary. But hey – we're only human.

Mostly Bs: Verging on the problematic, but still the right side of a problem. Nip it in the bud now, though, as it could go either way.

Mostly Cs: You need this rule like a newborn needs milk – urgently.

Mostly Ds: You're a complete Facebook stalker addict, and should think about going into the Secret Service, where your skills will make you less miserable.

Mostly Es: You're the most grounded, sane person around and definitely don't have even the whisper of a problem. I salute you.

The compulsion women feel to look up profiles of men that have hurt them is irresistible. We do it whether we still want to be with the guy or not; whether we even like him or not. Most of the women I spoke to for this book used the word 'addictive' in relation to their checking up of certain men on Facebook.

- A 2010 NBC Oxygen Media survey of 1,600 women (age 18–34) found 40 per cent of those surveyed self-identify as 'Facebook addicts'; but we don't how the people surveyed defined 'addict', how many of them are single, or how they manifest their addiction, i.e., in stalking or wall-posting etc. Still, almost half is a lot.
- Slightly fewer, 34 per cent, stated that they check Facebook literally first thing in the morning, before going to brush their teeth.
- In a poll of 1,700 people in the UK conducted in 2010 by people-search engine Yasni.com, 62 per cent of women – compared with 42 per cent of men – admitted to having looked up a former love interest online.

Lexie, 29, says: 'I hate Facebook for the fact that I can look at guys that I should be over but I'm not. Being able to see the latest photo of what they look like – it's torture.' It's not just former flames that draw her painful but undivided attention, but men who are hurting her in the present tense too:

'I really struggle when I like someone who is rejecting me. I can't stop staring at their profile, looking at all their wall posts, new female friends, their life beyond me. It's like in the Facebook movie [The Social Network], when Zuckerberg is staring at his ex's picture as a non-friend. I know that feeling well, like looking in the window from the cold outside.'

Ricky Emanuel, adult psychotherapist and head of child psychotherapy at Royal Free in London, and author of a book on anxiety, says that the impulse to stalk exes is often sheer masochism. 'Women have more of a tendency towards internalised pain, which suggests that they are therefore more driven by this kind of masochism than men,' he says.

Another friend, Maddie, recently raged that a girl she'd heard was dating her much-hated ex was a 'hag' because her picture – located on the Facebook wall of said ex – was obscured (she is holding a Pret bag in front of her face). The girl, of course, had no idea she'd become a figure of hatred for Maddie, whose existence on earth she knew nothing of. Maddie was merely throwing energy at a screen, at an image of someone with whom she had no relationship.

Women are all over Facebook, probing and posting. Sheryl Sandberg, COO of Facebook, has talked about the prevalence of women on social media sites; they are not only the majority of Facebook users, but drive 62 per cent of activity in terms of messages, updates and comments, and 71 per cent of the daily fan activity, according to the website TechCrunch (2011). Women have 8 per cent more Facebook friends on average than men, and spend more time on the site. According to an early Facebook team member, women played a key role in the early days by adopting three core activities – posting to walls, adding photos and joining groups – at a much higher rate than males.

The secret information gatherer

Every single woman I know does as thorough a search as possible on a man of interest, be it someone she's just met, or someone from her past she still wants to keep tabs on, for ego's sake, or as Ricky Emanuel says, because of masochistic impulses. Both types of Facebook stalking have negative, energy-draining results. Such a pastime invariably skews reality, presents a distorted picture, makes you feel like crap and, crucially, wastes time. Judging from my own experience and that of the numerous women I talked to for this book, combing other people's Facebook walls and websites for comments and pictures posted either by them or to them can take anywhere from 20 minutes to several hours a day. It's never a good use of time in that you never feel a sense of peace or achievement at the end of it. This applies for all protracted, pointless Facebook browsing, of course, but when it comes to men it is actually harmful.

My beef with Facebook stalking – and the reason I think it's counterproductive for women trying to build up self-esteem – is that when you find what you're looking for on Facebook (a life that doesn't involve you) it can only ever disturb and annoy you. Maddie felt enraged but there was nothing she could do with her angry 'hag!'. I feel shitty every time I see Jesse's beautiful girlfriend Lauren cavorting in the Californian sunshine. I feel like an idiot knowing the name of the mother and brothers of a guy I fancied but who didn't ask me out. And like a perv sending links of another non-starter guy's impressive guns to a curious friend.

Facebooking men is also just a big old slippery slope since it's very easy to hit 'enter' and end up making a deeply embarrassing mistake. Sarah-Jane, 27, told me of the horror she felt when she realised she'd posted some excited/pervy/imagine-us-married-style comment about a guy she'd gone on some dates with on *his* wall, by accident. 'It was just awful. It was beyond repair. Eight months later I'm still scarred.'

An alien, or wise person who has been living under a rock for the past 10 years, could ask:

'Why would you care so much about a world represented solely through pictures and words chosen for their social value? What's so compelling about that?'

The power of Facebook

One powerful argument is that Facebook uses Skinner box-style reward mechanisms that keep us coming back. The Skinner box, invented by B.F. Skinner at Harvard in the 1930s, is used for studying animal behaviour: the desired action gets a reward, like a piece of food, while the wrong one gets punished. It's such a powerful way to train animals that you can get dogs dancing in adverts and elephants walking on tightropes. But in the case of Facebook, we're the animals being trained – at least according to strident Facebook critic and technology essayist Cory Doctorow: 'Facebook uses the same mechanic [as the Skinner box],' he said in his TEDxObserver talk on Facebook, kids and privacy. 'It lavishes you with the attention from the people that you love, the more you disclose about your life. [They all seem to say] here's some social stimulus and some attention! The more you embroider your life, the more reinforcement you'll get.' Stalking is a search for the reinforcement of juicy information, rather than the craving for a 'like', update or message – but Doctorow gives a compelling argument for why Facebook is so powerful.

The ritual

Relationship therapist, Val Sampson, says Facebook addiction is about ritual – and who doesn't feel that a cheeky cyber-spying binge helps feelings of emptiness or uneasiness?

'When we don't feel right, we look to something to make us feel better. The ritual of logging on, of looking at messages and pictures, stimulates certain brain functions. It's some intellectual engagement, all those bright colours. If we're not feeling good, it can soothe us to some degree, but in life, our challenge is to make ourselves feel better internally in a positive way, not from the outside.'

There's another point to be made about that 'soothing' feeling: the distance between the computer screen and the face has been found to be very engaging for the brain; one possible reason is that it's the same or similar distance between the mother's face and a baby's when the baby is in the mother's arms. But that's probably about where a Macbook's similarities with your mother end.

The thrill

Another reason we're drawn to Facebook stalking is that it's titillating – could the half-naked picture of Richard, a guy I met briefly at a party and thought was hot, sailing in San Francisco be anything but? Once again I think Emanuel is onto something fundamental when he talks, very despairingly, about our 'infantile' culture of fizzy, instantaneous social and sexual excitement, which appears to have overtaken mature relationship building, especially among young people. Facebook satisfies our desire for the instant by saving us actually having to wait to get to know someone. In the place of 'getting to know' someone (or not), we can get the dirt on them – and anyone else whose privacy settings we can outsmart.

Research also suggests that the picture-led reality of CMC (computer mediated communication, of which Facebook is the most powerful example today) is not only *as* compelling as the real world, it is *more* compelling.

Under surveillance

Facebook's success is attributed to its 'stickiness' – that is, once you pop, you can't stop (as per Skinner box theory). A 2008 University of Bath study found that the number-one thing that keeps us going back for more is surveillance, of which the single woman's Facebook stalkery is one example. 'The primary use of Facebook was for social searching – that is, using Facebook to find out more about people who they have met offline,' it said. The authors didn't look at whether the surveillance was positive or negative, or exactly who was surveying who – only that people like to do it and that they allow themselves to be watched. 'It would seem from the present data that "keeping in touch" may in actuality refer to "checking up on regularly".' This represents an odd social shift in the way we perceive people, from whole, actual people we either know, don't know, want to know or are getting to know, to a sort of a weird 1984-style Big Brother's watching you, where we're all Big Brother and all under observation.

'The magnetism of Facebook is multi-pronged, particularly for women.'

In the case of the single woman, whose self-esteem may be extra vulnerable despite shows of bravado, partaking of surveillance of unsatisfied love interests has got to be negative. 'I've done that whole self-harming checking thing,' says Ruth, 31. 'It literally is self-harm, so I try not to do it now.' Recall Lexie's use of the word 'torture' earlier – these are strong words, full of pain. Which is not what the single woman needs as she goes forth with strength in the hostile world.

It's amazingly hard to put a lid on it, though. The magnetism of Facebook is multi-pronged, particularly for women. There's the desire to be on the 'Book', to post photos, to show other people what fun you're having and – more to the point – how good you look having it. The 2011 study *Cyberpsychology, Behavior and Social Networking*, found that women post around five times as many pictures on Facebook as men, competing for eyeballs. Stefanone lamented that female self-worth is still anchored in the gaze of others. And who among us hasn't instructed a friend to instantly post and tag a picture of us looking tousled and fun-loving in the hopes that guys, or a guy, will see it and think 'oooh'.

Keeping up with the Joneses

Then there's the allure of looking at what the Joneses are doing, which is particularly strong for women, and often includes a need to know what that guy who took you on three romantic dates then abruptly went silent on you last year is doing. A Stanford study that homed in on that post-snoop low is particularly illuminating. It showed that scrolling other people's attractive photos, bios, and upbeat status updates creates a grass-is-greener malaise that has a sizeable and measurable impact on mood. Alex Jordan, the paper's lead author, found that users were convinced that everyone else was leading a perfect life. Writing about the study in online magazine *Slate*, Libby Copeland makes an excellent point: that as a showcase for the most enviable parts of our lives, and our wittiest observations, Facebook invites a 'grass is greener' or 'keeping up with the Joneses' style of thinking. And, as she says, women are particularly prone to such thinking, quick to see other people's lives as painfully holding up a mirror to their own.

I can relate to that and I am sure some of the Facebook users among you do too. After all, we really don't benefit from seeing any guy of romantic interest live his charmed life – with other girls – on the screen in front of us. Especially when like a bunch of sad sacks, we've gone and looked for it.

Leonard Sax, a well-known psychologist and author, is also convinced that girls (women of the future) are particularly prone to a terrifying absorption in the Facebook world of self-selling and updates. In his highly acclaimed book *Girls on the Edge: The Four Factors Driving the New Crisis for Girls*, he hand-wrings about the 'cyberbubble' – the way Facebook draws teenage girls in, so that they're updating and posting late into the night, and can't break away to talk to people face-to-face or do their homework. Sax, who has written a companion book about boys and their disengagement from life, says boys tend to prefer video games to Facebook.

Digital overload

If the single woman is particularly tempted by the Facebook surveillance of men that aren't necessarily offering her what she wants, she's part of a much bigger picture of people struggling with the digital lives they've created for themselves. That we're all juggling numerous social media sites, email accounts, and incoming messages, like texts and IMs, is nothing new. But more and more, that frazzled feeling we get when responding to seven bits of information at once, that sense of 'Err, early onset Alzheimers?' at the end of the day when you realise there are eleven unsent, half-written emails open on your desktop, is prompting serious research. And what scientists are finding is that juggling incoming information all day can ruin our ability to focus, make us unhappy, negatively impact on our personal relationships and – what do you know? – create technology addictions.

Scientists found that each time you receive a message, tweet, or newsfeed update, your brain releases a squirt of dopamine – a neurotransmitter that helps control excitement. This squirt – they say – can be addictive, and without it people feel bored. So when you're on Facebook anyway, servicing your need for that dopamine squirt (and feeling that pang of disappointment when there's no red box at the top showing a message or update), you figure you might as well have a cheeky peek at Will, Jack or Tom's page. It's hard to tear yourself away and if you do, you want to dive back in again soon. 'Technology is rewiring our brains,' neuroscientist Nora Volkow told *The New York Times*, comparing the addictiveness of digital messaging to that of drugs and alcohol. Indeed, for many of us, once you pop you can't stop.

FAD

There is an actual disorder these days called FAD (Facebook Addiction Disorder), though not everyone takes it seriously, especially when you can google such terms as WAD (Widget Addiction Disorder), TAD (Twitter Addiction Disorder) and YAD (YouTube Addiction Disorder). Futurelab, a highly regarded marketing strategy consultancy, posted a blog with the six signs of Facebook addiction. It's tongue-in-cheek but contains some sobering truths. Reads one: 'Any notifications, messages and invites reward you with an unpredictable high, much like gambling.' All you have to do is google 'Facebook addiction' and over 46,100,000 results come up. (This is a mere snip, however, next to Twitter's 122,000,000 plus.) And most of the women I interviewed about Facebook use for this book used the word 'addictive'. The point is, if you find it hard to stop checking up on guys – or just checking up full stop – you're not alone.

'Facebook is the bane of our lives.'

I was having drinks with Sarah, 32, a pretty and successful businesswoman, and her equally pretty and driven friend Antonia, 31. Both of them are single and have been for a couple of years. Both of them have unsatisfactory men on the go in various forms (they readily admit to being in the grips of junk-food love). Sarah told me about this guy who won't commit to her – even though they've drunkenly confessed love to each other several times – because he has ex issues. When she found out he was going to Egypt with his ex, she immediately turned to Facebook. 'There was conflicting evidence,' she said intensely. 'I assumed they were back together and he'd been lying to me, but it said "single" on her profile. So maybe they were going as friends. I just don't know. It's driving me crazy.' To get to the ex-girl-friend's profile, she had to get another friend of hers to hack into her boyfriend's Facebook account, since he was the closest link. She hadn't felt better after researching the ex, nor has the information served her well, since she's still stuck in a drawn-out limbo with the guy. Antonia put it succinctly, if dramatically: 'Facebook is the bane of our lives.'

The itch we can't stop itching

As with Emma, I've never met a woman who feels better after a Facebook check-up on a man – except very rare occasions where someone's felt vindicated that her boyfriend has ignored wall posts from a perceived rival. The reason it makes us feel crap and erodes our self-worth is that Facebook stalking is an itch you can only scratch, but never soothe. The main reason for this never-ending loop of dissatisfaction is that you're not interacting with anyone; you're not after resolutions based on mutual exchange. You're just a voyeur, an impotent observer who ends up stuck with the emotions transmitted by looking at someone else's Facebook identity. As Emanuel puts it: 'This kind of voyeurism has an impact on your internal world: the infor-mation you're getting is somehow soiled and sullied – it doesn't make you feel good. There's curiosity that's healthy and there's intrusive curiosity, which is about a childish peeping through the keyhole, wanting to know what people are doing there, wanting to know everything. The first is adult, the second infantile. We all have a bit of both.'

Acquiring knowledge the right way – and we all know what that is, i.e., through healthy curiosity (talking to someone, reading books, googling) – is one of the great pleasures in life, and is even considered by the psychoanalytic world to be one of the fundamental human drives, alongside sleep, food and sex (see the work and theories of iconic early psychoanalyst Melanie Klein for more on this).

Alex Heminsley, journalist and author of *Ex and the City: You're Nobody 'Til Somebody Dumps You*, put it to me over coffee: 'Facebook stalking is not actually stalking – you only ever see what people want you to.' But Emanuel is convinced people are naive, and don't know how the information they post is going to be used, even though, following various hoohaas, Facebook's privacy settings have now been improved.

Jaron Lanier, a Silicon Valley programmer, is the loudest voice on the issue of Facebook-reduced reality. His central argument in his book *You are Not a Gadget*, is that not only does Facebook under-represent us but we start to under-represent ourselves for it. Scary, and possibly true.

So when Emma thinks she understands what's going on with her squeeze and his ex based on the text that goes in the boxes that Facebook has thoughtfully provided, she might be getting a false, reductive picture, and basing her emotional response on that. When I stalk a guy I like who is leaving me hanging, I'm not gaining understanding of him, the person – I'm only drawing conclusions from a series of information nodes that have been chosen by him to represent a certain image (as Lanier would say, that 'under-represent' who he is). A study about social networking called *Public Displays of Connection* is named very well,

I think – it captures how we perform relationships for our viewers, not necessarily how we actually are.

Wean yourself off Facebook stalking: actually doing it

In an ideal world, you'd go on a total Facebook diet first, like Phase One of the Atkins. Then, when you went back on Facebook, you wouldn't be *gagging* for the gratification of stalking; you'd have other things you could do, and Facebook wouldn't seem such a comfortable place to hang out for long stretches of time. It's always at the end of a Facebook session, when you're unsure what to do next, that you think, 'Well, I'll just have a little look at Jack's profile' – so the less time you're spending on Facebook in general, the less chance you'll be tempted into stalking.

But a total Facebook ban is perhaps too much to ask; indeed, while writing this chapter I've probably checked Facebook about seven times. It's not all awful – most of us quite enjoy certain aspects of Facebookery – and more importantly, you don't need another thing to worry about failing at (i.e., quitting Facebook).

BUT, the Man Diet requires that for some amount of time, you do go cold turkey on the looking up of men (hopefully never to return to it).

How to get the most out of this rule

1. Challenge yourself to a Facebook ban – within reason

What constitutes a ban for you depends on how much you normally check it. If it's every two seconds, cut down to twice a day. If every hour, once a day. If five times a day, cut down to twice a week. If three times a day, go nuts and see if you can do just one check a week, lasting not more than 15 minutes. When I talked to a senior psychologist in the NHS about this issue of not just stalking but also feeling the need to check Facebook all the time, she said she always recommends the adoption of a strict window of time. She asks people if they think they *could* limit Facebook sessions to twice a week. Asking yourself: 'Can I?' sort of shocks you into realising that it might be out of your control – which is a fairly sobering thought when you're talking about a social-networking site. Of course, it is within your control, you just have to try harder.

2. Expect your fingers to stray dangerously towards the letter 'f' – of course your browser will recognise what you're after instantly

When it does that, immediately take your hand off the keyboard and do something else with it – wave it outlandishly; flick some dirt; put your hair behind your ear. Anything to give your brain time to catch up and redirect. Soon you'll reap the pleasure of denial, à la hardcore diet whereby 'no pain no gain' leads to gratifying weight loss.

3. Ban mobile Facebook

Luckily, my iPhone is so old and decrepit I can't bear to check Facebook on my mobile, since it's so slow and faulty. I also prefer it on a bigger screen. You may have a better phone and be more wholeheartedly of the 'mobile' generation, in which case you're fighting the war on a double front. I urge you to do it. Mobile Facebook is also to be regarded with great suspicion because it is extra good for stalking – if you're friends with the stalkee, Facebook Places, a mobile app, can show you where they are *right now*.

Backups and substitutes

♟ *Get booze backups*

It's vital that you have an emergency backup ready and waiting when you come home drunk and twitchy. *Heat* magazine; *Sunday Times Style*; some delicious gherkins. A friend you can ring for a chat, preferably in America, where it won't be late at night.

If you're really struggling, I recommend Freedom, an application that locks you off the internet for up to eight hours at a time – set it before you go out and you won't be able to get online six hours later when you're drunk and destructive. On its website, macfreedom.com, you'll see a host of celebrity testimonies saying things like, 'Without freedom I couldn't have finished my book!' Well, with Freedom, you might have no choice but to wean yourself off the junk-food love that is Facebook-stalking men who give you nothing back.

♟ *Stuff your bag*

If you're a big mobile Facebook user, the handbag is your best friend. Mobile internet use mostly occurs when you're in transit or away from home, with a bag. In that bag you can put lots of much better distractions for those moments waiting on the platform or on the train, or in Starbucks for a meeting. Try an iPod with great podcasts (I like Dan Savage's *Savage Love* sex podcast and *This American Life* – both free), riveting tunes (hello Rihanna) or my personal favourite: a book.

♟ *Try this rule in conjunction with number five, Do Something Lofty*

That rule is all about finding something rewarding and enjoyable that has nothing to do with men or love or dating or singleness. So, ideally, you could just do a nifty switch – trade Facebook session for lofty/asexual activity session. If you've taken up something lofty that isn't interchangeable with Facebook browsing (volunteering, say), get a backup – such as a good book, cooking or a craft (knitting is great for this – you can lose yourself in soft woolly knots rather than mental ones). Or a blog or online newspaper you can visit instead of Facebook, that informs or enriches or amuses you.

How I followed this rule:

I started this rule by observing when and why I would check Facebook. It was usually when I was:

- A bit bored.
- Feeling empty; for example when having a 'Where is my life going?' moment that I didn't want to deal with.
- Feeling idle or restless.
- Wanting to dilute my focus on whatever I was supposed to be concentrating on by an aimless browse.
- In the mood for shit-stirring.
- Urgently curious; I just *have* to know what that person looks like on holiday, how much they party and how many friends they have. Knowledge is power, right?
- Feeling self-destructive and brave at the same time. 'I'll just see if my ex has a new girlfriend. I can handle it …'

Pre-Man Diet

I am actually very good about not looking up exes. It's too painful. However, I am terrible about men I've just met, am interested in, or have begun dating. I am also terrible about former big crushes.

Ex history aside, after meeting someone or developing a crush, or even just getting an email from someone who has piqued my interest, I can be like a wild horse charging for my laptop so that I can have a vigorous, private Facebook stalk. Hours can pass in this way, going through someone's wall – what they've posted, what others have posted – any mutual friends of interest, searching their friends for attractive women and so on. In fact, my friends and I have been known to boast about our stalking skills. And when you add in Google and LinkedIn, things can get quite spectacular. But did I ever make any discoveries I was grateful for? Not really. The main effect was that I could see how much fun these boys had, how many girls they romped with, and what a closed-from-me life they had (that's a known negative side-effect of Facebook). It sometimes made me feel weird on dates.

How I did it

When I asked myself the 'Can I?' question, at first I thought, 'Oh my God. No. I can't. That is really quite worrying.' Then, two seconds later, I thought, 'Of course I can. It's a simple matter of discipline. I am stronger than my desire to unhealthily, habitually cyber-snoop!'

I couldn't go cold turkey. I set myself limited time for checking Facebook – Tuesdays and Fridays. And by 'checking', I mean not hanging about on the site. If I had updates or messages, I'd read them. I wasn't going to let myself start looking up persons of interest – we all know where that leads.

How did I get on?

This was my worst rule: 9/10 on the difficulty scale. I failed frequently – I found it impossible to stick to checking

Facebook only twice a week. So I modified it to once a day. Even that I struggled with. But I did manage to change the type of Facebook checking I did. I pretty much stopped stalking right away – but I had to try really, really hard at night, particularly after a few drinks. Sometimes I would just give in, reeling in at 1am and desperate for some kind of junk-food love – exactly like when you want a kebab. I'd feel dirty afterwards – also like you do when you've had a late-night food binge. Sometimes these off-the-wagon stalks would lead to very unwise messages or wall writings – causing me to break another rule, Do Not Pursue, too.

But it was easier than a food diet, I found, and generally one binge would scare me off any more for a while. Remember: the key with the Man Diet, as with any diet, is not to lose heart, but to get right back onto it if you've binged on a big sloppy late-nice slice of chocolate-cake love.

What did I let through the cracks?

Assuming I wasn't in a particularly destructive mood, or inebriated, there were absolutely no men I felt necessary to Facebook stalk while on the Man Diet. Obviously there's a difference between looking people up and stalking – the former is one of Facebook's key functions. So yes – occasionally I'd look someone up. But it wouldn't be for stalking reasons; i.e., it would very likely be a girl, relative or colleague.

As for when I was feeling destructive or inebriated (or both), see 'How did I get on?' above …

And now?

It's bloody hard – I still have to fight the urge to look a guy up as soon as he becomes interesting (or after it's gone wrong). I crack every now and then – but over time, my desire to do it has lessened. I check it from once to 20 times a day, but usually for no more than two seconds. If there's a red mark in the updates section, I check it. If not, I click off. I do occasionally stalk. And it still makes me feel dirty. Overall, though, I've cut down on the amount of dead time and pointless voyeurism – that is, the attainment of unnecessary information – that is the Facebook contribution to junk-food love.

I realised that it didn't have to be Facebook I turned to. Going for a walk, buying a coffee, and flicking through a trashy magazine or newspaper online work just as well to pass the time than Facebook. As for that curiosity: Do you *really* need to know that information when you can only get it off a social-networking site rather than from the horse's mouth? It feels like you do – the reality is that you don't. And are you *really* going to be fine with new info regarding your ex's life? Probably not, unless it's finding out he's still infatuated with you.

SOS!

Like booze, Facebook is very tricky to leave well alone. If you give in and have a massive stalk, and now feel crap because you know a million things you shouldn't but have nowhere to go with them – and also like you've thrown your time down the drain – panic not. Instead:

- Learn from your mistake. What was the trigger that led to this bout of Facebook stalking? Was it feeling low, hungry, angry, drunk, unloved, bored? Select one or more of these and find another activity you can do when that feeling arises and try to remember to do it when it next strikes.
- Strongly consider investing in a programme like Freedom that locks you off the internet for up to eight hours. If you fall into Facebook's man-stalking clutches when you come back from a night out, set it before you go out.
- Ask yourself next time you feel the urge: 'Is it really going to make me happy knowing more about this person? Is it what I want and need?' If the answer is no, try hard to do something else instead. Which brings us to the next point.
- Find an alternative fun website to Facebook and make it a favourite (jezebel.com/nytimes.com/ perezhilton.com/heatworld.com and even Twitter

are some suggestions). If you feel that the itch to type f-a-c … into your browser is overwhelming you, just click on this site first and I guarantee you'll forget about the Facebook itch soon enough.

Rule Number

No Talking About Men

You need this rule if you …

🚹 Can't experience anything man-related without thinking of how you'll describe it to your friends.

🚹 Never process your love/sex life without recourse to a cosmo or five, and at least one friend to hear about it and offer advice.

🚹 Get the feeling your love life is a circus act and your friends are the audience.

🚹 Feel dull if the 'cupboard is bare' of stories.

🚹 Say yes to certain sexual or dating activities because 'at least it'll make a good story'.

🚹 Overanalyse every encounter.

🚹 Feel more, not less, obsessed with a guy after talking about him for two hours with your buddies.

🚹 Find yourself stumped for conversation when men are off the menu.

🚹 Feel that you're always volunteering graphic sexual info.

🚹 Assume that delivering amusing anecdotes of your single life is what people expect of you.

Goes well with ...

- Do Something Lofty
- Dwell on Your Sense of Self
- No Facebook Stalking
- Refuse to Have No Strings Attached Sex
- Know Your Obstacles

M y friend Rebecca had been single for a week, and had already grabbed the bull by the horns. She'd gone on a date with someone her friend had (already) set her up with, taken him home and slept with him. Unfortunately, he had sloping shoulders, bad acne and a sex style so aggressive she'd got cystitis. A week later she'd recovered enough to do it one more time with him, but she had to admit, she didn't fancy him. No matter: she moved swiftly on to a vague acquaintance who gave her her first taste of anal sex, but he had a girlfriend, and yapped unappealingly during sex, so that one was put down to five-too-many martinis. Then again, the German banker she drunkenly shagged on a private members' club pool table was no better: he had a co-habiting girlfriend. Putting taken men on the back-burner for a while, she focused her attention on a dull but good-looking – and very evasive – Catalonian. An idiotic Italian borrowed for a few hours in Florence, another German at a wedding, and a bevy of unsuccessful dates and crushes ensured she always had a topic of conversation during that first 'wild' single period.

What happened next ...

Well, I knew all these details about Rebecca because they were readily proffered – and not to an audience of shocked prudes, but to squeals of delight, disbelief, and in some cases, congratulation. Sometimes it even felt as though Rebecca was having the wild sex in order to tell us the story – the stories were such hits of adrenaline for her; her eyes took on a maniacal shine, her body language grew intense, her gestures emphatic. Eventually, Rebecca quietened down because she got a boyfriend. She went from over-sharing and over-entertaining to volunteering virtually nothing. A few months into the relationship, she said one of the things she had really noticed about her new status was how nice it was to just ... keep shtum about her love life and its every up, down and conquest.

So I say ...

Take a break from talking about your private tales of man action. As women, we'll never kiss this line of convo goodbye. But it can get out of hand and taking a break can really recharge your batteries and renew your perspective.

A culture of spilling all

When you're single, people want to know the details, and you're happy to oblige – at first. Then you feel that you really ought to, or you'll be letting the side down. Being single myself – and particularly at the beginning of this most recent period, when others were getting used to the excitement of my changed status – the first question almost every friend greeted me with was: 'So? What man news?' I'd walk into work: 'So, Strimps, and what did you get up to last night?' someone would say, with a smirk.

I'm a fan of a good story – almost as much as Rebecca, and have trotted out a good few too. But after an intensive period of man-related chatter, I began to be suspicious about the effect of routinely telling all to my friends – and many other people. It felt as though I was selling myself a bit; in denying myself the private domain entirely and morphing into a 'tell-all' machine, I began to feel … cheap, like (un)paid-for entertainment, and a bit of a clown, too.

I didn't like that it was becoming a social reflex, either and I was always scavenging for man news when I was out with friends. Let me be clear: discussing romantic and sexual matters with my friends is a permanent and posi- tive feature of my life – not to mention, as for most women, a natural one. Not only is talking the way women find comfort and guidance on a whole range of issues, it's how we work our problems out. I can't begin to imagine life as a typical man, whereby problems are kept in as a matter of course, and only released if teased out or forced out or via a bout of desperation or rage. Because often it's not until we open our mouths and articulate something that's bothering us that we can start to see the real shape of the problem and the possible solution. Asking you not to talk about life with your friends would be a punishing and ridiculous request – and it's not what this rule is about. When it comes to real issues, talking is essential for emotional health and happiness. But when it comes to general discussion about a specific area of social life – such as men – the benefits of talk can backfire (of which more later).

Natural, general life talk with friends is fine. But there's a line that I think the Man Dieter needs to draw between spilling the man beans over cocktails once in a while and dishing out some man-related anecdote or observation (sex, dating, rejection, crushes, texts, the agony of a drought all count) like a dutiful pony trotting round the ring.

The most demanding audience, of course, is the non-single one as they want to live vicariously through you.

'We're supposed to be telling "hilarious stories", it's like being a dancing monkey – you feel really bad about yourself when the cupboard is bare.' **Cara, 34**

Journalist and author Alex Heminsley makes a good observation: 'If you're married, the questions stop. You can't say: "How is your marriage doing?" But if you're single, the door swings open: "Do you do online dating?" and so on. It's everyone's business. I do find it shocking that my friends' husbands can say to me: "Are you getting any at the moment?", but I couldn't possibly turn that question around.'

The result of this pressure to delight and amuse is that we feel boring if we have nothing to tell. There's a real fear of being dull, and – in so being – not living up to the expectations of friends, hairdressers, mothers and the fun-loving, sexually voracious world in general. Annie, 27, recently single, told me she's very wary of people asking her about her single sex life all the time and finds it offensive. 'I have a friend who had an awful, scary experience with a guy and went off men a bit, whereas before she was always shagging around for fun etc. After she withdrew, her relationship

with her friends changed – she had always been the one
with the entertaining joke about who she'd shagged – when
she stopped, she felt some of her friends went off her. I'm
pretty sure they did.'

Let's talk about sex

Our assessment of what to tell and what to keep back has
changed drastically. After the frank experimentation of the
ancient world, with the coming of Christianity, sex became
a problem and a dirty secret. In the modern period, the way
this problem has been addressed has changed. Rather than
trying to keep sex hidden and silent, the modern means of
dealing with it is to endlessly talk about it (as per Foucault,
the god of social theory). The human body and its sexual
needs became the source of an enormous proliferation of
medical theories, conduct books, pornographic fantasies
and cautionary tales. And in this process, individuals were
forced to define themselves in terms of sexuality, to tease
out the riddle of their sexual natures.

The rise of the girly tell-all

Nothing has entrenched this more than the two most popular representations of single female behaviour of the past 15
years, *Bridget Jones's Diary* and *Sex and the City*. These
two books/films have greatly influenced our habits of disclosure, and showed that sex is anything but private. Even in
1991, Salt 'N' Pepa's 'Let's Talk About Sex' was considered
a provocative title; now it would be like calling your song,
'Let's Talk About Council Tax'. (Although Salt 'N' Pepa
weren't just talking about crazy, fun sex – they were big on
raising HIV awareness.)

Those of us who lapped up *Bridget Jones* and *SATC* were seduced by the cosy, compulsive, booze-infused chatter of Bridget and Carrie and co. For them, too, the quest for/question of validation through men is the motivating force. Bridget made confession not just a virtue but a source of unbelievable charm and cheer, with the honesty of her diary: her weight, her embarrassments, the sex with Daniel Cleaver. But the tone of her diary was pre-*SATC* and very pre-*Girl with a One Track Mind* – it's pretty safe; we don't hear about cock rings, anal, or any real kinkiness. When she's not reporting her sex life directly to the reader, she's recounting her get-togethers with her friends – those piss-ups with Shazzer, Jude and her gay best friend Tom, are the comforting glue that holds her sanity together.

But whereas Helen Fielding made the diary format delectable for the modern woman reader, Bridget's practice of divulgence is nothing next to the women of *Sex and the City*. Their sophistication and world-wisdom (read: sexual wisdom) is entirely bound up in their ability to retell everything with wit and frankness. This need to confess all, along with their sexuality, are the very keys to the women's identity. But, rather than promoting a positive outcome, their discussion revolves around women's sexual dissatisfaction, and entrenches it.

In his essay, 'Sex, Confession and Witness', Jonathan Bignell discusses the prodigious amount of confession and self-doubt expressed by the ladies of *Sex and the City*. There is so much of it, he says, that viewers are left with the strong impression that feminine identity is centred on lack and disappointment. After all, one of the programme's great recurring themes is the worry over where the next helping of sex is coming from.

Like the women of *SATC*, we talk ourselves into and sometimes out of sexual anxiety. It's also true that modern society is preoccupied with sex and romance-related anxiety, and nobody more acutely than the single woman. We oscillate between tales of lack and tales of excess; tales of triumph and tales of woe.

And who can resist the girls' brunches? They are a tantalising picture of female sucess: no sweatpants and fry-ups and hangovers for them. No. It's haute couture, beguiling headpieces and fresh fruit for the girls of a Sunday morning. At night, it's the best nightspots, delicious cocktails and a sense of possibility. I wanted those brunches; those cocktails – a tempting backdrop to disclosure if ever there was one. Of course, translated to real life, there's a lot of 'cocktails with the girls' – often very sweet, expensive ones – and the divulgences to go with them.

Why we do it

These days, most people aren't murmuring their deviant thoughts to the priest in a box at church, hoping to escape damnation. A good few, however, are sharing them proudly with a newspaper or magazine who will guarantee your five minutes of fame as long as your story is shocking enough. 'First person is what we want,' a senior editor at *Grazia* told me. It's the prevailing format for women's magazines and tabloid newspapers. In *Big Brother*, the dishing of intimate secrets is the main component of the inmates' quests for survival and, more importantly, fame. Naturally, the focus of tell-alls tends to involve sex in some way, be it in the shocking relationships relentlessly thrashed out on *The Jeremy Kyle Show* to the 'I was a hooker' brand of memoir that's recently appeared, and so beloved of our newspapers.

Where did this need to both consume and tell 'intimate histories' (as per the title of former call girl Belle de Jour's bestselling diary, *The Intimate Adventures of a London Call Girl*) come from? This is a massive question, beyond the scope of this book, but to skirt it briefly I think is helpful. After all, the complex, insistent way we talk about men is a symptom of a world in which you are what you tell.

The question of how we came to be sexual blabbermouths is tackled admirably by Essex University sexologist Ken Plummer in *Telling Sexual Stories*:

'Every invention – mass print, the camera, the film, the video, the record, the telephone, the computer, the "virtual reality" machine – has helped, bit by bit, to provide a veritable erotopian landscape to millions of lives. The media has become sexualised. Sex, then, has become the Big Story. From Donahue and Oprah … to the hyperselling of Madonna's Sex, a grand message keeps being shouted: tell about your sex.'

Sure enough, of all the topics in the world, dating, singleness, weddings, relationships, particular men and sex take up the most airtime among a wide range of people. Why is that? It's partly that sex and love cut to the core of our egos, wellbeing and happiness. But there may be social reasons

– that go beyond the personal – at play, too. Michel Foucault, the social theorist, provides one useful explanation. We all have a secret, he says, and in modern times that secret is understood or assumed to always be sexual. Think about it: if there's a puzzle, you'll want to keep trying to work it out. It's not necessarily that you're hiding anything consciously; but let's face it, our love lives are far from black and white. And they're ever-shifting. The more we look at them and think about them and talk about them, the more there seems to be to look at and figure out. And so on.

As Foucault says darkly:

> 'What is peculiar to modern societies, in fact, is not that they consigned sex to a shadow existence, but that they dedicated themselves to speaking of it ad infinitum.'
>
> History of Sexuality

The downsides to talking about men

Not only does talking 'ad infinitum' not solve sexual mysteries, it can create them. Caroline, 32, has been single for a year following a serious relationship. In the last year, she's probably not had one animated social conversation that hasn't concerned her admittedly numerous conquests. She gives off an anxious energy at the end of these conversations, but out of habit she finds it very hard to exclude the topic of the men that are in or out of her life.

Feeling free to be open with friends is a great joy – and a great help. But when social interaction becomes more of a habitual spewing out than a meaningful sharing of thoughts and experiences, it stops providing answers, and actually grinds you down. Researchers at the University of Missouri-Columbia actually found that talking about boy-trouble with friends can make girls (the study focused on teenagers) depressed and anxious:

> 'Excessively discussing problems [...] characterized by mutual encouragement of problem talk, rehashing problems, speculating about problems, and dwelling on negative affect [...] may cause problems to seem more significant and harder to resolve. This could lead to more worries and concerns about problems and associated anxiety symptoms.'

Girls 'co-ruminate' more than boys and lo and behold, the boys in the study came out in better spirits. Susan Quilliam, sex therapist and author of the new edition of Alex Comfort's *Joy of Sex*, has written that although girly tell-alls are so habitual for most of us that we'd hardly know what to do without them, we might actually be happier if we kept more to ourselves.

Recounting experience with a therapist can be life-saving. But making *everyone* your therapist (or just all your friends) is unhelpful; using other people to justify yourself is not nearly as good as being able to justify yourself from within. This is particularly true with sex.

Pyschotherapist Ricky Emanuel, for one, is staunchly opposed to indiscriminately bringing what happens in the bedroom out into the free-for-all of social chat: 'There's no better judge of the infantile than the need to share sexuality in a public sphere. Adult sexuality has to be actually private and respectful of the other's privacy; as soon as it becomes other people's business, it becomes infantile.'

Feeling free to confide the deepest sexual 'secrets' is an essential development in mental and sexual health care. But outside the realms of therapy and the prosecution of sexual crime, something's gone a bit odd. It's true that some people don't like to share personal details full stop. But the things many of us keep to ourselves tend to be things we're embarrassed about or afraid of the consequences of admitting, like sleeping with your friend's ex. Sexual acts or desires are either secret, or they're fair game; there's nothing in between. There's little sense of the sacred in our ideas of sex: in breaking sex down and trotting out the details, or trying to pinpoint what exactly happened, sacredness or specialness gets trounced and the experiences we're in such a rush to talk about become void. Rochelle Gurstein's impassioned history of the culture of public exhibitionism insists that in baring all, we lose sense of what's important. She goes so far as to call it 'one of the bitterest of historical ironies' that in making possible a liberal attitude to intimacy and sex, we've ended up shining a neon light on things that should be left in the shade. Indeed, she believes that our culture of sexual exploitation has 'stripped love of its value'.

'Girly tell-alls are great, but we might actually be happier if we kept more to ourselves.'

The competitive nature of the tell-all – the sharing of details, the enumerating exploits and the details therein (penis size, positions, number of orgasms, dirty talk) – takes its toll on self-esteem too. 'The quantitative view of sex – how many orgasms etc – says nothing about its quality. It makes people feel they're failures,' says Emanuel. 'All this confessionalism just stimulates the fizzy excitement and the voyeurism. If you've had a meaningful encounter, you wouldn't want to share it, and you'd struggle to do so.'

Emanuel is right: putting *meaningful* sexual experience into words can't easily be done. So when we're talking about our sex lives, the emptiness alarms should be poised to go off. Raymond Carver's book of short stories, *What We Talk About When We Talk About Love*, is a whole book devoted to the idea that you can't put love into words. 'It ought to make us feel ashamed when we talk like we know what we're talking about when we talk about love.' Sex is a different story; but how interesting is it when it's just the act?

Who have I become?
There is something else unsettling about the habit of spilling and dirt-dishing – first, the sense that you're creating a persona, and second, that you're trapping yourself in it. The more you tell wild stories of your exploits, the more people say: 'Wow, you're really living the wild life' and, eventually, 'You *are* wild' or 'You really are something!' Worse, you start to bill yourself as someone whose chief trait is the ability to talk about men.

Once you've been labelled thus, either by others or by yourself, your narrative must prop up this idea with your verbal performance. You learn what to tell and what details delight. You also perfect the subtleties of story delivery and how to cast yourself in them: skilfully painting your role as the sexual adventurer, the victim, the explorer or the libertine. Laura, 29, told me numerous stories while I was writing this book. After a while, I got a distinct impression that, through them, she was cultivating a persona: that of the surprised bystander, haplessly finding herself in positions of enviable sexual embrace. Another friend of mine is always the voracious predator who seems to leave her conquests quaking and unsure (and, as she paints it, running away as soon as they recover the strength). She, I believe, uses her stories to express anxiety about her particularly assertive brand of femininity. Some of us use our stories to seem empowered; unscathed; exciting.

Ken Plummer gives this idea the stamp of academic approval in *Telling Sexual Stories*: 'No longer do people simply "tell" their sexual stories to reveal the "truth" of their sexual lives; instead, they turn themselves into *socially organised biographical objects*. They construct – even invent, though that may be too crass a term – tales of the intimate self, which may or may not bear a relationship to a truth.'

Katie Price has gone so far as to create a double, Jordan, to embody scandal and sex. And women like Zoe Margolis of *Girl with a One Track Mind*, Brooke Magnanti of *Belle de Jour*, Catherine Townsend of *Tales of a Sexual Adventuress* and many more have made commercial successes out of their exaggerated online personas.

Pre-Man Diet, as I'd trot out my entertaining stories, I couldn't help but feel I was slightly on autopilot, with the distinct impression of delivering a script. At the time, I was writing an article for *Psychologies* magazine on attraction, and I mentioned the idea to some of the experts I was talking to. Turned out, there is a kind of self-scripting that can mould people. Psychotherapists usually refer to a script whereby people decide stories about their lives in childhood, then try to follow them towards whatever ending they envisioned. But 'script' can be as literal as saying, 'I only like men with blond hair' or 'I always get rejected' or 'I love sex!' These can limit you as much as a fixed life vision. It strikes me that a good deal of our storytelling ('So I went on this date …' … 'So I was like, "what are you doing with that pot of honey?"' … 'The sex was amazing' … 'I shagged him in a broom closet' …) is an ongoing, but not always helpful, script-writing exercise.

Cutting down on the man talk: actually doing it

'All we talk about anymore is Big, or balls, or small dicks. How does it happen that four such smart women have nothing to talk about but boyfriends? … What about us? What we think, we feel, we know. Christ. Does it all have to be about them?'

This is Miranda speaking, in Season 2, episode 1, *SATC*. It's a good question; and I'd like to think the answer is definitely no.

Now, this rule, as with all of them, is to be applied within reason. As I said at the beginning of the chapter, a blanket ban on man chat would be unnatural and possibly unhealthy. There are certain crises, like a break-up, a horrendous date or rejection, or an ex you're still vaguely obsessed with getting back in touch with that require advice and comfort. But as far as general chit-chat is concerned, we're changing our approach.

1. Get in shape – mentally and verbally

Talking about men is a habit for many of us – something we reach for as an easy, comforting space-filler, something that's easy for everyone to get on board with. Plus, offering and getting advice can be fun.

So to break a habit like this requires training ourselves to talk about things other than what we got up to in bed, or indeed, about men at all – whether we're frustrated at their lack, confused by their signals or overwhelmed by their appetites. We have to be firm in this resolve. Every time we feel a man-related comment rise to our lips, we do a mental shuffle. What else is there we can say instead?

2. Develop a filter

You need to confide in your friends. That's what they're there for. But you don't need to externalise everything as soon as you think it – or as soon as it happens. To observe this rule, choose carefully what topics require sharing. The following can be kept to yourself:

- early dates
- the details of sexual encounters
- horniness
- a hot guy you saw
- texts or silences from a man you're interested in or dating
- recent exploits

- potential men of interest
- the general character of a man you are obsessed with
- your ex

Topics meriting a blab

- feelings of definite pain or despair
- a major rejection, e.g. break-up
- the advances of someone completely unexpected

3. Impose a time frame

Everything in moderation. If you do feel that a man update is essential, get it out there in as few words as possible, nail down why something's got you down or why you're thrilled, and get what you want from your friends – that nugget of advice, that boost of reassurance, that backslap. Then close the topic before it drags you into a pit of indecision, despair or obsession (or a frenzied high), and your friends into a parliamentary advice-giving session. Twenty minutes should be adequate before you guide everyone on to brighter, more fruitful pastures.

4. Train your friends

Weaning both parties off junk-food chat is essential if we're to lift ourselves out of the co-rumination rut, bring fresh ideas to our heads, and leave us fresh for clear-headed assessment of a real romantic prospect when (and if) it appears. Crucially, we need to show ourselves how much more we're capable of. Take it from me: leaving men out of my social interactions had an instant effect on my bearing and self-respect. I stopped being the single girl with entertaining stories, and started being … a woman in my own right. You can only do this if your friends are on board – either consciously or subconsciously.

5. Show a reluctance to talk about men

I don't think there's any need to spell out that you 'don't want to talk about it'. Your mates might take this the wrong way, like you're being funny with them. It might also make them think something is really wrong, causing them concern, and lead to even more questioning. But most people are sensitive enough to pick up on a resistance to talking about a certain topic. If you've had a date, don't blab about it in advance, and don't raise it afterwards. If they bring it up, just sum it up in a breezy few words.

6. Distract them

It's not hard. You may think that getting your gossipy mates off the scent would require superhuman strength, but like anyone, they just want a good chit-chat. They'll soon forget about the 'So, what did you get up to last night' opener if you beat them to it with: 'Don't you think Twitter is ruining our brains?' or 'What's the best way you've ever cooked white fish? I need inspiration.'

7. Choose who you confide in

Even in a crisis, some friends will do more harm than good – even though everyone means well. I know a woman, Sue, who was on the counselling team for a friend during a sticky break-up. The friend got so flustered and confused by all the advice flying at her that Sue eventually told her to stop discussing it with all her friends and to choose one or two and very carefully. 'What I find bizarre,' says Sue, 'is how women share so much of this stuff with so many friends, most of whom aren't equipped to give good advice and just make the problem worse!'

What she means is this: Every friend has their strong points, but when it comes to man crisis management, choose the one (or ones) with the strongest relationship track record, the most honest style, and the busiest job. This way she isn't going to be tempted to draw the conversation out because she knows she has limited time with you and she'll want to cover everything efficiently.

8. 'So, what's the man situation?': how to respond

No matter how hard you try to be breezy and evasive, sometimes friends can't be put off this direct request for information. You have to handle this well not to appear like you're lying. Saying: 'Nothing' is too abrupt and, of course, it might be a lie. So use a decoy detail: 'Oh, nothing much sadly. There is this very hot guy who just joined my desk at work, though. Probably has a girlfriend!' Then turn it around: 'Didn't you say that guy you hate at work just got promoted? Tell me about that – sounds annoying.' And off you go. But beware: the kiss of death is opening the door wide with the wrong kind of 'nothing' – i.e., one that says, 'I'm depressed, let's talk about how there are not men in my life/no good men anywhere.' The key is in the fast turnaround to another topic.

9. Managing their expectations

If your friends count on you to be a font of man-related amusement, and stopping abruptly will be a big deal, then wean them off it over the period of a week. Be less and less interesting – in other words, cut down on the juice. You've been feeding them goodies. Time to empty the man-story cupboard until they know (or assume) it's bare.

10. Develop the art of conversation

The most passionate advocate of actual conversation, rather than just talk or chat, is Oxford scholar Theodore Zeldin. He begins his lovely little book, *Conversation*, with BT's 'It's good to talk' slogan. 'But of course that's only half the truth,' he continues. 'Nobody could say simply, "It's good to eat", without adding that many of the things we like to eat do us no good at all. If we used diet books for conversations, as much as for our meals, they would warn us off many different types of talk, and they would not find it easy to say where we could go to taste the haute cuisine of conversation.' Once again, food is a natural metaphor for our purposes: we need more haute cuisine, more sustaining, delicious talk, and less of the emotionally bloating, short-term highs that come from dishing the dirt on our sexual experiences.

11. Why conversation rules

Zeldin's passionate point is that conversation is productive and even electrifying, a major force of cultural improvement, but that 'talk' is not. '"It's good to talk",' he reiterates, 'is the slogan of the 20th century, which put its faith in self-expression, sharing information and trying to be understood. But talking does not necessarily change one's own or other people's feelings or ideas. I believe the 21st century needs a new ambition, to develop not talk but conversation, which does change people. Real conversation catches fire. It involves more than sending or receiving information.'

Zeldin is a romantic, but believes that real love can and should be founded on the exchange of ideas as conducted through conversation – rather than simply on eyes meeting across a crowded room. The books, film and TV of our culture represent love and courtship via lusty chemistry; but good conversations, he says, can cause and build love too. 'A relationship may start chemically or romantically, but conversation adds something infinitely precious to it.'

12. Remember; your singleness is an opportunity

If Zeldin is right (and I like to think he is, even if he is a touch idealistic), then we stand to have better romantic relationships by developing our conversational skills. Our single periods are the perfect time to practise them – we don't have to use our talk time thrashing out the status of our relationships; nor trying to convince the kids to eat their dinner. With practice, we can try to move beyond *ourselves*, and towards the more rewarding realm of our *ideas*. That's what Miranda was getting at in her outburst in *Sex and the City*, and it's what Zeldin puts perfectly here: 'Asking that same old question, "Who am I?" cannot get us much further. However fascinating one may think one is, there is a limit to what one can know about oneself. Other people are infinitely more interesting, have infinitely more to say.'

13. And finally: honour our foremothers!

We have a lot to talk about beyond our romantic or sexual discontents – and I can't help but feel we owe it to our foremothers to engage our brains more when we converse, and not to let the culture of 'you're nobody until someone loves you' sidetrack us into dead ends. Think of Jane Austen's caustic remark, no doubt betraying a yowl of personal frustration: 'Imbecility in females is a great enhancement of their personal charms, there is a portion of [men] too reasonable […] to desire anything more in woman than ignorance.' Or Mary Wollstonecraft, who rails against the entrapment of females in a world of trifles, in an age before girls were educated like boys: 'In youth their faculties are not brought forward by emulation; and having no serious scientific study, if they have natural sagacity it is turned too soon on life and manners. [Females] dwell on effects […] without tracing them back to causes' (*A Vindication of the Rights of Woman*).

We have every opportunity of 'scientific study' now, ladies, so let's show how much more we can talk about than who we did or did not take home, and how and why.

How I followed this rule:

Pre-Man Diet

As soon as anything of note happened with a guy, I'd take it – like a good golden retriever bringing back the stick – to my friends. This habit dated back to my teenage years, when anything that happened (happenings were indeed rare) seemed a massive deal.

As an adult, this habit meant that I was reporting everything – great and small; important and not. It was partly to share with friends, partly to gain their approval, partly because I relied overly on their advice and was afraid to advise myself. Which is to say, I stopped being able to process experiences by myself. And, as I talked about them with my friends, I started *over*processing them. So, a guy whose importance was minimal, or whose deed (text, silence, gesture) had been of small importance, would become a big deal simply because he'd been discussed as a matter of course, sometimes at great length.

I am good at telling stories and analysing, so my friends enjoyed my tales. Sometimes they led (and lead) to truly interesting revelations. When I started thinking about the Man Diet, it occurred to me that by talking all my experiences into the ground, I was ultimately losing touch with what had really happened. And often I'd leave these general man-discussions feeling anxious and ill at ease.

How I did it

First, I stopped jumping up like a circus dog to the ringmaster when asked: 'So, man situation?' or 'What did *you* get up to last night?' I just gave a brief answer along the 'nothing' lines, and saw that my friends were vaguely disappointed, but nothing they wouldn't get over in approximately three seconds.

Then, I started thinking twice about what I said regarding men, when it would have been my moment to initiate. Often, on very brief reflection, I'd realise I didn't actually want to talk about something. I'd start the conversation about something else. All it took was a second thought to change the course of the conversation.

How did following this rule make me feel?

Smarter, freer, happier. From the very first conversations in which I declined to take the bait from my friends, or started up a different topic, I felt like I was getting outside myself. That there was more to me and my feelings than men and validation. It's a great feeling. You feel yourself expanding and brightening, like a watered flower.

How hard was it?

5/10. It wasn't a breeze, in the way that catching yourself mid-habit is never a breeze. But it was actually an enjoyable rule to implement. I enjoyed feeling and hearing

myself (and my friends) talk about other things. One friend
is doing a master's degree in philosophy, for example, and
it was great to have air space to talk about that rather than,
say, the ok-ish lawyer that I'd been emailing. Pre-Man Diet,
the degree would have been utterly squeezed out, or at
least, put much lower on the list, than something
romance-related.

Everyone's friends are different. Mine were happy to talk
about other things, in general. And those that weren't –
well, I was happy to listen to them talk about their views,
experiences and reflections. My friends made it relatively
easy.

What did I let through the cracks?

Anything that felt genuinely important – a surprising and/or
interesting/amusing advance; out-of-the-blue contact from
an ex; a real quandary or sadness. But in the early stages of
the Man Diet, you will probably have less to report than
usual, because you won't be Facebook stalking, pursuing or
(if possible) getting wasted and having lots of no-strings
sex. I, for one, went through a peaceful, quiet patch – and
instead of complaining of a drought as usual, I just enjoyed
it and took it as a bonus that made following this rule
easier.

And now?

I am the world's biggest talker and – as you might have
guessed – relationships are a big thing with me. But

post-Man Diet, I am a lot more choosy about what I talk about, man-wise. The result is that I enjoy those conversations, when they do happen, so much more. That said, nobody's perfect. Occasionally I slip into phases where I hear myself moaning about men. Usually it's because I'm worried about something else – my weight, my looks, whether or not my biological clock is ticking – and men are a handy (but toxic) prism through which to think about these things. When I hear myself starting conversations with comments such as, 'Is my vibe really bad right now? I keep turning men away!' or 'Woah, that guy over there is so good looking. Way out of my league, though', I try to change the topic before I get too stuck in.

SOS!

Man chat is so ingrained in female friendships that a slip every now and then will hardly be surprising. Nor is a binge fatal (though it can lead to making mountains out of things better left as molehills). But if you find yourself panicking about not having anything interesting or funny to say, or you're reaching into the man store-cupboard of chat out of habit, spot that you're heading into junk-food love territory and do the following:

- List five things you've done in the last week that are vaguely interesting and have nothing to do with men. Read the list several times and update it as you go. Which leads to …

- Have genuinely juicy backup topics, but think of them in advance. Don't give yourself time to get sidetracked onto whether or not so and so is asexual, or whether that player who always compliments your rack is worth your time. Go straight in on work, diets, politics, parents. The urge to talk about the player will dissipate. Promise.

- Go out and do something powerfully anecdotal that has nothing to do with men. You could take your lofty project (rule five) and ramp it up a notch. Joining a dinner party cookery course will instantly give you lots of new material as well as being perfect for the Man Diet. So would doing a 10k run, learning to use a powerdrill or investing in the stock market.

♄ Identify the man-mad friends, for whom romantic status is the be-all and end-all of conversation, and be prepared. It sounds drastic, but perhaps don't make plans with these girls for a week or two, until you've re-centred. When you see them, not only will you be met with: 'So, any cute men?' but you'll be most likely to worry about coming up with non-man-related conversation with them. If you are going to see them, the key is not to be taken off guard.

Rule Number

Do Something Lofty

You need this rule if you …

- Think or talk about men out of habit – either in a dull moment on your walk to the Tube or when meeting up with friends.
- Find it easier to talk or think about some aspect of your love life than anything else.
- Pore over anything from a text to a parting kiss to an ex's new girlfriend for hours at a time.
- Make things far more complicated than they need to be through rumination and analysis.
- Feel like men are your full-time job.
- Start talking about that guy *again* or complain about the single life and your friends seem a little bored.
- Wish you had something new and challenging in your life – apart from a guy with communication issues.
- Want to rediscover that you're a good, clever, driven person first and foremost – rather than a singleton.

Goes well with ...

- 👤 Dwell on Your Sense of Self
- 👤 No Facebook Stalking
- 👤 No Talking About Men
- 👤 Take a Break from Internet Dating
- 👤 Take a Break from the Games

C hristmas 2010, and Kara was worn down. There had been a slew of unsatisfactory man encounters – two hot guys on holiday in Egypt who had refused to use condoms at the 11th hour; a one-night stand with a lawyer that she'd thought would become more but didn't; a wrangle with an attractive German at a wedding with no follow-up; a sommelier she kept trying to ask out to no avail; and a Norwegian, the only guy who was up for seeing her on the regular, who made her brain ache with boredom.

These were the facts. Then there was the analysis – by the time she and her friends had finished addressing the seeming cornucopia of men in her life ('I don't have lots of men! They're all crap or don't like me!' Kara would protest), her head would be buzzing with all their exclamations, instructions, pep talks, questions. It was a full-time job sleeping with a handful of men – not for the time the men took up (for that was woefully short) but for the amount of mental space they took up. She kept thinking back to them: Was the sex good? Had they not been in touch because of something she'd said? Was she becoming a slut, or enviably experienced? Was

she damaging herself emotionally without knowing it,
or gathering valuable wisdom? Had she looked fat while
on top of the German, since it was after a big meal? Did
some of them even still think about her?

What happened next ...

After a while, the inverse relationship between time spent
thinking about and discussing men, and the time she actually spent with said men, got her angry. She'd start sounding bitter. She'd say things like 'Well of course, no man ever
fancies me!' and her friends would protest wildly. She would
bring most conversations around to herself – and men.
Somewhere between a performing monkey and an old lady
who can't get over the milk being delivered half an hour
late.

Kara could hear herself becoming a bit obsessive – not to
mention negative – but she couldn't stop. It was like she
was in man mode; only alive in relation to men, only interested in talking about men, only animated by them. It
always happened after or during periods of intense sexual
activity – everyone wanted to dissect it, herself included.
But she didn't like the feeling that everything else was
getting squeezed out. And the talk, analysis and the rest
wasn't actually helping matters, it was just making her
sound bitter. When she concentrated at work, she felt good.
That is, when her mind was completely elsewhere than
herself.

During the Christmas break, she decided to do the polar
opposite of thinking or talking about men. She started reading on the plane to the States, where she was going to see
her family. At first it was boring. She struggled on though,

proud to be even holding Tolstoy's mega-tome among all the other passengers either watching reruns of *Family Guy* or skimming the airline magazine. By the time the plane flew over Iceland, she was actually beginning to enjoy it. By the time she landed, she felt like an intellectual.

But on a real, genuine level, she felt like she'd had a break. A better kind than if she'd just vegged out with the *Twilight* series. This is because her brain had been working hard on something other than where her next date was coming from – and for several hours, too. Obviously when she was at work or talking to her mother on the phone her mind was busy, but it wasn't a nourishing busy, just a stressed busy. Over the course of a six-hour flight, she'd become naturally preoccupied with a story beyond her own and Prince Andrew was beginning to obsess her mildly in that Russian aristocrat way they have. When she got off the plane, her mother

'She decided to read War and Peace. *Take that, bitches, she muttered to herself as she packed the huge tome in her hand-baggage.'*

complimented her on her 'clear eyes' and said she seemed happy. Kara chuckled – realising she wanted to get back to Prince Andrew and his stupid but beautiful princess Anna more than she wanted to check email or Facebook for any developments with the Hungarian barman she'd met the night before she flew out.

So I say ...

Stop the flood of junk-food love by diving into something totally different: something asexual and preferably lofty.

There is no one 'lofty' – different strokes for different folks and all that. By 'lofty' I mean worthy, substantial, challenging. It could be cultural, like reading about art for an hour a day, or it could be social, like volunteering a few hours of your time each week for a local charity or going to an exhibition to see something that you wouldn't normally find space in your diary to do. *War and Peace* worked for Kara. You might find offering to walk your aunt's dog lofty.

For this rule to work, your chosen activity has to have the following qualities:

1. It must take you away from yourself completely
When doing your lofty thing, your attention must be entirely focused on what you're doing. You will naturally forget yourself and that's the key. Anything forced, that doesn't truly absorb you, won't work.

2. It must be a positive (not neutral) activity
That is, it must make you either engage with something higher, whether it be the literary gods), or the gods of doing good.

3. It should help improve you
When I first tried this rule myself, I thought bodily improvement would count – dieting, working out and so on. While I still think that when done sensibly, turning your body into a project is a good way to re-channel your energy, I now don't think that bodily improvement alone counts. To really benefit from this rule, your mind, soul or conscience needs to be improved through some kind of enjoyable challenge,

be it physical, intellectual or social. I hate boot camps and boot camp ideology, so when I say challenge, I really do mean an enjoyable one.

It can be a tiny challenge – like getting through the boring bits of *War and Peace*; a medium challenge – like deciding to learn the history of French cinema; or a big challenge – like spending time with needy children when you're terrified of kids. It depends what you like. I am always grateful for big challenges once I've done them, but I usually don't feel like undertaking them. Small challenges that I enjoy – like cooking a meal for my elderly relatives – are just fine. You might be one of those people who has never run a mile and within a year has completed the London Marathon. In that case, it's all about big challenges for you. The marathon is a good one, by the way, because you're not only challenging yourself big-style over a long period of time, but you're doing something lofty in raising money for charity.

4. It should widen your world

Anything that can make you see the world with more wisdom, insight or compassion counts. Learning is the key here. We learn constantly, consciously and unconsciously. Some people's jobs require a steep and very conscious learning curve, but for most people jobs don't provide this in the way that the Man Diet requires.

So choose how you like to learn, and be open to unexpected learning. If you like to imbibe info straight off the page, ask your cleverest friends for some books they recommend on a topic you're interested in. Go to the library and see if you can get them. Ask your friends or respected colleagues for blogs or websites they like – and make them your favourites. If you like to learn through doing, then there is an almost endless choice of activities you can do, you just have to choose an area and get googling.

What works for me: the book cure

Whenever I've felt sucked into a particularly thick wodge of junk-food love, it's books that yank me into a different headspace. Fiction in particular (or a brilliant companion like this one is, naturally!) is the surest way to get me out of any rut. Because without even realising it, I suddenly care more about what's going on in the story than in my own head.

Summer 2010, and I'd had a particularly rough few weeks and was feeling a bit low about life, love and the universe. I was spending far too long complaining and feeling glum. So I forced myself to pick up the second Stieg Larsson (of Millennium trilogy fame) book and get stuck in. Within half an hour I was a different person. I cared about what happened to Lisbeth Salander more than my own troubles. Without any conscious effort, my spirits lifted and I started noticing the world around me instead of the world inside my head. The sun on my shoulders, the breeze in my hair, the cute crinkles in the faces of my friends when they laughed all struck me as rather lovely instead of being invisible to me.

Now, I've talked about loftiness. How could reading Stieg Larsson be lofty? It's not. But it's a start. Once I'd wrested myself from self-absorption and improved my mood, I was ready to get stuck into a range of other books. My mind began crawling over stories that took me from 20th-century Russia (try Simon Sebag Montefiore's easy-reading

Sashenka for a gripping novel that will teach you all you need to know about Stalinist Russia at the same time) to 19th-century rural Britain (Thomas Hardy's heart-rending *Tess of the D'Urbervilles* will put all your romantic woes in perspective – and then some – while presenting a smashingly drawn portrait of farm life at the end of the 1800s. No, I didn't think I cared either).

Other books that have made me forget my woes, improved my mind through historical learning and their wonderful use of language, and left me emotionally fired up include ...

***Daniel Deronda* by George Eliot:** Daniel is both gorgeous and a difficult nut to crack; Gwendolyn, who falls for him, is a beauty who marries for status and money and suffers for it. Lots of strange and accurate Jewish lore and exploration of heritage, ranging from country manors to London alleyways.

***London Fields* by Martin Amis:** Not everyone loves old Mart. But I do. He is the most creative wordsmith alive – but only his old books, like this one, are both electric and gripping. This is a London murder story: Keith Talent is hilarious; Nicola Six is haunting, Marmaduke the baby is terrifying. You'll be grateful that a) you aren't married to Keith and b) you don't live in Amis's pre-nuclear London, with its low sun boring into the residents' eyes at all times.

***Portnoy's Complaint* by Philip Roth:** Roth's first and horniest book. You think you have frustrated sexual desire? Try Alex Portnoy on for size – at one point, he masturbates behind a billboard advertising chopped liver en route to his Bar Mitzvah lesson. He also masturbates in his sister's lingerie.

Neris and India's Idiot Proof Diet: OK, OK, it's not lofty, per se. But this is way more than a diet book – it's about denial, self-esteem, the lies we tell ourselves, and most of all, it's a bloody good argument for putting the excuses aside and 'being all you can be'. It sits on my bedside table at all times. India Knight's voice is your voice and my voice, in this instance. Jolly pictures of pants, cheeses and lipsticks are a bonus.

***1984* by George Orwell:** Maybe you had to read this in school. Somehow, it bypassed me. But at one of the most unpleasant emotional phases of my life, I picked it up and began missing my Tube stop I got so into it. There's so much to lap up – 'doublethink', 'telescreens', 'Room 101', the whole weird world of Big Brother in a post-apocalyptic, totalitarian Britain. The love story at the centre of it all is weird, poignant and finally, devastating. This is high on the lofty scale because it's an important book, whose words and concepts come up in lots of discussion even now.

Just go with the flow …

Books are my bias. But doing anything positive that makes you forget yourself (don't even think about going near drugs or booze!) is widely recognised to be powerfully good. The concept that supports this best is 'flow', the brainchild of the man with the world's most difficult name – Mihály Csíkszentmihályi, a psychology professor. The idea of flow is used across many fields of psychology, and those immersed in it experience an energised feeling of full immersion in an activity. So to cut to the chase, flow is when you feel full focus and involvement in an activity and a sense of success in the process of it.

Crucially, flow means that the pleasure of doing has won out over the chaos of feeling. According to Csíkszentmihályi, when you're in flow, emotions are not just contained, but they're perfectly channelled towards the task in hand. When you're caught in depression or rumination, you are 'barred' from flow. It's exactly then that you should seek to attain it, though.

You might be wondering if you've experienced flow before. Well, I can tell you that you have. In fact, we all have. As children it happens all the time. You know that completely focused look toddlers have while poking something new and strange? Or learning to walk? That's what we have to aim for. Of course, as adults it's harder to achieve real flow than just finding a new toy – and most of us can already walk. We have to find something we love actually *doing*, which is rewarding in itself – and it can't be eating kebabs, downing wine or staring in the mirror.

For true flow, I'm not even sure that reading counts. Reading is a form of doing, but not in a strict sense. Ideal flow activities are playing an instrument, performing or practising a physical challenge, teaching, giving someone a manicure, sewing, cooking, training a dog. You have to be so into your activity that you stop being self-conscious; instead you're aware. Often, time will feel distorted; like an hour passing in a minute.

> *For our purposes, it means that the men who are dragging you down emotionally simply vanish into the horizon. Meanwhile, your strong, true and energetic self surges to the fore, making you feel like a million bucks.*

Use your great brain for more than analysing men: it deserves it ...

We have brains, and we can use them to amazing effect. Thinking creatively is the best use of the heads we were born with – whether in problem solving, applying a new maths formula to some financial issue at work, or finding seemingly impossible props for your kid sister's university play. It's all brain work that doesn't involve looking in the mirror, scheming to make a man keen, trading man stories with friends, or deciding who to reply to on a dating website – and is all the better for it. In fact, studies have shown a significant positive relationship between happiness and creative endeavour. The feeling that you are in control of what you do, rather than being controlled by it, strongly enhances that positive relationship.

Lisa Bloom, a graduate of Yale Law School and a regular pundit in the US, recently came out with a book called

Think: How to Stay Smart in a Dumbed Down World. In it she tries to light a better path for women today, who she feels are on one hand excelling more than ever before at work and university, but on the other, getting more and more obsessed with and addicted to reality TV, celebrities and looking in the mirror. Women have fallen off the intellectual path, Bloom says, and the book offers solutions to 'Reclaiming the Brain God Gave You'.

Applied to the Man Dieter: whether you're a reality TV junkie, can't stop staring at pics of Cheryl Cole in a bikini or spend far too much time talking and thinking about men who don't deserve the honour, it's time to increase brain function. We're trying to rise as high as we can go given our natural strengths, not engage in the thankless task of fitting ourselves around what men may or may not be thinking. This is all about vigorous brainpower and positive activity.

More to life than love?

His book is far from sexy, but I like very much what the late psychologist Anthony Storr has to say on creativity, and the worth of getting involved in the lofty and/or asexual. He argues that interests that go beyond the self can be a source of happiness purer than romantic love – an extremely controversial statement these days. Storr blames Freud for making love and sex the benchmark of human fulfilment, resulting in a widespread conviction that the most important thing in the human world are romantic relationships. Indeed, he says that interpersonal/social relationships are too weak to support the massive amounts of stress and importance we attach to them; 'the burden of value' we put on them will lead to breakdown. Storr challenges the assumption that only intimate realtionships will make us truly happy and that if they aren't doing so, there must be something profoundly wrong with them. Translated for the Man Dieter: if you don't have a partner, there must be something wrong with you, a feeling many single women have expressed to me.

OK, they're a little beyond our scope, but Storr points out that some of world's great thinkers turned down romantic fulfilment and families – Descartes, Newton, Spinoza, Nietzsche, Kant. They're men, though, so they'd have been seen as noble thinkers suffering for their art, whereas historically, single women are generally seen to be frigid or diseased. But let's look at a few of the women who remained unattached in order to pursue other forms of greatness; it's a plump and inspiring list. They include the pioneering sociologist Harriet Martineau (1802–1876), who boasted of being 'probably the happiest single woman in England'. She proclaimed: 'My business in life has been to think and learn, and to speak out with absolute freedom what I have thought and learned.'

Barbara McClintock (1902–1992), winner of the Nobel Prize for Medicine in 1983, also chose to never marry – her business was to devote herself to research on genetic mutations. Margaret Brent (c.1601–1671) was a colonial landowner and attorney for the Governor of Maryland and a very early feminist. No man needed. Elizabeth I remained famously virginal, choosing a metaphorical marriage to her subjects: 'all my husbands, my good people'. Lise Meitner, genius nuclear physicist, was Germany's first female physics lecturer, appointed to the post at the University of Berlin in 1926. Man free.

And let's not forget poet Emily Dickinson, novelists Jane Austen and Anne Brontë, the feminist Gloria Steinem, explorer Gertrude Bell, sign-language pioneer Helen Keller, former Secretary of State Condoleezza Rice, and, of course, Oprah. Florence Nightingale also had her mind on higher things, turning down a marriage proposal because 'I have a moral, an active nature which requires satisfaction [...] I could be satisfied to spend a life with him in combining our different powers to some great object. I could not satisfy this nature by spending a life with him in making society and arranging domestic things.'

I'm not saying that we're all cut out to be nuclear physicists, poets, queens, secretaries of state, pilots and novelists. And the key difference between us and most of the women mentioned is modernity – we don't have to choose between wifehood and career fulfilment. All the same, the list is worth noting because it shows:

- Throughout history, there has been a startling connection between being a truly trailblazing woman and not being married.
- Many successful women felt that they were freer to do their thang without a man in their lives, and, like Florence Nightingale, not willing to compromise a different kind of lofty 'satisfaction' for any man.
- These women derived the chief meaning in life from doing and thinking, not marrying and breeding.

- It is possible to be mega-fulfilled without ticking the hubbie and kids box.
- We respect them not because they are single, but because they attacked life with so much interest and determination.
- We don't need to denounce sex and love in the attempt to become truly great. But, like these women, we should give our best selves free rein to be creative. For us this might one day include having a partner – after all, unlike many of these women, we're not likely to end up with a patriarch who expects a martini or equivalent in his hand at 6pm every day and all his ironing done. But what the Man Dieter should do *now* is give her creative energies a kick up the arse.

It's old-school and deeply uncool, but whenever I find myself Facebook stalking, plotting, feeling rejected, or feeling like I have an itch to scratch with some pointless dalliance or other, I turn to Storr's *Solitude* for inspiration. Basically, when I feel that junk-food love is engulfing me, I read the lines about how pursuing your interests – from stock speculation to piano playing to gardening – can make you happy. Happier, indeed than many an intimate romp.

That's right. From *War and Peace* to gardening to share trading, the horizon for the Man Dieter is vast, if we'll let it be. Now's the time to think about that hobby as a carrier pigeon breeder.

So how do you embrace something lofty?

When you're feeling caught in a pattern of junk-food love think, the idea of hauling yourself into a different head-space where men don't exist except as cheerful friends or acquaintances can seem daunting in the extreme. After all, there may be a guy who's messing with your mind to such an extent you feel totally powerless. As discussed in the Take a Break from the Games chapter, men are bizarrely good at wrapping you in emotional knots. We all know that awful butterfly feeling where you're afraid to seem keen, afraid to displease him, but can't wait for his next text or email because, frankly, you're hooked on his inscrutable coldness or paradoxical mixed signals. A guy doesn't even have to be hot or particularly charming to get you hooked – he just has to play his game well.

'A guy doesn't even have to be hot or particularly charming to get you hooked – he just has to play his game well.'

When you're in this labyrinth, getting out seems impossible. We all have friends who can't get over some guy that's never going to agree to properly go out with them. Hell, I've been in many unreciprocated love-knots, where a guy has me obsessed without ever offering anything. I know the feeling of thinking the world has basically come down to my obsession with him. But it is possible to want to *try* to lift yourself from this energy-sink hole, and to do it too. Trust me – I've done it, even though I'm far from being one of these pragmatic 'I'll just think about something else' people.

Count yourself lucky if you're free of one of those endless and confusing situations right now. If it's a simple matter of getting the mind off men in general, or forgetting certain men in particular – like the four unsatisfactory characters you've shagged recently that have made you wish you hadn't – then you'll be fine in two days.

Doing something lofty: actually doing it

1. Pick a lofty area you'd like to focus on

These tend to be: athletic, community, intellectual, artistic, crafty, musical, bookish. Remember, it has to fulfil certain criteria (refresh yourself with the list above), so if it's athletic, there has to be a charitable element; if bookish, something that expands your horizons, either linguistically or historically. If artistic or crafty, it has to be active – you have to be doing it, not buying it. Same with music: doing, not just listening (unless you've launched yourself on a music-appreciation programme).

A reminder of good lofty activities likely to bring about flow: gardening (for your grandpa), training dogs, helping kids, writing something with a purpose, playing an instrument or trying to learn one, getting stuck into a quality book (not strictly part of the flow vision, but never mind, it works for me), volunteering in any field (apart from terrorism), giving makeovers to women at homeless shelters.

2. Decide how much time you're going to give your activity

Let's be honest, you work hard and need to have enough time to party and wind down after a long day or week. But you don't need *all* your spare time for quaffing cocktails and sitting on the sofa watching *Jersey Shore*. Be realistic. Is it something you can do a little bit of every day, like training for the marathon? If it's an academic project, then you can easily do, say, half an hour a day on the Tube or, better yet, when you get home before switching on the TV. If it's something more community-oriented, it'll take a bit more work. Start by googling. Then send an email. If you don't hear anything, follow up with a phone call. Offer yourself a couple hours a week. Imagine how good you'll feel when you step out with your mates of a Saturday night.

3. Decide what your junk-food love addiction is

It might be:

a) One guy that's not giving you what you want and taking too much brain space, not to mention making you frown more than smile.

b) Brooding on singleness and low quality of available men in general.

c) A few guys, all of whom are mediocre but none of whom you can bring yourself to get rid of.

d) Sex. Or more specifically, your sexual performance and worries about how it has affected recent shags.

If a), you need to go in heavy, and be brutal. Start immediately. Don't wait for things to improve, because they won't. To get yourself in a position where you can start your chosen activity, dive into a book that has no obvious comparisons with your situation. Grab a thriller, to yank you in.

Once you start reading, and later, training, cooking, playing, gardening, whatever your lofty activity is, shut off all electronic devices. The last thing you want is interruption from him. At the times when you'd normally try to find him on Facebook or start texting him, grab your book-weapon and get stuck in.

If you're b), adopt a brisk approach. Set a time for starting – say, a week from now – and line up your ducks so you can get stuck in. Set up a substitution whereby the time you normally devote to brooding or bitching becomes the time you either do, work on, or talk about your new activity.

If you're a c), same rules as apply to b). Instead of thinking about those guys, or getting in touch with them, bring yourself back to your project. Or, if you're suddenly overwhelmed by some bad-for-you attention, adopt some of the strictness of a) and reach for the nearest thrilling book.

If you're d), your self-esteem needs a big boost. Start with a project guaranteed to bring validation quickly – if you have any elderly relatives, ring them up right now and arrange to go round and do something nice for them. The feeling of good person-ness that will flood you will make you see that your sex performance hang-up is probably out of proportion with reality. Then, decide to study up on feminism, to get a firm grasp on how you are among many women who worry about their sexual situation – and find out why culture has led us to compare ourselves to porn stars. Your brain will expand, and you'll give yourself the chance to say: 'I feel this way because of culture, and I have the power to change it.'

4. Bring others into your new lofty activity

Start talking about what you're doing and you won't believe how many other people either have similar interests, know someone who does, or can recommend things. This process is fun, exciting, and does everything the Man Diet is supposed to do. Bring on the new, curious, mind-expanding you.

How I followed this rule:

Pre-Man Diet

I always had something on the boil – a book, a writing project. But they just fit into whatever else I was doing and I didn't make the mental effort to embrace them as a tonic to man-related furore. I didn't carve out time for them – they just kinda happened, or didn't. The word 'discipline' is far from sexy – but I like it. I had no discipline about my lofty activities – in the same way, I had no discipline about when I talked about or pursued or stalked Facebook potentials.

How I did it

I thought of the meatiest, scariest book on my shelf and I decided to read it. It was *War and Peace*. Aside from work, finishing *War and Peace* was to be my main priority. It took months and made me feel extremely smug and lofty and engaged in the finer things in life – snobbery aside, it really helped focus my mind on something gratifyingly non-social.

How did it make me feel?

Very concerned with the fate of Natasha Rostov and Prince Andrew. Also comforted – there was a clearly defined bulk to work through, 1,400 pages to be precise. There was a Saturday evening towards the end of reading the book. My flatmate was going out to the pub for the Champions League Final – and instead of going with her as I was vaguely tempted to do – I said to myself: 'I find watching football really boring, no matter how many eager-beaver men are crammed in the room with me. I am going to stay on the sofa and read *War and Peace* solidly for three hours.' I did so, and felt so unbelievably nourished by 9pm that I went out into the night with a glow people actually commented on. I felt good that I'd made an assertive decision to do something literary instead of social. And I felt good as a result of having concentrated on one thing for three hours. Whatever it is that floats your lofty boat – from gardening, to poetry writing, to volunteering at Oxfam – I think you'll find the same.

How long did I keep this rule up for?

Forever, I hope. OK, so I finished *War and Peace*. But I'd so enjoyed the way it had shaped my mental life that I soon set about another challenge – learning to knit. In one form or another, I've not only kept this rule up, but it's felt like a life saver at times and pulled me out of potentially dark or unproductive spirals. Who knows what I'll do next. Reading's a constant and my first port of call, but maybe it'll be wine tasting or babysitting my neighbour's toddler, if they'd trust me (it'd certainly be a challenge).

SOS!

The most likely wagon pusher-offer here is the idea that you don't have time to do your lofty activity. If you've stopped doing yours for this or another reason, then consider these points:

🚹 You DO have time. Promise. When you're going through a busy patch it can seem like there's no time at all left in the world and never will be. Not so. It'll pass and it's your job to spot when a new time slot emerges where you can fit in your lofty activity – otherwise it'll just get layered over with non-lofty and possibly man-oriented activities.

🚹 Try something new. Are you done knitting your scarf, reading *War and Peace*, taking a cooking class, or is the dog you've been walking getting too feisty? Well – there's a lot more where that came from – be imaginative.

🚹 Keep up the good work! You're doing wonderfully – and if you've let it slide and find yourself giving undue mental energy to the 'man sitch' then get back on the horse.

🚹 Dive straight into a juicy book – a thriller, a classic, whatever – just to get your mind back off yourself and into another world.

🕴 Go on a diet (only if you need it). I'm not joking – the moment I joined Weight Watchers I only had thoughts for Pro Plus Points – forgot about men entirely. Just saying.

Rule Number  6

Take a Break from the Games

You need this rule if you ...

- Are terrified of seeming too keen.
- Force yourself to wait at least two days before replying to any text.
- Pretend you don't like a man when you do and – even when he shows he likes you – have trouble relaxing/ believing him.
- Are 'drawn to arseholes'.
- Would rather see a guy behaving offish as mysterious and a challenge rather than just someone stringing you along for a useful bit of ego boost.
- Try to match every nuance of his communication with something a bit more challenging.
- Think every relationship or date operates along power lines, i.e., with a 'winner' and a 'loser'.

Goes well with ...

- Do Something Lofty
- Take a Break from Internet Dating
- No Talking About Men

W e sat there, momentarily silent, deep in contemplation. It had been a night and almost two days since Helen had gone on the date with Tony. They'd met in a bar, Helen taking a chance and striking up a conversation with him. With his sandy, close-cut hair, enormous build and noisy laugh, he'd been irresistible to her. So it was a brilliant result that, after she'd asked if she could steal his chair, he'd dived right into the spirit of things and chatted with her for an hour.

The date had been brilliant and Helen was sure she was in love. They'd parted with the best smooch of her life and she was absolutely convinced he'd be in touch. Naturally, she was absolutely dying to message him.

What happened next ...

Trying to act in her best interests, I strongly cautioned her against it. It was the rule, hard and fast, that he had to get in touch. But it was more specific than that: he would be playing by the rules too, playing the game, and men always waited till the third day before getting in touch. 'You're right, you're right,' Helen said, firmly tucking away her

phone and closing down her Facebook. I don't know how
we both knew so clearly, without shadow of a doubt, that
this was the rule, and that it spelled out a game we absolutely had to play, but we did. Helen did not break down,
even though she was absolutely gagging to, and – just as I
predicted – the next night, she got a text from Tony.

Now, Helen was moderately pleased – after all, he'd got
in touch. She'd have preferred a phone call. But the content
of the message was encouraging enough: he'd had a great
time, and was she free later in the week to go to a film? She
wanted to reply immediately: 'Yes, yes, yes, what time,
where,' but again, instinctively, held back. Waiting a few
hours was easy – should she push it any more, she
wondered? It was agony, but we all thought 'yes', followed
by less generous-sounding thoughts like 'Let him stew'.
Finally, the next day, by now convinced that she'd waited
too long and he'd have gone off with someone else, she
replied. After a few more dates, it didn't work out – Tony
turned out to have ex issues.

So I say …

'Give it a break. Step away from the games.'

Helen's story is a simple example of obsessive, counterin-
tuitive game playing that dominates dating today. Having
spent years playing them, coaching and receiving help from
friends also trying to do the 'right' thing, I've arrived at the
conclusion that nothing amounts to more pointless stress in
the single woman's emotional periphery than the game
playing of (usually unpromising) early romance.

So why do we play games?

There are genuine, clever and rational reasons for game playing. At its best, it demonstrates a certain level of emotional intuition – when the right time to do certain things is; how to make the other person feel comfortable. After all, barging in, passion first, all cards on the table can easily set off 'scary scary scary' alarm bells.

But rather than being the art of well-meaning courtship, whereby each participant has a chance to show their understanding of social cues, it's become a competitive sport of who is going to show their keenness cards first – and thereby lose. Dan Savage, whose sex podcast and column, *Savage Love*, are among some of my favourite things on the internet, gave a rosy view of game playing in an article in Forbes. In it, he argued that games are an important way to show you are capable of being a good partner. Fail to play the game right, and you're less likely to play the larger 'game' of life right. Games, says Savage, are a way fo showing you're in tune to someone else's needs, moods and sensitivities. Which is exactly what we require in realtionships.

He's right, to a degree. But I'm not sure exactly what these subtle, personality-predicting games are that Savage is referring to – what I see in women from 18 to 35 is a contest of who is going to show their keenness cards first.

'I know for sure that I have sabotaged relationships in the past by trying to play it cool – being all aloof. I was hiding everything, even from myself. The fear is always of being that crazy girl, you don't want anyone to think you're too attached; which basically means crazy or insane.'

Celia, 34

That Celia is perpetually knotted up in a game of romantic cat's cradle is hardly surprising since she feels that 'the worst thing you can do in our society is think there's a future. But of course if I'm sleeping with them I want it to go somewhere.'

'We're supposed to be a clean slate, with no sexual history, whereas guys aren't. It's exhausting. There's nothing more lame than thinking about the future. I can't remember the last time I liked someone without that feeling that if you do something wrong, you can fuck everything up. There's like this line you can cross to screw up your future, I feel.'

Frances, 27

It seems that women have by far the most to lose by playing the game wrong – whereas a man who shows he's keen displays masculine confidence which is attractive (not least to me). Interestingly, a sizeable number of men who I interviewed for my last book said it's 'great' when the woman asks them out. So I took their words at face value and went on an asking-out spree to really quite depressing effect. Now, it's not that the men were necessarily lying when they said they like to be asked out. Rather, I think they liked the idea of it but when it actually happens, it puts them off. I've pushed this one to the limits with my own actions (I like to take control), and I have to conclude that in the majority of cases, being proactive doesn't really help a woman's cause in the early days.

Or maybe we're just not getting it right when we ask men out. Interestingly, social scientists have found that not only is game playing higher stakes for women, women just aren't as natural or as good at it as men are. So much for all that 'men are so straightforward/men are simple creatures' talk that circulates.

Janet Kwok, of Harvard's department of human development and education, has surveyed numerous studies on sexual or romantic game playing: 'Game playing seems to appeal to those who have high sensation-seeking (i.e. they like physical stimulation) or who want a short-term dating strategy in order to keep more people at a distance and date more people. Perhaps it's not a surprise, then, that game playing seems to be more popular with men than women. One study found that the more sexual partners you have had, the more "games" you play (such as refusing to commit or having multiple partners simultaneously) and that men are more likely to endorse these kinds of behaviours.'

Bridget, 29, has no doubts about who is to blame for the world of mixed signals and stressful game playing: men.

'Very few are immune from the disease known as game
playing commonly affecting rising numbers of men in the
dating world. Wanting honesty and clarity from these men
often results in being tarred with the "needy" brush. Or
worse the "possessive psycho" – and can you blame us?
The sort of person, like my ex, who sends you a list of
potential wedding guests while sniffing around Facebook
flirting with other women – backup plans? – are more
common than you think. Game players love the chase and
will spew out grand gestures as needed – they thrive on
conquest and have ash-cloud-sized egos.'

It's a shame, but as long as the sexes feel at romantic logger-
heads, games will continue to be toxic – more like battles or
guerrilla warfare than anything leading towards mutual
understanding. It is slightly depressing that women are still
governed by the sense that unless we hide our real wants,
we'll be wrong-footed. That in order to appear attractive to
the opposite sex, we must play a game we don't particularly
enjoy. I'm not sure men enjoy it either, but they seem
awfully good at it.

'A lot of people do see dating as a game, and not to be
sexist but I blame the guys! Us girls think that in order to
keep a man interested, we should play hard to get, wait at
least half an hour minimum before responding to any
message from them and not sleep with them until at least
the fifth date. Buy why? If we like someone, why should we
have to follow the rules? Because otherwise we'll get
nicknamed a stalker or something ridiculous and the said
guy will end up running a mile!' **Jess, 27**

The original game player versus the modern PUA (pick-up artist)

Modern-day pick-up artists cite Casanova as their hero, and why wouldn't they? He is the most famous seducer in history. One of the top practitioners of pick-up artistry, Adam Lyons (of Attraction Explained, which he runs with his wife and former pick-upee), once explained to me why a guy I'd been seeing for three months had never allowed me to relax, get close or – God forbid – even say the word 'girlfriend'. 'He's a Casanova. He was a dork in school, never got any girls, then decided to commit himself to getting as many women as possible. He learned all the rules, studied up, and didn't stop till he perfected them. Now he just goes through girls, trying to heal those wounds from high school.'

But what the Lyons and their cohorts don't make clear is that Casanova's whole approach (and spirit) was drastically different from today's repellent tricksters who go by sad names such as Mystery, Papa and Style.

Ian Kelly, *Harry Potter* actor and author of *Casanova*, a *Sunday Times* biography of the year, knows more about that master of love's 'technique' than anyone else on earth. As he told me over tea at the British Library (one of the best places in London to perv or observe modern flirting, not to mention talent), he is very keen to distance himself from the idea that Casanova 'was playing a game that someone else doesn't want to play, let alone know they're playing. It would be a game of two or more players – nothing manipulative, seductive or "pick-up" in the modern sense.'

The games Casanova and his cohorts played lacked the seriousness that we give ours – which might be why they were more fun than ours are (which are just exhausting, albeit less dangerous). Kelly notes that the 'frivolity of the game, which was without consequence but rather an elegant pastime, is not necessarily valid in north American cultures. We tend to invest everything with a lot of meaning, perhaps because we see it as a transaction, either financial or sexual.'

Poetry, art and costume were essential parts in the charm-game they played. If you were really looking to marry a girl, you'd follow a set procedure quite apart from mask-wearing and poetry-reciting, beginning with leaving your card at her house, which would then be given from mother to father, who would then permit mother to give daughter the go-ahead to see the suitor.

But the real fun was in being frivolous (not, of course, if you were a woman who fell in love with a prize seducer and got pregnant).

> 'We have this rather dismissing term for it in English –
> "flirting" – as if it's something we do when we're 14. It's
> naff. It completely denies how much goes on anyway
> between two people. So when you start dancing, so to
> speak, the question becomes even more "what do we
> mean etc?" The answer to that might trouble people more
> now than it did.' Ian Kelly

There is something the modern PUA, as pick-up artists are known, have picked up from Casanova – a passion for artificiality, for setting the stage. 'The best analogy is food,' says Kelly. 'Even rustic food takes a lot of work to make it appear like that. It takes imagination, artifice, to make a splendid meal. That's something like the 18th-century game of love. It's theatrical, but not arch.'

Games gone wrong: pick-up artistry and other purveyors of junk-food love

Flash forward to the modern celebrity pick-up artist, who has reared a whole segment of vile faux-seducers. As Neil Strauss, most famous of them all, puts it towards the end of his interminable book *The Game*: 'Nobody had understood the potential of this whole pickup community, the bonding power of dudes talking about chicks. We had manicures, we had mansions, and we had game. We were ready to infect the world like a disease.'

He said it, not me (but I'll say more later along the same lines). What would Casanova say? 'Well, this idea of going out to con women – it's risible,' says Kelly. 'He'd have said: "Why would you not go out there in the spirit of all being in it together, as an elegant game to play?"' My guess is because one stems from a cultured, sophisticated desire to engage with the world and the other comes from the squashed, damaged products of American suburbia, desperate for validation.

In recent history – that is, the time of our adolescence and adulthood – there have been three books I blame for the rise of artifice, suspicion and 'poker facery' in dating:

1. *Men are from Mars, Women are from Venus*, by John Gray (1992)
2. *The Rules: Time-Tested Secrets for Capturing the Heart of Mr Right* by Ellen Fein & Sherrie Schneider (1995)

3. *The Game: Penetrating the Secret Society of Pickup Artists*, by Neil Strauss (2004)

The idea of 'mutuality', as imagined by the vegetarian socialist Edward Carpenter at the turn of the 20th century, is laughably far away from the world views of these books. But the authors hit a jugular and not only spawned millions of adherents each, they informed a generation of romantic angst, felt most sorely (though not exclusively) by the single woman who was (and is) trying to get on with life with or without the noisy ticking of her biological clock.

Gender planets?

Men are from Mars asserted that in understanding the differences between men and women, couples could make their relationships work better. It's true that women and men have differences, but they aren't always the same ones, and seizing polarising generalities and applying them to relationships spells trouble. (Relationships historian Marcus Collins talks fiercely about the 'evergreen parlour game' of crying 'sex war' in his excellent book, *Modern Love.*)

The book helped some people, no doubt – it was a best-seller, after all. But unfortunately, it was the title that stuck, and permeated the modern consciousness, even giving rise to a hit song called 'Men are from Mars, Women are from Hell' by Four Year Strong. So instead of focusing on the model of marriage whereby both partners are equally equipped and motivated to understand each other, we got a soundbite that hammers home our differences, all the way through, from the drinks we like, the movies we watch and the fights we have in bed. Those differences basically add up to this: women want to talk, and be loved (could that be why we like pink drinks?); men want to be quiet and escape conflict. It's hard to know whether this is true or not, because there's very little other discourse on offer that I can think of.

The single woman's scary straitjacket: *The Rules*

The Rules is a different story. It does not even try to sell a line of 'understanding'. It is purely game, pure distortion of character, and preaches intense discomfort (if not pain) as mandatory in both the female and male experience of getting together. Although according to the authors, the men actually enjoy the pain of constant rejection and iciness (perhaps because men are better cut out for game playing behaviour, as above), and it's just the women for whom such behaviour can feel like torture. And yet the book has

> '*Women want to talk, and be loved; men want to be quiet and escape conflict.*'

left more of a terrifying imprint on the female psyche than perhaps any other book on the topic (before *He's Just Not That Into You*, that is). As *Time* magazine put it: '*The Rules* is not just a book, it's a movement.'

So deeply did it penetrate American culture that thankfully, it started to spawn books encouraging more natural behaviours, like showing men that you like them – *Jane Austen's Guide to Dating* by Brit-in-New York Lauren Henderson is one such example. In it she thanks her favourite author, who she claims to reread frequently, for providing her with alternatives to the terrifying and restrictive culture of game playing she found in Manhattan.

The lingo of sport, la-la land and trickery pervades *The Rules*. 'What are The Rules?' authors Fein and Schneider trill.

'They are a simple way of acting around men that can help any woman win the heart of the man of her dreams ... You do the Rules and trust that one day a prince will notice that you're different from all the other women he's known, and ask for your hand!'

If the point of *The Rules* wasn't clear enough, the authors – one of whom filed for divorce in 2000 – hammer it home in language of need, possession and manipulation: everything but honesty and genuine pleasure. 'The purpose of the Rules is to make Mr Right obsessed with having you as his by making yourself seem unattainable. In plain language, we're talking about playing hard to get!'

But it doesn't stop there. The list of how to be attractive leaves little natural behaviour left for the marriage-seeker. Classic instructions (thanks ladies!) include the following.

> *'Don't be burdensome.'*
>
> *'Don't bore him with details about your day or your aches and pains.'*
>
> *'Men must be conditioned to feel that if they want to see you seven days a week, they have to marry you.'*
>
> *If you're sad because a guy has treated you like shit, or dumped you: 'You brush away a tear so that it doesn't smudge your make-up and you move on! Of course, that is not how you really feel.'*
>
> *And, for those of you tempted to display a sense of humour: 'Don't be a loud, knee-slapping, hysterically funny girl [...] when you're with a man you like, act ladylike, cross your legs and smile. Don't talk so much. Wear black sheer pantyhose and hike up your skirt to entice the opposite sex!'*
>
> *Perhaps the rule that stuck in most people's heads was this one: 'Don't call him and rarely return his calls.'*

No wonder that for reams of single women, the legacy of *The Rules* is one of fear, discomfort – and an addiction to game playing.

Lauryn, 31, is a classic product of post-*Rules* dating. Her testimony is full of the 'lose, lose' frustration it engenders.

'To my mind, the game is one in which we are meant to find the perfect balance of being indifferent yet accommodating of someone new in our life when he presents himself. We must present a front that we are living a full and complete life with an active social schedule with friends and prospective admirers as well as a fulfilling professional life. Yet, somehow within all this we are meant to find time to integrate a new man into our lives, all the while acting like we don't need them there.'

'You aren't meant to express eagerness at seeing someone,' agrees Holly, 29. She says:

'I read The Rules unfortunately, and I've never forgotten how it tells you not to stare at men, not to see him more than once a week and to always end phone calls first. And despite all efforts at empowerment, the onus is still on the man to contact, as we are inundated with the idea that if they don't it is because they are not interested.'

Maria, 28, who was also in on the conversation, adds:

'The problem with this particular game is that at some point you have to drop the disinterested act and that's the part I find difficult. When you do that? At what point? Don't we just seem flaky as women if we present this ideal of being impossibly busy and fulfilled and then drop things off the schedule for a new man in our life? And what is the perfect balance between being sexually empowered and slutty? Men don't want to hear that you aren't dating. God forbid you admit to a long stretch without sexual activity, but

women still feel pressured to not make themselves too
sexually available. It's an impossible balance.'

Be cool, be a bitch – just don't be yourself

Why Men Love Bitches is another bestseller; but it basically rehashes what *The Rules* said, only using the word 'bitch' to define (seemingly) independent and confident. As Argor says in the book's sequel, *Why Men Marry Bitches*: 'The worst thing a woman can do is see a guy every night of the week. That's how she becomes his good-time girl on his "reserve list." What will happen is, the guy will start coming over at nine o'clock and then he'll leave by ten-thirty. If he gets access or what he wants from her anytime he wants it, he won't have to lift a finger to keep it going.' Sound familiar?

Despite their popularity, books for women about rules are fairly pointless. Janet Reibstein, a visiting professor in psychology at Exeter University and co-author of *Sexual Arrangements*, says:

> *'People are trying to codify what happens in courtship, but*
> *there isn't a simple answer to any of these things. Probably*
> *there is a kind of elusiveness that strengthens courtship, but*
> *making it into rules etc is ridiculous. Game playing is*
> *exhausting – you can lose yourself.'*

Of course, that's exactly what Ellen Fein and Sherrie Schneider, authors of *The Rules*, want you to do. 'You may feel you won't be able to be yourself, but men will love it!'

And finally: it's a man's Game

If *The Rules* attacked women from the inside by entrenching a game playing culture that denies women's selves, then *The Rules of the Game* did something that is more sinister. Women playing by the Rules want power over men in order to get closer to them; men playing the Game want power over women to 'fuck and chuck' them. *The Rules* dedication reads like this: 'To our wonderful husbands and great kids.' *The Game*'s dedication is this: 'Dedicated to the thousands of people I talked to in bars, clubs, malls, airports, grocer stores, subways, and elevators over the last two years. If you are reading this, I want you to know that I wasn't running game on you. I was being sincere. Really. You were different.'

Crucially, what *The Game* did was set a precedent and carve out the contours of a vile 'community' centred around scoring tens (hot women) and back-slapping. Weirdly, 'the Game' is so widespread that you may fall foul of its adherents (I have). Pick-up artists claim to do what they do because they used to be dorks (in other words, that they are coming from a position of weakness so that we can sympathise and applaud them). But the whole operation is based on pure misogyny – that 'hot women' are the only women (the rest excite scorn), and that sex is the only usage for them. See the hot woman, trick her into liking you, bed her,

> *'Crucially, what* The Game *did was set a precedent and carve out the contours of a vile "community" centred around scoring tens (hot women) and back-slapping.'*

and job done. The operation leaves zero scope for natural development of feelings through natural, spontaneous behaviour because it's rooted in manipulating surfaces, i.e. getting women of 'perfect ten' calibre appearance to agree to sex, preferably threesomes. The men are more than happy to overhaul themselves, too: author Neil Strauss shaved his head, got piercings, fake tan and laser corrective surgery. But all you have to do is look at any PUA forum to see bone-chilling hatred of women. For example, the top story on www.pickupartistmindset.com was this:

> 'If a girl accuses you of using a line, especially right after your opener, she's not going to fuck you. It simply won't happen, no matter how much you think you can recover. It'd be like trying to sell an SUV to an environmentalist. Chances are she came out to make men feel small and get free drinks, so therefore you must go over the top and put that bitch in her place. Here's what you should say: "Well it got me laid last week with some slut. I don't see why it shouldn't work again." Enjoy the embarrassed look on her face as she stews in silence trying to think of a comeback. Then turn your back on her. She'll think twice before saying that nonsense to another man.'

Because the woman recognises that a PUA *is* using a line, and is not interested in him, she's a bitch, a slut and deserves to stew.

Here is how men who want to play The Game should proceed, according to Neil Strauss, aka 'style':

Step 1:   Select a target
Step 2:   Approach and open
Step 3:   Demonstrate value
Step 4:   Disarm the obstacles
Step 5:   Isolate the target
Step 6:   Create an emotional connection
Step 7:   Extract to a seduction location
Step 8:   Pump buying temperature
Step 9:   Make a physical connection
Step 10:   Blast last-minute resistance
Step 11:   Manage expectations

Target, disarm, isolate, extract, pump, blast? Women have evidently become the equivalent of terrorist hideouts – they must be forcibly blown into submission, before being contained so that they don't get any pesky 'expectations'. Warfare is the preferred metaphor – and so while the sexes are operating at their best-yet frequency, a far from harmonious atmosphere pervades the sexual landscape. In the current obesity epidemic caused by junk-food love, the ruthlessly game playing brotherhood is the equivalent of every late-night kebab you'll ever have, put together.

You may or may not find yourself embroiled with men like this. But for many women, to date has become to play games – often quite exhausting ones. It's not always anyone's fault. But taking a break from them will give the emotionally hard-working single woman a welcome break.

Ditching the game playing: actually doing it

Over the years I've played around with different game playing tactics, more game, less game, and I've arrived at this
formulation:

> *Game playing in the very, very early days, before the dating
> has got going, is less of an issue than it is as things get
> going.*

But even in the very early days, you can respond immediately with impunity. You can say, 'That was fun; would be
great to see you again' with full freedom. In fact, the less
false you are in your communications, the better your vibe,
and better the sense of self and wellbeing that you're
communicating, and the more naturally independent you
seem. This is merely a healthier, more authentic way of
achieving what game playing is meant to give you: power.
Only it's the 'I want to be around this person' sort of power
rather than 'This person is a total mystery – what the hell
are they thinking?' power.

The other thing is this: everyone gets one credit. Say
you've been upfront in your texting – replying immediately;
initiating the odd text. The credit applies to the situation
where the guy hasn't responded and you want to communi-
cate twice in a row. You can do this once – it's fine. Twice
and you're probably beginning to be obsessed with his
mysterious silence. It's gone from being open about wanting
to continue being in touch with them to wanting to crack a
mystery – the code of his coldness. The latter is pointless

more than anything else: resist the urge to exceed the single credit because it won't lead anywhere good and not because you'll embarrass yourself by breaking a key rule. And let's be honest: it gets tiresome sending messages that garner no reply.

I've done it many a time – but by last December, I'd learned my lesson. I had had a very enjoyable sleepover with a Google engineer I'd bagged at their office Christmas party (my friend had invited me). I had liked him due to his very cute looks and wry sense of humour. I had assumed – since I am obviously awesome – that he'd be in touch. On the Tube Ride of Shame (for him – the sleepover was at my house) the next day, he'd asked for my number. I heard nothing. Later in the week I sent him a light and airy email with one question, the signal he should write back. Nothing. I went through a range of emotions: consternation, denial (maybe he hadn't got my email??), anger. But the whole time, I knew he had received the email, and that he wasn't getting back to me because he wasn't into it. I got over it – and that was that.

Here are some pointers to help avoid game-oriented discomfort, whether you're prone to misreading actual coldness for mysterious possible interest, or you can't stop dating men that play with your mind.

1. Recognise yourself as a game player

Taking a break from games is all about *spotting* yourself game playing – which can be harder than you might think. You might be doing it either out of habit or in response to a man's mixed signals. You can't read a man's mind, or always correctly guess his intentions, but you can recognise when you feel uncomfortable or artificial or forced.

I'm not recommending you go nuts and start calling up everyone you fancy and telling them you love them. Some degree of control is still necessary – but this time, it's control that is going to be good for you, not control exerted to trick men or save yourself from seeming too keen.

2. Make a decision and stick to it
When you catch yourself doing something like counting the hours before allowing yourself to respond to a text, either reply right away if you feel like it, or hold back because you are genuinely busy or not that bothered. Believe me: nothing bad will happen.

3. Learn to cut loose when he starts messing with your head
As for when a guy you're seeing seems keen by dropping little suggestive tokens – 'I miss you' texts from Paris, toothbrush bought and coyly presented for your overnight stays – and then counteracting them with long periods of silence, weird comments like 'I can't possibly have a girlfriend now' and general unaccountability, you need to clear out. You're being played with like a kitten by a reader of *The Game* – what PUA Adam Lyons would call a Casanova, or rigorous woman-tricker. If you start saying to yourself, 'But he said x, y, z – it was so sweet, so why is he not x, y, z?' act on it instantly. It means you're in a game you probably don't want to play, and a game that only he will win, unless you default.

4. Be brave. Be natural.

Think of how you are with your friends, male and female – natural, open, yourself. They love you for it, and being around them is stimulating and nurturing, not stressful. After you part ways with them you don't wonder or worry about the signals you gave off. These friendships are a fundamental, positive part of your life, right? For the period of your Man Diet, see what happens if you push your friendship behaviours right through the complex doors and alleyways of dating. A few of the doors could slam. But tiptoeing through them, guided by false restraint and guesswork, wouldn't necessarily get you where you want to go. On the other hand, being yourself, acting on your wants, and showing you're not embarrassed about either of those things, is going to get you there more safely and in better shape as a woman who knows her mind and herself.

For a period of time, you'll get a chance to rediscover the joy of relaxing as yourself. If dates fail, so be it. If nobody fancies you, fine. Their loss. You will be so much more vigorous, energetic and clear-eyed at the end of it. Game playing has turned toxic and now we need to detox.

How I followed this rule:

Pre-Man Diet

I went in phases. Sometimes I thought games were everything – and forced myself to stick to Rules-style ridiculousness, like not replying to his text for ages. But I'm not a natural at games. So I'd try to play them – most games boil down to not seeming keen – but ended up confused and confusing. But even when I wasn't playing hard to get, there was always a morbid fear lurking of seeming too keen; always something holding me back, something stifling myself in their presence. I worried *a lot* about games: whether I should or shouldn't play them; whether I played them right; whether they worked; whether I screwed things up by not playing them enough.

But the other half of games is spotting game playing men. Pre-Man Diet, I was frequently taken in by gameplaying men. The worst was a guy called Marios, who – I later found out – was employing pick-up artistry to make me attached, but never intending to date me properly. Others would blow hot and cold and I'd spend my whole time scratching my head and poring over the mixed signals. It was exhausting, and often offensive.

How I did it

I caught myself a) playing games and b) worrying about playing the game right. This is easily done. More importantly, I spotted when men were playing games, which is what they do while deciding if they want you and for what purpose. All banter but no date? Cut the cord. As soon as there was some weird inconsistency between a guy's keenness when we met (references to the future, cuddles), and his keenness when we were apart (no contact, me having to finagle him into the next meeting), I just stopped responding to his texts. You may have a different style of cord-cutting, but remember: we're not looking to get ornate and scheming.

How I felt

Slightly stern, ever so slightly holier-than-thou, but freer and more relaxed. My patience for bullshit took a nosedive. What before I might have tried to figure out, or assumed was just a guy being awesomely mysterious – I now dismissed as tiresome and also bad for my brain and vibe. Trying to figure out what's going on between you and a guy when it's not clear is a massive drain of energy and often futile. Doing this rule means you don't pay attention to anything that isn't clear. That's a massive relief.

What I let slip through the cracks

From men: only things I didn't realise at the time were games, like craftily worded texts adding up to nothing. From me: not much. As soon as I felt myself getting even vaguely obsessive and suspicious, the 'negative game energy' alarm bell would sound and I'd back away.

And now?

Well, as I said before, my natural ability to conceal my true feelings and thoughts is woefully low. However, I'm not a sociopathic blabbermouth either, so I would rather be coy and quiet than sucked into a game. Since I adopted this rule, I've tended to retreat into silence if I'm in doubt. It may not be ideal; but I just don't want to be caught in power struggles because I know I'll end up losing. The result is I obsess much less over texts that aren't nearly as fascinating as they appear. I waste less time, in other words.

SOS!

You can have the best will in the world, but if a game playing guy ensnares you, you can find yourself doing a merry dance. If you've fallen foul of one, or are generally finding yourself in a matrix of stressful guessing and suspense, don't panic. What's going on is that you've allowed a game player (or your old habits) to get you back into it all without you even noticing. Games are tricky like that. Here's how to regain equilibrium.

- Be aware. Simply notice that you're playing games, or have been sucked into one. That's the first step. Then you can extract. How you extract is up to you – it depends on what the situation is (first few weeks of dating, pre-dating, etc).
- Read Neil Strauss's *The Game*. It will send useful shivers down your spine: useful because the book is so vile, such a horrible extreme of artifice, you'll be running from games as fast as you can. The same can be said of *The Rules*, a book that terrified many a woman in the 1990s and remains widely distributed today.
- Let go. Games are dragged out when you know things aren't going to work out, so you'd rather

pretend mixed signals and bad behaviour are just masking real feelings. They probably aren't, so just walk away and breathe a big sigh of relief.

Rule Number

Do Not Pursue

You need this rule if you ...

- Go after men you like the look of – but get depressed by rejection.
- Pursue more than you are pursued.
- Find that over 50 per cent of the men you pursue don't return the compliment in the way you were hoping – one-night stands excluded.
- Become a wild beast of a man-hunter as soon as you've had a few drinks.
- Get furious at the suggestion that pursuit works less well for women on all levels.
- Are a drunk dialler/texter/Facebooker.
- Spend a good part of your hangovers wishing you hadn't jumped a certain guy.

Goes well with ...

- Cut Down on the Booze
- No Facebook Stalking
- Dwell on Your Sense of Self

I'd gone for a work lunch with a friend of mine at quite a posh restaurant. I was hungover, truth be told, and had indulged in several servings of junk-food love that week. But, as so often happens with JFL, the more you have, the more you want. When the sommelier came in to chat wine (we settled for Diet Coke), I noted a very cute Italian accent. I also noted a 6ft 1in well-built man in a suit, with a shock of dark hair, tanned skin and brown eyes like bullets. Despite not wanting wine, I concocted many reasons why he needed to stay in the room with us. I had a lot of questions. He happily provided answers. He was friendly. I cursed my choice of apparel: black sweatpants, a baggy jumper and my glasses.

Later, I decided that my newspaper urgently needed a profile of the hottest sommeliers in town. I emailed him a witty, flirty email (having taken his card and not, as normal, lost it). His reply, which came several days later, made me swoon. I found it hilarious, ador-able, and flirtatious. But then, Pierce Brosnan has flirted with me before – to flirt is not to want.

I kept the back and forth going, sometimes even doubling up emails. I started to drop by the restaurant

– and there he'd be, smiling and ready with a cocktail on the house for me and my friend (about seven of my friends were dragged there in total to view the man).

Each time, I'd swear there were sparks flying, that his eyes were saying what his mouth wouldn't because he was at work, and then eventually I'd leave, waiting for him to get in touch. But he didn't, so I continued to pursue. I invited him to my book launch party. He couldn't make it. I kept dropping by. I suggested we do the interview on sommeliers over drinks at London Bridge. He didn't get in touch – until I volunteered to come and see him at work for it. We sat on a bench outside while he talked about life, love and the universe and I listened and, sometimes, took notes, feeling oddly depressed.

Then, in a joyous fluke, I ran into him at Green Park Tube station. I was looking good – dressed and ready for a night out. He said I looked 'beautiful'. I nearly died. I was on my way to review a restaurant and told him so. As he got on the Tube, he said: 'When are you going to invite me to review with you?' I'd mentioned this in the past to him – as he'd expressed (just polite) envy, but he'd never committed. Encouraged to try again, I emailed him with the offer of a restaurant review I thought he'd be flattered by in the extreme: Hakkasan. And you know what? He didn't reply. It was the rudest thing. But the poor guy probably knew no other way to make the point that he wasn't interested and that if it had seemed otherwise it was only unthinking Italian flirtatiousness, convenient for sucking up to a journalist.

What happened next ...

Drunk and on my way back from Hakkasan, I dragged my friend into his place of work and confronted him over his no-reply. He was relatively unapologetic. I saw him for what he was (in relation to me), walked out and promptly got over him.

The rejection had taken its toll on me, though. As I know from my last book, men are anything but straightforward in the way they reject – they are terrified of confrontation and would rather keep the ego boost of a back-burner keen bean than offend her outright. This means that unless you're vigilant, you can end up being rejected without actually admitting to yourself or fully realising that that's what is actually happening. For the period I was chasing him, I felt like I was desperately trying to scratch an itch I would only be able to do if I could reach my hand a tiny bit further. I felt hopeful and buzzy – but was going on nothing. And I made a bit of a fool of myself (you can argue over 'a bit'). It wasn't good for me – it was blown up and became an Episode In My Life, but one where nothing had actually happened.

And it rankled because around the same time I'd taken an active approach to several other people. As with the sommelier, I'd decided I liked them and got stuck in – how could they be anything but thrilled to receive my attentions? The fact that they had other stuff going on in their lives (like women) or the chance that I simply wasn't what they were looking for, I kept out of mind. I was like a blind woman trying to hit the piñata and, of course, I failed, and the bat ended up hitting my own head.

The result was that I began to feel:

a) like a fool
b) unattractive
c) cursed

It was an ultimate low. I was swimming in junk-food love and I needed to clamber onto the warm, clean sands of the Man Diet. I needed to see clearly, and regain self-confidence and perspective.

So I say ...

'Men can woo women but we can't woo men.'

First let's define pursuit. For women I think it's a bit subtler than for men. As the guys I interviewed for my last book confirmed: men can woo women but we can't woo men. Most of know this and don't go around sending flowers and calling repeatedly, saying: 'Let me take you out for dinner.' But what we *can* and often *do* do (well, if you're anything like me) is see a guy we think is attractive and make it very obvious that we think so. We may give him our most seductive eye across the room, then go over and talk to him. This is already some degree of pursuit – but often it's groundwork and they'll pick up on it. If they don't, we may well commence real pursuit by asking for their number or literally proffering our own. The chances are they won't get in touch and you will. Then they'll either not reply or you'll meet up but there will be some issue – he's not that into it, he's seeing some-one, he's not that great. Mostly, it's that he's not particularly keen because you did all the legwork. If we were going to get really *He's Just Not That Into You* about it, we would conclude that if he really had been keen, he'd have asked for the number and used it. If a guy asks for ours and uses it, we might come round. If we do the same to him, he won't.

Liz Tuccillo, co-author of *He's Just Not That Into You*, articulates the wall that independent-minded, sexual women continually run into with men. 'Are you telling us that we have to just sit around and wait? I don't know about you, but I find that infuriating. I was brought up to believe that hard work and good planning are the keys to making your dreams come true. [...] The guys get to pick. We're just supposed to put on our little dresses and do our hair and bat our eyes and hope they choose us. [...] Really, in this day and age, the hardest thing to do for many women, particularly me, is nothing. We like to scheme, make phone calls, have a plan. But guess what: my way? Has sucked. Hasn't worked at all. I've never had a successful relationship with a guy that I've pursued.'

Here's a list of pursuit behaviours you have to drop for the Man Diet detox. It's not a strategy to get him to go for you – it's just a strategy to claw back self-sufficiency and a sense of self-worth.

1. Thinking, 'Oh, I'll just send him a text – maybe he lost my number or has been really busy.'
2. Ogling a cute man. As in, you're having a conversation with a friend, and you interrupt with: 'Oh my God, there is the hottest guy over there', and then stare him down. Not allowed.

3. Going over and striking up a conversation with an attractive man.
4. Asking an attractive man for a cigarette or a light when you know you have an ulterior motive.
5. Offering your number/email even if he doesn't ask for it.
6. Getting in touch when he plainly could have contacted you, pretending to yourself that he might have just been busy.
7. Contacting him more than once in a row, thinking that you can win him round. You can't.
8. Scheming – i.e. leaving your number for a guy at a bar, or behaviour similar to this. Particularly dangerous when around waiters.
9. Facebook-friending a man you met that you think is attractive. A sure way to look like a stalker …

Whether you want a relationship or not, I'd say you *always* end up feeling worse when you've been the chaser – be it at the bar, for sex, or for casual 'seeing each other'.

None of these behaviours will necessarily result in out-and-out rejection. But the silences in response to your text post-sleepover (especially when said sleepover is initiated by you), the sense that if you weren't driving things they wouldn't be going anywhere, and the questions you ask yourself about *why* they aren't driving things forward, all leave you feeling empty, hungry, anxious and sad. It is in exactly this state that people reach for the pizza or the biscuits, making things worse and worse (as any dieter will tell you) the less satisfied they are. It is exactly the same with men, and the common modus operandi of the pursuant woman is 'I need another one to prove that I *am* attractive' or similar.

Take the Daniel Craig lookalike bouncer I drunkenly seized on one night recently at Shaka Zulu, a club in Camden. Yes, he was wearing a yellow fluorescent jacket as he did his rounds. He wore one of those ear microphones. He could have been anyone – a criminal or a nutcase – but for some reason I liked him, went for him, and bagged him. Naturally, having been the aggressor I got what I wanted, but not for long. He'd been nicer and hotter than I predicted and I wanted another meeting. But no reply to my text the next day. Since it was not to happen (I know enough about the male mind to read the signals accurately), I felt low and sad. But I quickly turned my attention to the next bit of junk-food love to get my mind off this one. However, catching myself in dire need of the Man Diet, I pulled back on the behaviours that so quickly spiral out of control: getting in touch with unworthy or unwise past partners, going out and getting hammered, and trying to do the same thing all over again. Instead, I stayed in a few nights and did some Man Diet-friendly activities:

- 👤 I read a good book.
- 👤 Gave up the booze and nights on the town for a bit.
- 👤 Visited my grandpa.
- 👤 Skyped with my brother.

Bingo. Straight away I was back on track and starting to feel better. What's a Daniel Craig lookalike next to the joy of unfettered, glorious womanhood? Exactly.

Pangs of rejection: worse for women?

Research indicates that rejection is worse for women than men. Of course, men I've spoken to about this have said they don't like rejection one bit. But they rarely feel low in the way we do when we've been left in the cold (especially after sex). Their ego takes a hit, but they're socially trained from a young age (some say 'hardwired', though I'm suspicious of that argument) to be more aggressive in their approach and, inevitably, to deal with the percentage of 'no' and 'you're a scumbag' responses that get thrown at them. One study found that women reported stronger negative responses to rejection – for example, if her partner wanted less sexual contact than she did – whereas men reported more experience in handling refusal.

Whether women are *really* programmed to be pursued and not to pursue, we certainly *think* that's the case. It is the social norm, even though the original biological arguments of women being the more passive party have ceased to be so pressing. Pregnancy and infection are easily controlled now. And while some attribute male pursuit to testosterone, women have testosterone too. Still, women are self-conscious about pursuing men.

Whatever dregs of chivalry are left in culture dictate that men *do* and women *wait* and *receive*, although the ironic thing is that this changes drastically as soon as a relationship gets going. Women are more likely to be seen as obsessive and desperate when they pursue a guy – a remnant of the kind of thinking that sees women as spinsters, or frigid, or desperate and so on, based on prejudice rather than reality. So despite the fact that we may feel like doing so, when we do it, we not only feel the stress of possible or real rejection, but we feel like we've stepped outside social norms too.

So pursuit is a stress-fest and a junk-food love danger zone. I am not in favour of enforced female passivity, as it seems deeply unfeminist. But I know from lots of experience that being assertive with men is a wounding, courageous path. And in order to build up your strength, you need to limit the knocks.

Maria, 27, told me about a guy she liked. She spent the whole night trying to attract his interest. Nothing happened, so she sent him a message on Facebook saying: 'You're really cute. Want to go for a drink?' He eventually came back to her with some excuse and declined the offer. 'In the past I'd have actually cried about this,' Maria said. 'But now I feel kinda used to it and just move on. When you pursue as much as I do, you get hurt a lot. It still sucks though and I always feel shit about myself for a few days after. But I can't stop myself.'

Rejection actually hurts

A neuroimaging study, where participants lie inside an fMRI machine, found that regions of the brain activated by social pain are similar to those found in studies of physical pain. Janet Kwok, who studies human development and education at Harvard, observes that:

> *'For women, that pain could be worse than for men: recent*
> *research suggests that women experience more negative*
> *emotions following sexual rejection than men do because*
> *women who ask for sexual contact proactively are viewed as*
> *"promiscuous" whereas men who act similarly are instead*
> *percieved as "aggressive". To be sexually rejected, then, is a*
> *serious affront because it presents a greater threat to self-*
> *esteem in a cultural context where men are believed to have*
> *a greater sexual appetite than women.'*

This is a useful point, though I'm not talking about the feelings relating to the physical sex act. I'm talking about the related but more general feeling arising from: 'Hello man. I like you, here I am' and the man implying he can take it or leave it.

For example, Emma, 33, was trying to get over a chronic game player she rather loved. She went to Greece on holiday and met someone there. He was gorgeous and romantic, and she was quite into him, so she made it known she wanted to see him back home. He seemed up for it, but when they got back Emma contacted him asking if he was still coming. He never replied – and she was crushed. She felt:

a) like a fool
b) to blame
c) obsessed with finding out what she had done wrong

Emma told me:

*'What really made me feel shit was that I made it clear I
liked him, then texted him when I should have just left it. His
silence was like a big fat slap in the face. I couldn't stop
thinking about what I'd done wrong or if it was something to
do with my performance in bed, or what.'*

Women and men usually have different motivations for
pursuit, so the rejection can feel all the worse for us. We
may pursue for sex, spurred on by some drunken notion or
simple carnal need. Or we may pursue knowing we want
more. But if we find we like the person we've bedded, and
they're in any way interesting or civilised, we usually
wouldn't mind seeing them again. Having had sex with
them counts in their favour, *increasing* the feeling of wanting to see them again. Sometimes, in a wrong-headed
attempt to rope them into something
more, we'll sleep with them. Monica,
31, who says she initiates with men
most of the time, says: 'Men see a package but they don't always see me. I use
my looks to attract them and I always
think, maybe if they see me/sleep with
me, they'll like me. For who I am.'

*'Women and
men usually
have different
motivations for
pursuit, so the
rejection can
feel all the
worse for us.'*

Men, on the other hand, may pursue
us for sex, and even when we turn out
to be amazing, the deal is done and
they're on to the next one. Having had (casual) sex with
them usually makes it less likely they'll want to see us again.

Sex, hormones 'n' more …

Now, I get squirmy at those statements saying that women *always* want love from sex and can't relish the act in itself, whereas men just gobble up the 'in-and-out', then it's job done. It makes us seem pathetic somehow, and it's also plainly not true. But if we don't like the guy we're sleeping with, or we aren't attracted to him, or there's something creepy or off-putting about him, we're probably not going to enjoy the sex that much. We probably won't settle into it enough to come – unless he is a master of the art. Men, however, can generally get off – they have that setting whereby they can basically use any woman as a masturbatory aid. So if we do have a truly erotic or satisfying sexual experience, we probably genuinely find the guy attractive, and we will probably feel more lovey and less 'wham bam' about the experience after.

The attachment hormone

You've probably heard of the hormone oxytocin in relation to women, sex and attachment. Actually, it's primarily released after distension of the cervix and uterus during labour, and after stimulation of the nipples (by a baby), facilitating birth and breastfeeding. Oxytocin is also released in connection with orgasm and physical pleasure – adding a sense of trust, attachment and bonding after the sexual exchange. It is released in men, too, during sex, but it seems that more is released in women (results aren't particularly conclusive about this). Whether it's down to good old oxytocin, or other factors, women tend to exhibit greater attachment after sex than men. Hence the bad feelings caused by rejection when the guy doesn't call or doesn't want any more connection.

Of course, oxytocin is meant to be good: it is associated with happy feelings. But studies have shown that single women have less oxytocin overall than women in couples. It also found that those women whose oxytocin levels dropped in association with negative events – rather than keeping an even keel – were more prone to relationship anxiety and depression. I think it's interesting that single women have lower levels of this happy-lovey hormone over-all than coupled women because it means that when we do get turned on or sexually intimate with a man, we experi-ence a relative spike. Every spike has an anti-spike, and when it comes to the sexual anti-spike – i.e., rejection or dissatisfaction – things can get very gloomy indeed.

He thinks I'm ugly!

When a guy rejects us we often question our attractiveness first. We care a huge amount about being considered attrac-tive. And if you're really considered attractive, why would a man not want to go out with you?

While men are investing more in skin-deep beauty (Moob Tubes, slimming boob tubes for men to wear under shirts, were among ASDA's bestselling items when they came out), appearance and sexiness has nowhere near as extreme an effect on male self-esteem as it does on ours. Women put a huge amount of care, anxiety and work into their physical appearance and attractiveness. Even if we don't put in tons of effort, most of us would crumble if told we were too fat/ thin or had bad skin by a man we were even vaguely inter-ested in. Telling a man he's too skinny or getting fat doesn't usually crush him or end the relationship. But if a man so much as mentions our bodies in the sack, many of us either drop him on the spot or feel chronically bad.

We're also conditioned to expect more overt attention from men relating to our appearance. Whistling builders, pervy men in clubs (or anywhere for that matter) and general looks of lust when we're dressed up are the norm from adolescence. In fact, if a man *doesn't* respond to our looks when we've tried, it can be taken as a bit of an insult.

'Telling a man he's too skinny or getting fat doesn't usually crush him. But if a man so much as mentions our bodies in the sack, many of us feel chronically bad.'

In *Female Chauvinist Pigs*, Ariel Levy interviewed a bunch of young women about sex. The most striking aspect of these interviews – to me anyway – was how absorbing their personal appearance was to them. Since they made looking good their very raison d'être, you can imagine how crushed they'd be if someone rejected it. Discussing her experience in high school, one girl spoke briefly about her career aspirations, but the topic that elicited her greatest passion and most prolonged attention was her own appearance. Her obsession with how hot she looked, she confessed, was largely bound up in making guys like her. And making guys like her, specifically through her looks, was the key to her self-worth. While she freely admitted to this link, she seemed wholly uninterested in examining its problematic nature.

Naomi Wolf's *The Beauty Myth* hammers home the pathological depth of women's attachment to their appearance – the long and the short of it being that we can never be beautiful enough and thus, as long as the myth of beauty's importance persists, we'll always feel lacking and uneasy. Now, I'm not saying that all women are completely obsessed with looking perfect at all times, nor that their primary validation comes from being considered hot by men or women. But female attractiveness is such a deeply ingrained part of society that we *all* worry about it more than most men.

For one thing, there's lots to be done. Whereas men generally don't wear make-up or have too much choice in clothing, we can use any amount of skincare, make-up, scent and clothing in various combinations. Not to mention the work we do on our bodies. Some biologists might say that women are supposed to attract a good mate and so need to be more attractive than males. But peacocks and other animals are an interesting exception – the men must work harder and be more attractive to get the female interest. Women have never found passive men attractive; passive women have always been attractive.

'The pursuing female's problem is seeing too much.'

Our appearance is massively important; our personalities come second, initially at least. When we meet a guy and go after him, we're proffering our best spin on our appearance. Best clothes, best make-up, cutest shoes, most alluring scent. So after all that, if he isn't interested, it hurts.

And when a woman asks, 'Am I ugly?' she won't be satisfied – however positive the answer – until another man comes along and proves that she isn't. But that's a junk-food love pattern and we're weaning ourselves off of that kind of thing.

Which is why we're not going to put ourselves at the mercy of the male stamp of approval for a period of time. We're not going to send out any male-bound boomerangs whose loss in the bushes can make us feel truly rubbish. We're going to stop trying *completely*.

Giving up the pursuit: actually doing it

1. Go temporarily blind

The key to this part of the Man Diet lies in the opposite of 'seek and ye shall find'. Stop seeking. You won't see, and you won't be inclined towards action either. The pursuing female's problem is seeing too much. Seeing the guy. Seeing how fun it would be to bag him/sleep with him/go out with him/introduce him to your friends. Seeing how well you get on. And thus seeing how impossible it will be for him not to like you.

But this vision isn't as reliable as we think it is, nor is it going to be helpful to you right now. Scanning the room is a habit. Especially when you're single, you're on acute alert for potentials. Many of us have our radars activated and ready to go whenever we step out the front door, especially on a night out. There have been so many times when I've said: 'Oh my God, did you *see* that man?' to a married or coupled friend – a friend who would formerly have been onto him like a hawk – and they've responded: 'What? No! Where?!'

Channel that blindness and become that person. When walking down the street or into a bar, stop looking for men or monitoring men's reactions to you. It's a matter of eye control. Wear metaphorical blinkers, like a horse. On the street it's perfectly easy to look straight ahead, at the floor or at all those fascinating buildings along the way. In the bar, keep focused on the people you're with. Every time you feel your mind wandering and your eyes scanning the room for attractive men, bring yourself, eyes and mind, back to the person you're with.

If someone sees *you* and comes over, you can evaluate their attractiveness and proceed – in accordance with the Man Diet, of course – from there.

2. Dress comfortably and don't go out feeling like you're a man magnet. Keep it plain and simple.

I find that it's when I go into the world feeling like it owes me a great big 'DAAAAAMMMNNN! Aren't you HOT?!' that I get into trouble. When you dress up, particularly in clothes that put you physically ill at ease (hello poorly fitting strapless bras and skyscraper heels) – you expect things. You feel like you can have your pick and you get miffed if nobody chats you up. More to the point, you feel like the least you deserve for squeezing your feet into skyscrapers is some bloody recognition.

So if you just go out in genuinely comfortable clothes that are more understated than your usual razzle-dazzle gear, you'll find it easier to be in the moment as 'You', rather than 'Man Magnet'. This will make it easier to concentrate on your friends, and will make your urge to go up to some dude less simple. You'll think: 'I can't go up to him without my armour.' And that is a perfect reason not to.

3. Be strict about electronics

Not every woman has the temperament or urge to approach men themselves. But every woman, when she sees, dates or sleeps with someone she rather likes, is tempted – in the absence of contact from his side – to send that text, to ask him out for a drink, to do *something*. It may be subtle ('Hey, it was really nice to see you') rather than overt ('Drink tomorrow?'), but it is still pursuit, and it's still putting yourself out there. And it still feels like hell when you don't get the reply you were hoping for. The temptation then is to keep going until you get a response – after all, maybe he didn't get the message; maybe the dog ate his computer or phone; maybe he had a sudden bout of diphtheria and was rushed to A&E; maybe he just has a terrible memory and needs a quick prompt …

Basically, it's easier not to have that temptation in the first place. A big part of the Man Diet is allowing yourself a period of withdrawal; the blinkers should mean you don't have to face the urge to pursue. If somehow a guy falls through the cracks, and into your bed, I implore you to fight the urge to pursue him. Meditate. Go out with friends. Read. Watch a movie. Whatever it is, when the fingers twitch, make them do something else. There's a minute chance that getting in touch when he hasn't will lead to where you want. But it's infinitesimal. Believe me, I've tried.

And finally ...

Here's a tricky question. How do you deal with:

a) Horniness
b) The presence of enticing men?

Horniness is a tough one; it sits abstractly on your brain and heart, making you all jumpy and full of adrenaline, or it makes you down and hopeless.

It comes and goes so if you can live with it for a while, and commune with your vibrator and the other things in your life, the edge should naturally fall away. Once the Man Diet is over, it'll be back in a better, juicier and more fruitful form. I promise.

As we all know, horniness is greatly accentuated by booze. As serial pursuer Meera, 31, told me:

> 'When drunk and horny, all sense goes out the window. I'm like a five-year-old: "I want now, I must have now." The next morning I'm like, "Oh, Jesus, why?"'

If you can keep the booze under control (see rule number two), you'll make your life a whole lot easier. Drink, sure, but don't do it to let off steam when that steam is horniness. Because you *will* do something that ends in junk-food love feelings. Or at least, you're much more likely to.

As for the presence of enticing men, repeat this question to yourself: 'Are they really that enticing?' If a man is not showing much interest in you beyond civilised chat, ask yourself if you really want or need to give yourself so ardently to him. Is he actually worth the trouble? He has a pretty face and some good attributes. Fine, but that's still not enough information to make you abandon your Man Diet. Men are really worth it when they see how great you are. If he isn't particularly showing that appreciation, I say his enticement is limited.

Lucy, 30, told me that if a guy doesn't like her, she's more likely to like him. 'I tend to go for people who don't find me attractive – that makes *them* more attractive. It's about low self-esteem because you tend to think you don't deserve the attention. A lot of girls go for guys who aren't right for them. Someone becomes attractive because they don't want to go out with you – you respect that. It makes them cooler!'

By now you'll spot a severe sign of junk-food love poisoning. This rule is designed to get you out of that self-esteem-bashing rut of pursuing (inevitably) the wrong men. Lucy tried it out for a while and guess what? She has been much happier since she stopped worshipping the men who saw nothing to worship in her. But to get to that stage, she just had to put the brakes on her habit of pursuit and showing she was keen. She's already feeling much stronger and prouder and at peace. She'll be ready to dive back in better and stronger soon. As will you!

How I followed this rule:

Pre-Man Diet

OK, I will come clean and say that I was a big pursuer. Worse than most people. But then, pursuit was a natural extension of certain aspects of my character that are less pronounced – and sometimes more – in most women today. They include wanting to take things into my own hands, not seeing why I should just sit there when I want something, and – of course – the 'me like, me want' train of thought.

I went up to men I thought were attractive – frequently. I went through a phase of devil-may-care contacting and number/email-asking. Words are my preferred mode of attack, so I sent industrial quantities of emails and texts I shouldn't have. Two glasses of wine would make me think a 'bold' message was a good idea. Yes, I was bad.

How I did it

I simply stopped doing all of the above. Even when I was tempted. Sound too easy? Well, it would be if you weren't in the zone. But I *wanted* to take a break – a break from all that expended, chaotic energy, much of it bouncing back negatively. Being in the zone came first, not pursuing came second.

How I felt

A million times more relaxed, and as though a burden had been lifted. Letting go the whole question of 'should I or shouldn't I' was a huge relief. When I was out with friends, I was much more present with them, since the possibilities of what could be *if only I went over and talked to that guy making flirty eye contact* ceased to be of interest. Hot guy at five o'clock? Not my problem. Dude took my number and hasn't texted? Already forgotten.

What I let slip through the cracks

Nothing for quite a while. It's fairly easy to get this rule right, because all you have to do is … nothing. But I have fallen off the wagon a few times, assertively making myself known to gentlemen in bars and so on, or – while online dating – IM'ing like mad anyone who looked fit. Instant feedback has been negative, though (men aside, I've felt somehow humiliated and regretful after these fits of impulsive pursuit), and I've clambered back aboard the wagon shamefacedly.

And now?

I sometimes give in to certain impulses, knowing I shouldn't – just as one does when one's on a food diet and the fried chicken is winking away at you across the street. I regret it pretty sharpish. But I keep the Man Diet in the back of my head at all times, so I'm usually able to recover from any episodes of unhelpful pursuit fairly quickly.

SOS!

I fell off the bandwagon several times on this one, only to be painfully reminded – like a dog straying over an electric fence – that it's best to stick to it (sorry for brutal image).

Basically, what can happen is you go for a period of time observing this rule perfectly. If this period overlaps with a strange dearth of male interest, you'll start to figure: 'oh come on, clearly I need to pursue a guy! This is getting me nowhere.' Well – it is getting you somewhere. It's helping make you a whole woman, confident in her personhood.

However, if you've fallen off the wagon because you're just gagging for some sex, and you achieved your goal through pursuing a man in some way, then good for you. Just be realistic: no expectations allowed. If you feel rubbish afterwards, don't beat yourself up about it. Just take it as what my friend Diane likes to call a data point: useful info about yourself for the future.

Rule Number

Take a Break
from Internet Dating

You need this rule if you …

- Are sick and tired of internet dating. Specifically:
  - creeps winking and perving at you, and attractive
    men ignoring you
  - dates without chemistry
  - dates with freaks
  - IM chats of a very low calibre
  - the constant, daily rejection that is a necessary part
    of internet dating
- Can't control the time you spend on there – i.e. you're
  always browsing.
- Have actually started to think of men as products to be
  shopped for.
- Feel like you're hitting your head against a wall.
- Stay up late waiting for people to IM you, then resent
  feeling tired the next day.
- Already Facebook stalk – internet dating is like stalker's
  paradise for you.
- Find it exerts a slight yet constant negative pressure on
  your mind.

Goes well with …
- No Facebook Stalking
- Dwell on Your Sense of Self
- Do Something Lofty
- Take a Break from the Games

Alexa, 29, describes herself as a 'dating fiend'. She's been on eHarmony for a year and a half, is beautiful, intense and always single. Recently, she met a guy online (one of the vast quantities who are drawn to blonde hair, green eyes and a slim frame), and thought he seemed all right. She agreed to meet up with him (Jake), hopeful but wary as ever. He was wearing a T-shirt that said 'Not too fancy' on it. 'Oh, a word tee,' thought men's fashion expert Alexa. 'Great, another one of those gay-metro guys.' The date began with a lot of generic exchange of information, but then she realised they actually had quite a lot in common. 'Plus he works super-hard in finance, so he's driven,' Alexa explained to me. They ended up having a three-hour dinner by Liverpool Street, near his office.

He appeared to be able to handle it, and she thought: 'I really like this guy.' They go on two more dates, and on the third date, she sleeps with him. But then 'work' kicks in. That it really kicks in, Alexa has no doubt, but it kicks in like an excuse, too. She starts making excuses for him: 'He's in the middle of this crazy period for *work. I happened to meet him right in the middle of this period. For the first few weeks we're dating the deal he's working on doesn't close.' Alexa notices that he won't make any plans and though she's trying to be flexible and supportive, it's beginning to drive her crazy.*

Six weeks in, they've seen each other six or eight times. One Saturday morning she rings him and he says he's going to a farmer's market with a neighbour, then the gym, and would she like to come? She doesn't, particularly. Later on, he calls her. 'I really like you, but with work being so crazy, I don't have the bandwidth to do this. What I want to do is take a hiatus and when the deal's closed I'll call you.' Alexa says: 'Fine, great.' A week later, thinking of him, she sends him a message: 'Thinking of you.' His reply is 'Much appreciated' to which she puts it out there: 'Any chance of the hiatus being over any time soon?' Him: 'It's not a hiatus from you, it's an opportunity to focus.'

What happened next …

Having been told to f*ck off as clearly as possible, Alexa went back online. She felt bruised, but she was used to this kind of crappy weirdness. Another one had bitten the dust. Five hundred people had viewed her profile since she'd logged on the day before, 20 had winked at her, and she began idly surveying the next batch of potential dates. She felt sort of crappy that she was back in the sea of perving, checking out, winking and chatting. After all, Jake had been promising, kinda. The next guy probably wouldn't even get this far. Then she noticed something that really made her feel shitty: Jake was online, and had been for some time. He was on a hiatus, but not from other women, evidently. She tried to tell herself that he might have just had a quick browse to relax, but a week later she saw him on another date at the same bar they'd had their first one. Work had let up? Possibly. But it was doubtful. More like another 'failure'. And he wasn't even that great.

Alexa, still single, frustrated but hopeful, put it to me like this: 'There's this notion about the internet, that there's this unlimited amount of potential dates. But we're treating people like they're disposable. There's always more. People get pickier – they think: "I didn't get exactly what I want because I didn't put the right search terms in." But I'm not sure you can ever perfect the search terms.'

Don't get me wrong. I know two couples getting married this year who met online. Many friends of mine have had good times, good relationships and great sex thanks to online dating. It's so lacking in stigma now that in some parts (OK, mostly in the US) you seem a freak if you're *not* online.

So I say ...

'For all its massive upsides – romantically and otherwise –
the internet is a sea of junk-food love.'

If you're feeling like you've been chewed up and spat out by internet dating sites, the best thing you can do is to take a break from them. Why? Because this will allow you to take a break from:

- Endless choice
- Having unattractive men perving at you
- Banter that goes nowhere
- Being rejected by people you don't even like
- Feeling like you're failing
- Guys more interested in shagging than relationships

Do it ... but don't believe the hype

Dating websites are just another platform for meeting people – the good, bad and of course, the ugly. Online dating sites work via a numbers game: you browse, view, poke, wink more people, and will probably end up with more dates than if you left it to real life. But most of those dates won't go anywhere, according to a piece in the *Wall Street Journal* last March, and the press releases fail to say that most people won't find what they're looking for online. Chicago psychologist, Kate Wachs, and author of *Relationships for Dummies*, told the paper that online daters were suffering from burnout as a result of how tiring online dating has become.

'Big dating websites like to report statistics about the number of marriages they've spawned, giving the impression that they are literally happiness machines.'

Big dating websites like to report statistics about the number of marriages they've spawned, giving the impression that they are literally happiness machines. Carl Bialik did a nice little write-up for the *Wall Street Journal* in 2009 about inflated marriage stats. He noted that eHarmony claims credit for 2 per cent of all US marriages, based on a survey it commissioned. Match.com (US) laid claim to 12 engagements or weddings per day, but then took back this number. Plenty of Fish's chief executive and founder, Markus Frind, estimates his site generates 100,000 marriages each year.

Bialik found that academics were sceptical of the research. One of the academics he cited, Eli J. Finkel, a social psychologist at Northwestern University, said that data coming from online dating sites should be taken with a large pinch of salt until their studies are peer-reviewed in the same way that proper academic papers are. Mark Thompson, a former executive in the online dating trade, believes that television ads showing lovestruck couples describing how they found their perfect match online should carry warnings that such outcomes are far from typical.

Even *The Economist* cautions online daters to be sceptical – a special feature on the topic quoted industry experts saying that online dating stats can be misleading. For example, one pointed out that a site's total number of profiles may be mostly composed of inactive, rather than active members. When you add in the fact that most online daters want partners within a 30-mile radius, the pool shrinks still further. Another cautioned daters that happy endings from romantic forays online are certainly unusual. Despite those gushy ads on TV (and the gushy stories we hear from our friends, all of whom know someone who met their husband or wife online), most people don't meet The One.

So, what we know is that there is a lot of choice online. But we don't yet know the precise number or kinds of relationships that all that choice leads to, or how internet dating affects *most* people's self-esteem – or how it affects men and women differently.

Too much choice?

'Choice' is one of the most cherished words in our society. It's freedom's sidekick, after all. Thank God; I often count my lucky stars I was born when I was and not a century earlier where choices were limited to 'What do I name my fifteenth child?' and 'How best can I serve my husband?'

But as with all good things, too much can be a mixed blessing. I'm not for a minute saying we should get offline for good, crawl back into caves or hark back to 'the way things were'. But with all these extra tools at our disposal, we need to be extra clever and wise in the way we use them or else we start to feel rubbish.

Many, if not most, women reading this book will have tried online dating. It's a good strategy and far better than sitting around moaning. But it has occupational hazards. And I think the biggest one is too much choice of an unhelpful variety. The phrase 'Water, water everywhere and not a drop to drink' isn't far off the mark here.

Or, if we keep with the food metaphor, canapés everywhere but nothing to eat. Lucy, 32, who has also been single long-term and on Match.com for a year, is fed up with the feast of flesh:

> 'There's always hotter women than you round the corner:
> online dating is a buffet, right there. It's a buffet of faces;
> you're bombarded. It's like in the US, you can buy any coffee
> you want, any sandwich, and always wonder if there's
> anything better. Guys are being emailed bulletins of other
> girls who they think might be better. You never feel happy
> with what you've decided. It's like me trying to choose a
> hotel for my holiday.'

There is choice within choice – there are hundreds of dating websites in the UK at the time of writing. Badoo, though you may not have heard of it, is the internet's most success-ful hook-up/dating service, with nearly 130 million members, and gaining 300,000 users a day. That's a dizzying amount of choice. Each site has a different reputation, advertising campaign, target audience and the all-important algorithm – eHarmony, for example, uses a patented 'Compatibility Matching System' requiring members to answer 258 ques-tions to join.

Then there's the endless choice of how to present your-self – are you a 'social' or a 'heavy' drinker? Are you look-ing for love but tempted to tick the 'looking for activity partners' box? If you admit to loving Tarkovsky films will you attract pretentious pseudo intellectuals? Do you want to write a long and passionate bio or a terse and clever one? Some people can't handle doing either, and outsource their dating profiles to professionals who will make them shine, and manage the banter up until the first date. Seriously.

Studies have found that too many online options can actually 'lead to more searching and worse choices in finding partners for romantic relationships online.' That is, by having many options available, users' ability to weed out the less suitable options is reduced. This could be because having a huge amount of options may increase the work your brain has to do to make judgements and choices, so you make more errors.

And more choice is not always more info, Prof Janet Reibstein, author of the relationship study, *The Best Kept Secret*, says:

> 'There is less information when you're meeting people on the internet – verbal and other cues, for example, which play a crucial role in attraction. But the numbers online are enormous to make up for it. So although there are far more times you can feel wounded, you have more of a chance of getting a hit.'

You're not the only one who doesn't (always) find it a bed of roses

Lots of women feel that because we're going online, things will be different, but in reality we wind up in similar situations as we would in a bar. Many feel angry that despite signing up, dating is still frustrating. It's like a massive bar that you can step into from the comfort of your sofa. Says one friend, Kat, who closed her account after getting 1,000 views overnight but only one approach, from a 21-year-old Vietnamese wife-hunter:

> *'The number of guys viewing my account was stupidly high,*
> *yet the number of guys who approached me for a date was*
> *seriously low – and so few of those were in any way normal.*
> *It essentially felt like going to a cheesy bar and having lots*
> *of men looking but not approaching you. I didn't like the*
> *idea of all those people having access to images of me and*
> *information about me so I closed my account. Glad I gave it*
> *a go, but never again!'*

Sally, 33, says:

> *'You feel like you need to do something since there are no*
> *men about. Then you start meeting these guys online, and*
> *you'll say, well he's a complete cock, he doesn't do the*
> *profession you want, but there's something OK about him,*
> *then he ends up treating you like crap anyway. You give*
> *them a shot, because everyone says to, you try to be*
> *pragmatic, then they shit on you. This is very common in*
> *online dating. It's the ultimate insult – when someone you*
> *don't even like rejects you.'*

Others are less negative in their experiences, of course, even if they haven't found their soulmate online. But I think Sally, Kat and Lucy are capturing something that a lot of women experience, namely: disappointment and a sense of being slightly insulted over and over again.

Tougher on women?
I know some of you won't agree with what comes next – many women find the dynamics of the internet to be good for self-discovery, meeting new people around a busy work

schedule, having good conversations and making friends (and, sometimes, babies). But if you're reading this chapter, you're probably not having the best time online – or you want to know how to make it work for you better.

So, forgive me if this doesn't apply even remotely to you or you violently disagree (but there's a general consensus among the women I spoke to that the choice offered by the internet is better for men, less good for women). Caroline, 33, who has been on My Single Friend and Lovestruck for two years, says: 'There's just too much choice for men. It's like a sweet shop: "today I want a polo, tomorrow I want an eclair".' The result, she feels, is that men use websites as a massive pool of potential shags, whereas the women online, particularly in their thirties, are earnestly seeking a partner. In other words, there is a mismatch in intent.

With all its potential sex and risk, the internet is the perfect male playground. Vivienne, 32, agrees: 'The amount of choice makes it so easy to cheat and for men to get an ego massage. It's the infiltration of American style. Men are inherently greedy; they want to spread their seed. The internet increases the number of people to date. But choice takes away happiness.'

Choice, as I said earlier, is an essential part of freedom. I'd much rather suffer from too much than too little. But what Vivienne is driving at is that choice of potential *partners* feels wrong if treated like choice of potential *purchases*. Dan Ariely, a professor of psychology and behavioural economics at Duke University, USA, and author of *The Upside of Irrationality*, is very down on treating human beings 'as if they are goods'. People can't be defined according to tick-boxes and attributes, he argues, in the way that a pair of headphones can (obviously). And no matter how well someone describes themselves, there's no accounting for that spark of romance. Joanna, 30, agrees with Ariely. 'I did Guardian Soulmates for a while but gave up. Everyone presents themselves identically. They all like (controversially) Sunday lunches in pubs, going to festivals, curling up with DVDS – were I not utterly superficial, it would be impossible to discriminate.'

My question is: has Ariely ever tried online dating? Because I think if you're going to bash it, you should try it and I know he's been married a long time. Ellie, 29, has certainly tried internet dating. She comes on strong, but brilliantly, so brace yourself:

'The internet has ruined dating and made wimps of men. Men are rude because they can be. They won't follow up because they don't have to. There are no consequences to their being a c**t. You don't email anyone to follow up. You pretty much know that every girl on there is single and hasn't had sex for a while. So if you act like you want a relationship, a girl will shag you quickly. Men use it for sex and women get taken in – there are men on there who want relationships but they are such social misfits. If you're a nice, normal guy, you don't need the internet, but girls do, because there are more of us.'

There might be a mismatch in the way (some) men and (some) women *use* online dating. But the sense of mismatch doesn't end there. For example, Lucy's main frustration is that even online there are reams and reams of perfect-seeming (or at least, attractive) women and few decent men. 'The power balance is even worse online because there are so many fewer [good] men than women,' she told me recently while we were scoffing burgers and beers.

The bummed-out feeling that there are only disappointing men around is a junk-food love feeling. Online dating can magnify this feeling. Which is why the Man Dieter should step away from it temporarily to rebalance and regain perspective.

If you want to look, you have to be looked at …

The other weird thing about online dating – which is why it's great as well as freaky – is the sense of being looked at. Women respond differently than men to being sized up and checked out – it can give us an ego boost, but the line between flattery and feeling violated is very, very thin. Veronica, a Match dater for two years, told me something with great passion (on our third glass of house white vino) that stuck with me: 'Minging men were winking at me. 65 year olds. There were so many f**king minging men winking at me. All those mingers made me feel violated.'

I've overcome fear and snobbery and gone online myself: Jdate (three guys, seven dates, zillions of emails and IM chats including with the likes of 'Naughtyboy 1234' who likes to get straight to video, which I decline) and Lovestruck (five messages, zero dates). I also found it weird that people were checking me out and winking but not doing anything more. I felt exposed in the extreme – flattered and horrified too. Also insulted, like: 'Why are *you* looking at me?' But unlike in a bar, you can't sneer at them. You have to let them stare and assess all they want.

Then there's the fact that you don't quite know *who* is looking at you. It's well known that people fudge their profiles to get more hits. (Not always massively, though, since the threat of being shown up on a date is a deterrent.) As Marina Adshade, an economics professor, argued on her BigThink blog: 'Everyone can find at least one good picture of themselves. And if everyone puts their very best picture on their online dating profile (and why wouldn't they?), then anyone trying to estimate the distribution of attractiveness using dating profile pictures will almost certainly overestimate the average level of attractiveness for people of that gender who are searching on that market.' In other words, people put up their best pictures, so most online daters are in for some kind of rude shock.

OkTrends, a blog run by OkCupid, an online dating site, reported in 2009 that users routinely fib about things such as their height and wealth (men) in order to boost their chances of being contacted – women are more likely to fudge weight or body type.

Caroline adds: 'Our mums would be eaten alive if they were out there.'

Taking a break from internet dating: actually doing it

Suspending your membership is easy. But if you don't want to give it up entirely, here's how to cut down on junk-food love online ...

It's funny, but I wouldn't be surprised if – just as the internet dating scene became socially mainstream in the easily embarrassed UK – a backlash happened. We follow the US in most things, from fast food to dating. So I was interested to see this headline in the *Wall Street Journal* recently: 'Scary New Dating site: the real world', which suggests that a critical mass of people are hitting the online dating wall and being sent back to square one, i.e. real life. 'Online dating is a lot of time for very little return,' says a brand manager quoted in the piece.

Whether you think online dating is just great, or totally awful, if you're channelling junk-food love vibes, here are a few ways to manage your dating life online to help achieve the goal of the Man Diet: more you, more smiles, less crap – men, feelings, sex. Period.

1. Set boundaries (and don't accept crumbs)

Be clear about the difference between online and offline. The biggest challenge with anything social and online is actively making yourself unavailable – if you're anything like me, you'll have half a dozen or more tabs up at any time. Forgot to close Facebook? Next thing you know, Unhealthy Mixed Signal Joe from last year is popping up, all over your green dot. Same with online dating. If you even forget you have your site open in a tab, you can be reading *The New York Times* online and suddenly Elliot456 'wants to chat with you!' Great for Elliot456; not great for you or your focus. (Did you know that focusing makes people happy and losing the ability to do so makes them depressed?) So remove yourself from the bored whims of dudes idling online, just browsing and killing time, since their interruptions are one of the purest forms of junk-food love. In the first instance, if they want to get in touch, they can send you an email or message.

I'm not saying don't chat – clearly IM is one of the big features of dating websites and can be fun/important if it's good. But set boundaries around when you do it – if you fancy a dirty browse and a random bout of chat, give yourself half an hour or an hour to do it. Best not let it spill into your day at random. When you're online, be online, but give yourself a certain amount of time. Then get off.

Therapist Val Sampson talks about 'being represented by all these availability symbols,' adding that 'boundaries are linked to self-esteem. At the moment, it's very important to set them.'

2. Banter when necessary

But move it to a live chat before you start to feel like it's going nowhere. Alexa, who as we know is a bit of a pro, says: 'I like banter hovering around the date itself. But I hate when it becomes a substitute for actual conversation, face to face. As soon as it does, I say: "Forget this chat – I can't wait to see you in person soon." They're like, "OK, cool."' Val Sampson says: 'There's nothing wrong with a bit of online flirting; it can be exciting and fun. But it can't be a substitute.'

In her book *Alone Together: Why we expect more from technology and less from each other*, MIT digital scholar Sherry Turkle interviews a typical young man who will do anything to avoid talking on the phone. He prefers texts, email, IM, anything. She makes a good point about how people who are always online, always have a green dot, start to fear real-time communication. As Turkle observes, with some sadness: 'If you feel like you're always on call, you start to hide from the rigors of things that unfold in real time.'

3. Don't be nice

In this case, be like a lot of men, who are far more brutal about who they do and don't fancy or see as potentials. If you hate when guys start messages with 'Heya! lol' then do not proceed with the conversation. Life's too short. If a guy seems OK but you just know his gelled baldness will repulse you in the flesh, bin it. Don't feel guilty!

4. Make your logged-on time productive

Choose some decent criteria (not just 'He's cute and I suppose I could shag him even though he looks like a player and is seven years younger than me') … and get aggressive. Spend half an hour solidly winking, messaging and hotlisting every single guy who meets your criteria. Sit back and give it 24 hours. Log back in. You might find only one of them has responded. But the chances are, he'll at least be worth your time sending an email and maybe more.

5. Swear off mobile/location-based hook-up or meet-up sites

Industry insiders say they're the future of social networking and online dating, but I say, who cares? For the duration of your Man Diet, ignore apps and sites like Badoo, Floxx (where you can alert others to an attractive person near you), Blendr (a new non-sexuality-specific 'version' of gay pick-up app Grindr), and Flirtomatic (members exchange flirty messages for free). These are the kebab shops, KFC and Millie's Cookies of love: they are built to give you short-term highs but are not helpful to the Man Dieter who needs to wean herself off junk-food love lows. Badoo, if you're not one of the hundreds of millions who use it, is the biggest buffet of ready and willing people out there (Nabucodonsor: 'Quiero meet kiss laugh con una chica, 24–32'; Londonboy 'wants to get down and dirty with a girl, 22–26'; Feri 'wants to practice kissing with a girl').

6. Grab a good real-life experience

Remember Sherry Turkle and the 'rigors of real time'? Well, get out there from behind your screen and remind yourself how different, and fun, real-time face-to-face meetings are. I'm not talking about seeing old friends. I'm talking about things like attending a talk, then asking the speaker a question at the end. Or going to a bookshop and chatting to the guy (or girl) behind the counter about new deliveries or the dire state of publishing. If you're in a bar and the waiter has an interesting accent, ask where he's from. (In that situation, I'd have a hard time not flirting. If you can flirt and enjoy it without wishing you could ask him out or vice versa and then getting all hot under the collar about it, then do it.)

7. Sign up for a hobby you like that MAYBE includes men

If you're hell bent on meeting men right now and don't want to even temporarily ditch your online membership, then make sure you're *also* trying to meet them in the real world too, by *doing* rather than *browsing*. There's a hilarious line in Helen Gurley Brown's *Sex and the Single Girl* where she advises those women who feel that they aren't meeting enough men to get employed (as clerks or secretaries) at 'garages, missile launchings and live-bait barges'. If you can find the equivalent of 'live-bait barges' (whatever they are), then you're golden.

It's not easy, tweaking online behaviour. The 'you've got mail!' thing is so embedded in our brain's reward system that it can be as addictive as gambling. But you can do it, bit by bit. A little discipline, a little pulling back, and you might find that you end up shedding a few pounds of junk-food love.

How I followed this rule:

Pre-Man Diet

I didn't do much internet dating. I did a bit, though, and exerted no control over when and how and with whom I chatted. I got caught up in banter with anyone vaguely attractive who tried – never mind that they were hoodlums or idiots. I'd check it like I'd check Facebook in the pre-Man Diet days – compulsively, just to see if there was any action or developments. Of course, 'developments' generally meant a flirt, or wink, or three new people who had 'checked [me] out'.

What I did

I was so fed up by the amount of unplanned time I was pouring into it, Facebook-style, and the comparatively small return I was getting (one or two chemistry-free dates; a few decent bits of banter), that I basically stopped enjoying it and lost the compulsion to go on it. Other people obviously find internet dating great fun.

How I felt

Like I was well rid of it, in part – if I'm honest – because of my pride. But sometimes I wondered – and rightly so – what I was missing by being stubbornly anti-web dating. Real life was not offering up goldmines of eligible men, and many of my friends were meeting online, so I wondered if I was doing the right thing. Short-term I felt I was, but long-term, I wasn't sure.

SOS!

Back on internet dating? Has a friend convinced you to try another site? Fine – I'm not saying don't waste your money. Here's what I suggest.

- Go crazy in the first week to get it out of your system. Set up a couple of dates – and, possibly, meet the man of your dreams. The initial frenzy is not a good time to be strict with yourself. But after a week, or as soon as you feel those old feelings of frustration or dismay creeping in, cut right back. How to do so is outlined in the chapter.
- Don't use the site just because you paid for it. If it's making you feel edgy right away, stop checking it. The occasional interesting message may come in, but you can pick those up every few days. Be very selective about when you go online, and don't forget to be brutal about saying no to people who don't appeal. Time is money, as it were.
- If you keep getting emails from an existing account saying so-and-so has contacted or winked at you or whatever, go ahead and check it. That's fair enough. I mean, only the inhuman could withhold. But if you're reading this SOS because you're back on obsessive checking again, then return to strictness: limited periods of time checking. And I recommend avoiding unsolicited IMs.

Rule Number 9

Dwell on Your Sense of Self

You need this rule if you ...

- Often feel truly lousy due to the man situation – whether because of things not working out or because of long drought periods.
- Can't imagine how you functioned before you went out with the man who recently broke your heart, or you feel like a break-up has totally hobbled you.
- Take rejection as a sign that you are not good/worth enough.
- Beat yourself up about your singleness.
- Are quick to self-deprecate.
- Feel boring when you have no 'stories' to tell.
- Panic daily about the clock ticking.
- Hate that your friends are all married and you feel like a loser at their weddings.

Goes well with ...

- Do Something Lofty
- No Facebook Stalking
- No Talking About Men
- Refuse to Have NSA Sex

Dwell on Your
Sore Eyeball

J enny, 32, a journalist, had just completed the
assignment of her life. She'd really brought home
the bacon this time, she told herself with pride.
She'd gone far and wide to get people to dish the dirt on
a fashion label that turned out to be utterly corrupt, and
involved in all kinds of things like child labour and
sexual abuse. It was dynamite and she scored the front
page of the biggest weekend paper.

On seeing the results of her work, she was utterly
thrilled, feeling that unique rush that having your
name in the paper can give you.

She went out to celebrate that night with some friends.
They got drunk, and she ended up taking some guy
home that said, in a diner at 4am: 'Will you at least let
me put it in your arse?' She decided to take him home
anyway – and though she did not grant him his desire,
she did sleep with him and discover he had rather a
good body. And wasn't as awful as all that. When he left
the next day, she felt the tingling of hope that he'd ask
for her number and actually use it.

By 4pm, feeling hungover as hell, she began to feel
down. Some guy who'd propositioned her arse at 4am

had been granted access to her boudoir. And despite the glaringly obvious fact that he wasn't worth any emotional bandwidth at all, his silence and carelessness were making her feel really down. Even the thought of her splash in the paper the day before only provided moderate mood-boosting.

She had an account on eHarmony. She logged in – only losers had winked at her. One guy might have actually been a criminal. She felt worse.

The next evening, she attended a dinner party some married friends were holding. Everyone was really congratulatory about her story. But it wasn't long before they were quizzing her about her romantic status. She couldn't help but feel that to them, the most interesting, if not important, aspect of her was the fact that she was single.

She left feeling worse than ever. Instead of feeling utterly on a high about her achievement, her prowess as a journalist and all the other things she was good at and people loved her for, she felt reduced utterly to a man failure. A single woman, first and foremost.

Interestingly, the lower she felt in general about 'never finding anyone', the more she dwelled on the guy from Saturday night. She didn't know why she was dwelling; if it was because she felt she'd slept with someone bad, or if it was because she wanted him to get in touch anyway, or the fact that both were true.

What happened next ...

I met up with Jenny for drinks later that week. I spent about half an hour hammering home the following factoids: Jenny is brainy, Jenny is successful, Jenny is brilliant fun, Jenny owns her own house, Jenny is attractive, Jenny is free, Jenny is talented, Jenny is kind, Jenny makes her family happy.

After talking about these facts for a while, the awful anal man's importance – which felt like the frosting on a cake of junk-food love – fell away and the cloud began to lift. The man stuff, and the single question, was a vortex of negativity with no resolution. The achievement stuff was positive reality. Jenny left in better spirits. We talked the next day – she said that once the initial black cloud of bad feeling had been lifted, which was fairly easily done by my hammering home *the facts* of her fabulousness, her self-esteem rose again and she became focused on being who she is rather than who she isn't with.

What this rule's about

Trading the first (man failure) for the second (real, concrete achievement) is seriously comforting. It also paves the way for a healthier perspective that puts sub-par men and sub-par encounters further down on the scale of importance. (They are only important – sometimes very – in teaching us what *not* to do.)

It can also help soothe broken hearts. When you've broken up with someone, you can't always see how you'll ever feel like yourself again. You feel like you're missing a limb, half your brain, whatever. You've lost something you loved, and the person you became with your ex – more sacrificial, more moody, more serious, whatever – is no longer required. You can't shake the grief before it's ready, but you can remember that you *are* a person, a whole person, despite feeling like half of you has been lopped off. This rule should help you in that process, and should help control spirals of despair if kept in mind as often as possible.

Modern woman: a cross-breed

We're at this weird point in history where we – as women, and as single women – are gaining power and exploiting our hard-won opportunities more than ever, and enjoying freedom without truly prohibitive downsides. Far more women than men go to university; 2006 figures from Universities UK show that women students outnumber men (57 per cent of university students are female) across all subjects, including engineering and physical science; 2002 was the first year that Cambridge University accepted more female than male undergraduates. In Ivy League universities in the US like Yale, there are more undergraduate women than men and, in his speech at graduation last year, the President of Yale addressed 'the women and men of the class of 2011'.

'You're nobody until someone loves you' – Stanford, Sex and the City

Single women are on the rise, cohabitation competes with marriage, and divorce rates are at 50 per cent. The cosy idea of the housewife and the happy neat nuclear home has been largely blasted to pieces. One in three kids experience the break-up of a family. Prime Minister David Cameron is obsessed with restoring the traditional format, having recognised it has all but slipped away. 'Think of any big social problem we face – from crime and welfare dependency, to ill-health, drug addiction and educational failure – and more often than not, it comes back to the family,' he wrote imploringly in *The Sun*.

So you'd think the old idea of trying to find a life partner with which to breed would be obsolete.

It may be going that way, BUT …

The single state is still far from being an easy social place for women to dwell – why else would the memory of Bridget Jones's pulverised, traumatic singleton-ness linger so poignantly? 'I blame Bridget for feeling like a single charity case,' says my friend Margaret, 30. Both she and I had, by chance, been rereading the book, having first devoured it at age 16. 'It set up a whole generation of women with major angst about not finding the one,' she put it as we headed for our second bottle of wine. Then there's all the negative words for single women 'past their prime' (spinster, frigid, sad, for example) vs similar words for men (err, bachelor). It's moved on from there – we now have 'bachelorette'.

But the modern single woman is still a very strange cross-breed: Strong and Independent, but also In Need of a Man. Beyoncé put her finger on it with her song 'Single Ladies'. On one hand, she's looking hot on a night out, men buzzing around her, and she's finally enjoying being single. On the other, she's angry her ex didn't claim her with a wedding ring. The single woman in this song seeks to be owned and carried to some magical destiny (referring to herself and what she has to offer frequently as 'it'). Hard to know why the song's called 'Single Ladies', really.

This song, which I've enthusiastically danced to a million times, is a micro-symbol of something bigger – that identifying oneself as a woman, *regardless* of romantic status, is rather alien in our society. Look at the obsession with Jennifer Aniston – the poor girl might as well have no acting career, for all that we care. I think she's actually pretty good at acting, but when you think of her, it's more likely to be in terms of her post-Brad single sadness and various failed flings. *Grazia*'s front cover 2 June 2011 said it all in big bold letters: 'FINALLY, Jennifer has found THE ONE!'

Ladies, I'm asking you not to think of yourself – even a little bit – in terms of whether you have *finally* found the one. That 'finally' says it all, doesn't it? It says: 'We've been waiting for something of *real* importance and now it has arrived.' It's just this kind of thinking – all those words that come with 'finally', like 'I never' or 'When will I?' or 'One day' – that make us feel like each romantic blunder is a failure of our very selves. It's not. Because we are much more than that.

We've hurtled forwards since the 1960s, of course. But there's still a touch too much of the 'Feminine Mystique' about – if you weren't paying attention in history class, feminine mystique is the concept Betty Friedan cataclysmically lambasted in her book of the same name in 1963. Friedan's point is that this 'mystique' is a hoax that results in women being confined to the sexual role only, as wives, mothers and housekeepers, as their true calling. It's a different world now, but the sense of feminine mystique – that we're really creatures looking for hubby – is still in the air.

Indeed, over the past year there have been several articles in popular sibling freesheets *Stylist* and *Shortlist* noting a regression of the genders back into traditional roles. Men want to be like alpha male Don Draper from *Mad Men* – all five o'clock shadow, big bones, cool suits and sexual conquest. (Thankfully, the articles stopped short of saying women want to be like depressed but beautiful housewife Betty Draper.)

'Being single is a job, but it's a secret job'

So says my friend Ruth. And so say the authors of 1990s dating bestseller *The Rules*: 'For long-lasting results, we believe in treating dating like a job, with rules and regulations.'

Well, I say we don't have time for *another* job. Aren't we busy enough with work and friends and hobbies and trying to do the right thing?

Of course. But as you'll have guessed, busy-ness isn't the actual issue. It's this: that if you're allowing singleness to swell to job-like proportions, you've neglected the art of being happy in your own skin, and you aren't taking full stock of your own unique set of blessings and challenges.

So when you feel yourself agonising over dates, trying to stay in the game with four under-appreciative guys at once, freaking out about your weight (i.e. how will guys fancy me like *this*?), compulsively checking your internet dating account every time you receive a 'wink', going on disastrous blind date after disastrous blind date … it's time to read this chapter. And in so doing, remind yourself that you're far more than single or not single – you're a friend, sister, daughter, aunt. You're an employee or a boss. You do things, you make money. You help people and make them smile.

We feel so much better when we remember that, and putting those achievements ahead of romantic status. You might be thinking that this rule is closely related to the Lofty rule. It is – but its purpose is to provide still another way to achieve the Man Diet's goal: *Feeling* your total person-ness. While Do Something Lofty provided urgent measures to take your mind off fruitless man-ruminations and cut down the negative feelings that this engenders, this rule requires a more thoughtful, mindful approach and is probably best read after Lofty.

Getting into the 'Me as Person' vs 'Me as Single Woman' zone – and why it's hard

Being single is a big deal – to your friends

It can be hard to remember you're far more than your single status or your last date. You have to really work at it when all around you, friends, family and media seem to be obsessing about the questions: Do you have a man in your life? If not, why not? If so, what kind of man? When's the wedding? Or, if you've recently changed status, the million little lights that go on in your social network; Facebook can help things along by putting a broken red heart on the newsfeed if you change your relationship status to single. Alex Heminsley's book, *Ex and the City*, carries the humorous sub-head: 'You're nobody 'til somebody dumps you.'

Holly, 31, feels like her single status is a huge deal. She says:

*'There's a real social stigma to being single, especially from
your late 20s. It makes it more difficult to attend weddings.
You get pangs of worry that you'll end up alone; that you'll
forget how to compromise and become quite selfish.
Especially at my age, when you're over 30, there's this sense
that you're sort of being left behind; having a boyfriend, or
a long-term partner, is associated with growing up. Being
single, you feel you're a child, somehow behind.'*

Mary, 30, adds:

*'You feel undesirable, like there's something wrong with you,
like you're half mad. People tell me – "just settle, just settle,
you're too picky!" But in reality, the longer you go without
sex, the more you consider randoms.'*

Ruth, 30, also feels that it's hard for people to get over the
fact that she's single:

*'People will constantly ask: "Why are you single?" Friends
will demand: "Why aren't you dating Jeremy or Derek?" or
whatever; they're just listing off the other friends you have
that also happen to be single.'*

As the girls say in the *SATC* episode, 'Bay of Married Pigs':

Charlotte: 'I hate it when you're the only single person at a
dinner party and they look at you like you're a …'
Carrie: 'Loser.'
Miranda: 'Leper!'
Samantha: 'Whore!'

Greener grass

But those people could possibly be a bit jealous. That, or misguided, thinking the grass is always greener. Samara O'Shea, a blogger who has been single for six years, made a clever observation in a piece for *The Huffington Post*. It is assumed that single people are looking for a partner, she wrote, and while this is often true, the assumption is based on the idea that life is better in a relationship. In a relationship, everything is rosier, right? Wrong. The full range of emotions you can feel as a single person – including loneliness and boredom – can be felt in a relationship too. And the wonderful things you can feel in a relationship, like warmth, validation and even ecstasy, can be felt when you're single.

Or, depending on the way you tilt your head, maybe the grass is a little tiny bit greener on the single side. A 2009 study by the University of Nevada, Las Vegas, found that heterosexual women do worse at work than lesbians, earning 6 per cent less than their queer sisters. This is because, it is thought, the desire for a husband – or indeed having one – puts women on a subconscious slow track. Either they think he'll earn more anyway – and that's what they want – or they're subconsciously holding out for a greater role in housework. Well, by the time we reach 30, there's no slow track for us. So, if we take lesbians as a promising example of the man-free, we are in for the bigger bucks. Mary, a lawyer in the City, read the study and commented: 'See? Having men on the mind limits productivity for women!' Which is to say: being able to truly see yourself as *far* more than your relationship status – in terms of real things like skills, productivity, people skills, joie de vivre – could even boost your pay cheque.

Forget the fairy tales, sisters – you're the happy ending
If you buy into fairy tales, you buy out of making your own destiny. You see each date, or relationship that didn't turn out as you wanted, or dry patch, as dips and troughs and peaks on your ski lift to the peak where a big wedding cake figurine will be waiting to top off your now-complete happiness.

Instead, we want to recognise that we contain all the ingredients, already, for a fully fledged fairy tale. We can do good, we can achieve, we can help the people we love and like enjoy life more, we can make the world better or we can just have enormous amounts of fun. Hopefully, one day, that full version of being will *include* a man – but it needn't be on hold without one. I say: if you're waiting for the prince that will complete your fairy tale, you're casting yourself as the Rapunzel-style maiden in waiting. Why not, right now, imagine yourself instead as an Amazonian warrior queen, oozing her own power, magnetically pulling people towards her, so complete that she has enough to go round for all her minions.

Despite the vigour, independence and warrior-queen-like potential of the modern woman, the idea of the fairy tale ending – with Perfect Man coming along and sweeping you off your feet – still runs surprisingly deep. It's hard not to think in terms of The One coming for us if only we wait long enough and in the right way. Google 'He's the one' and about twice as many hits come up than for 'She's the one'. And there could be a whole other book written (if there hasn't been already) on the swathes of pink and princess outfits that await baby girls.

On the page ...

American publishing, in particular, hurtles out books telling you how to get your fairy tale ending (or how not to, or why it hasn't happened) at a rate of knots.

Amazon is full of books called things like:

- *When Fairy Tale Romances Break Real Hearts*
- *Project: Happily Ever After. Saving Your Marriage When the Fairy Tale Falters*
- *When the Fairy Tale Fails: How Women Today Can Create Their Own Happy Ever After*
- *Happily Married With Kids: It's Not a Fairy Tale*
- *Happily Ever After: The Fairy-Tale Formula for Lasting Love*
- *Realistically Ever After: Finding Happiness When He's Not Prince Charming*
- *You're Not Snow White, and Life's Not a Fairy Tale*

It's no coincidence that the daddy of them all, *The Rules*, appeals to women using the language of courtly love and fairy tale: 'Trust that one day a prince will notice that you're different from all the other women he's known, and ask for your hand!'

On TV ...

Even *Sex and the City* opens with the classic fairy tale beginning: Carrie's voice intoning: 'Once upon a time.' And though Carrie is the ultimate free spirit, she wants the knight in shining armour the whole time, Big – and gets him. Charlotte is much more open about her romantic fairy tale. It's to the credit of the programme that it's not quite as straightforward as that. What appears to be a fairy tale – i.e., her wedding to Trey, with all those lovely tartans – doesn't actually add up to fairy tale. But Charlotte gets her knight in shining armour in the form of a dumpy bald lawyer; as Miranda gets hers in the form of dopey Steve. Carrie ends up with the most knight-like man – he is literally Big, rich as hell, and instead of having a white charger to scoop her up in, he drives a black town car that whisks her home the first night they meet. And let's not forget her jaunt to Paris in the footsteps of the Russian artist Aleksandre, with whom she is hell bent on finally getting her fairy tale in the most 'romantic' city in the world. Poor old Aidan, with his dog and his fried chicken and his lack of interest in Napa Valley wines and haute couture, just wasn't prince-like enough. When he tried to be her man in shining armour, offering her a sign of his love and fealty in the form of an engagement ring, she puts it on her neck instead of her finger.

More recent TV phenomena, like *Desperate Housewives* and *Mad Men*, grab us precisely for the way they pervert the fairy tale. They tease us with it – and, like cats reaching for the dangling string – we keep clawing back for more, thinking we might get it next time. The more we watch, the more jarring but deliciously captivating it is to see how far off the happy ending things seem to be heading for Betty and Don Draper, or Joan, or, in *DH*, Susan and Mike.

At the movies ...

And you probably don't need me to point out that the whole 'true-love-leading-to-amazing-wedding' trope is everywhere in the movies. Hollywood studios are experts at servicing (or is it helping along?) the American fixation with happy endings – and I for one rarely have the power to resist its shiny, glossy rom-coms and dramas. Why? It makes you feel good.

Fairy tale endings are everywhere from a film about an accidental pregnancy involving a gorgeous, successful woman and a scruffball, fat, loser man (*Knocked Up*), to the Natalie Portman flick *No Strings Attached*, in which a woman who prefers sex to relationships is revealed as truly deranged and messed up, not least for turning away Ashton Kutcher (they have a point). She comes to her senses – at a wedding, no less – and they wind up together, on the marriage track. *Love and Other Drugs* does the same thing, only here Jake Gyllenhaal's character ends up saving Anne Hathaway's headstrong MS patient, despite her intense aversion to that set-up and his occasional doubts. Plenty of other films (that I have enjoyed, believe you me) charge towards the 'happily-forever-after with perfect man' ending like there's no alternative – *27 Dresses* and *Never Been Kissed* are two I've enjoyed. *Bridesmaids*, the absolutely brilliant anti-romance of 2011, hilariously and painfully show the agonies of being a single woman in your thirties while all your friends are either married or getting married. It's a triumph for female friendship, and bashes wedding madness and the cult of fairy tale firmly over the head. But even in *Bridesmaids*, the happy ending is a love story for the single girl.

Wedding madness

On one hand, jamborees of casual sex are perfectly allowed, even encouraged in our society (which is much better than the alternative). But on the other, we are also absolutely obsessed with weddings. Take wedding dresses. They're a source of hysterical interest and prompt massive spends – just think of Kate Middleton's, for which her parents forked out 100k. In fact, just think of that whole wedding. It was amazing, but what was even more amazing to my mind, was how passionately the whole world cared. Everywhere from Laos to Connecticut I had conversations about it. It's all in good spirit, of course, but the flip side of this wedding furore is that for women, it is hard not to feel pressure to pull off your own fairy tale – and in high bridal style.

The intensity of the conjugal fairy tale knows no bounds (strange when you consider divorce rates, particularly in the US). The TV show *Bridezillas* is one of the biggest deals on US TV, and let's not forget *The Bachelorette/ Bachelor* and *Joe Millionaire*, *My Big Redneck Wedding*, *A Wedding Story*, *Say Yes to The Dress*, and *Rich Bride, Poor Bride*; and in the UK, *My Big Fat Gypsy Wedding*. *Brides* magazine is a must-read for millions of women. The US wedding industry is worth $40bn; the UK's is more like £6bn. According to a 2008 wedding survey by *Brides*, the average overall cost of getting married in the UK is £22,858 (up from £21,901 in 2007. Couples in London and the South East spend on average £23,932 on their weddings). That's a hell of a lot.

Marianne, 28, a post-grad at Princeton University, paints an intense picture of marriage in the US, where it is truly the holy grail. 'You worry you have an expiration

date,' she says. 'For me, unfortunately, it's about achievement. I went to Harvard, now I'm at Princeton. Marriage is
the next step. I feel like I want to get this one out of the
way. Once I've finished my PhD, the degree I care about is
marriage.'

Don't get me wrong – I have no beef with wonderful
weddings, and wouldn't mind having one myself some time.
But I include all this wedding stuff to show how powerful an
idea the 'happily-ever-after' one is in our culture.

Janet, 30, notes that her craziest nights out now are hen
dos.

> 'And there's this worship of the hen going on. It's like
> getting married is the be all and end all, as if it makes a
> woman a goddess that we all have to bow down to. It's
> insane.'

Could it have to do with cold, hard cash? Possibly: bestselling author Jonathan Franzen has expressed disgust at
materialistic love. 'You can all supply your own favourite,
most nauseating examples of the commodification of love,'
he told graduates at his commencement speech to Kenyon
College, Ohio. 'Mine include the wedding industry, TV ads
that feature cute young children or the giving of automo-
biles as Christmas presents, and the particularly grotesque
equation of diamond jewellery with everlasting devotion.'

He sounds a bit grumpy here. But he wouldn't be the first
to give a convincing argument that the commercial needs
of advertisers and manufacturers are the *real* backdrop to
everything from female insecurity about weight and ageing
(buy diets and creams and surgery!) to the big, fancy

weddings we feel we really ought to have. The further from that seeming holy grail you are, the more a woman feels like milk going bad in the sun unless someone gets her to the altar on time. It is in just such an environment that women need to step back and try to base their success or happiness on who they are as individuals – not on how far along in the fairy tale they are.

And finally ... the online onslaught

So you know you're single and need to do something about it. You get online, and the websites spout their own urging messages at you (quite apart from the people you get in touch with). 'Love is Out There. We Can Help You Find It' and 'A Better Chance at Love', says eHarmony. 'Start Your Love Story' urges Match, using the fairy tale idea of a tale, with a beginning, middle and end. Stressful emails from JDate come emblazoned with: 'Show Him You're a Great Catch'.

Suddenly, you're even more stressed about your status – your website is haranguing you to get on with finding your prince. Updates and bulletins pop up by the minute, offering tips on how to be better and more attractive and who might be your match. Many people have a wail of a time on it, but there's no doubt that internet dating can raise social anxiety and make you even more edgy about being single.

It can be brilliant, but it can make you feel a lack where you don't have one. It can get you exactly what you're look-ing for, of course. But for now, we want to feel like we've got what we're looking for already, in ourselves. (Rule overlap alert! If you're taking a break from internet dating

266 THE MAN DIET

– rule eight – you're ahead of the game here. Cutting down on your use of dating sites will help block out some of that *noise* that gets in the way of our ability to acknowledge ourselves as people, not women Desperately Seeking Men.)

Dwelling on yourself as an individual: actually doing it

1. Acknowledge yourself

It sounds simple and boring and the kind of thing Americans would do on emotional workshops in Oklahoma. But Americans have the right idea, because it's important and it's hard. Judy Bud, a psychotherapist, says: 'People don't acknowledge themselves nearly enough.'

So, how to acknowledge? Start by thinking of anything you're pleased with, whether it's a challenge at work, home or socially. It could be a good deed. Or a job well done. Or something you were worried about but that you still got through, like a board meeting, or a family reunion. It often takes an active effort to even remember these things. We're so used to being self-critical that we actually block out things that deserve a pat on the back – even from ourselves. So, first of all, remember something. Then say to yourself, even though it'll feel cheesy, 'Yeah! I did that. That was good. I deserve a pat on the back.'

Repeat this mental exercise once a day. It's a lot less sweaty and annoying than going to the gym.

Many therapists advise clients learning the art of self-acknowledgement to actually pat themselves on the back, physically. Just reach over and give yourself a cheering tap a few times. You can do it quite subtly, so that you look like you're scratching an itch rather than a mad person. This enables a bit of back-patting in public should you think of something while out and about.

You might have heard of affirmations, another therapeutic suggestion whereby you write out something uplifting and positive that you also think is genuinely true about yourself, and once a day, you read it out to yourself a few times. This works really well for some people, particularly as the power of words can be so strong that your brain follows their lead. Basically, you talk yourself into seeing your whole being in a zen-like way.

My favourite, however, is The List. Simply open up a Word doc or get out an old-fashioned piece of paper and pen and write down as many positive things you've done as you can think of. If you want to throw in some general positive things about who you *are*, go ahead. But I always think being specific about deeds or accomplishments is a better way in. And if someone like your mother or aged aunt or brother has told you recently how much they love you, note that down.

2. Ignore your mother

Don't ignore how much she loves you and that you need to be good to her (within reason; I'm assuming the average mother, i.e. somewhere between infuriating and wonderful, rather than a monster). But mothers get very preoccupied about their daughters being single. They can get obsessed, in fact. They grew up in a different time, a time when single women over age 27 were dangerously near to being spinsters with cats, in danger of ending up poor creatures rotting alone and penniless without a man's salary. Let's not forget accusations of frigidity, barrenness and misery. So it's understandable how concerned they get, particularly if their hopes for grandchildren rest in your hands. But they can make you feel really bad about it, and with one or two ill-timed comments, reduce all your other achievements to your woeful (to them) lack of man. It's not helpful. But if you steel yourself in advance, you can just about ignore the topic when it comes up. Or shock her with some other bit of news that distracts her. Or say: 'Look, I'm completely sex starved. What do you want me to do?' That should get her to pipe down.

3. Develop an aware, critical eye

As I've spent a good deal of this chapter showing, we are surrounded by things and people saying:

MAKE YOUR FAIRY TALE HAPPEN NOW!!!!

and

WHERE IS YOUR PRINCE, EXACTLY, SWEETHEART?

We absorb most of this – along with cartloads of other information – without realising it. But it's quite gratifying to make a conscious attempt to monitor headlines and ads and even subtler things, like film plots and conversations that are telling you something about being single. I'm not advising you to get angry every time you see a Jennifer Aniston headline. But start to notice every time you see something directed towards you – be it probiotic yoghurt, jewellery, skin cream, glossy magazines, or film – that's all about fairy-tale romance or sex and you'll start to see how much of it there is. To avoid being driven insane by it – and thus to follow this rule effectively – simply recognise that all this stuff is about marketing and commerce, feeding off old ideas about femininity. It's not there because it's reality. Then pat yourself on the back for not having been driven insane, and for being pretty grounded despite glitches (such as those leading you towards this book).

4. Pick role models

It sounds cheesy beyond belief. But when the bulk of the women we see in music videos, movies, magazines, fashion shows, reality TV and even *Forbes*' Rich List (think Lady Gaga) are characterised by their hot bodies, turbulent love lives (or very successful ones, e.g., Kate Middleton, as was) and crazy clothes, you need to strive to remember there are famous women out there who have made it completely independently of their appearance, clothes or sex appeal.

Pick three or four and buy their biographies, if they have them. Just having them on your bedside table will have a beneficial effect because you'll subconsciously register them every time you go to bed. Read them, or skim them, if you can. Do anything cheesy you can think of – get these women as your screensaver. Get posters and actually hang them up.

Some women that inspire me ...

Ayaan Hirsi Ali – *Infidel*, the story of her escape from an arranged marriage in Somalia to Holland, and from tribal Islamic life and female circumcision to political infamy in Europe, is completely inspiring.

Hillary Clinton – go figure. Hillary could have allowed Bill's indiscretion to hold her back. But no. People hate her, then they hate her for trying. But she keeps her eye on the ball and has got to the very top of what is, unfortunately, a man's game.

Tzipi Livni – the dark horse of Israeli politics, and another example of a woman scaling man-made walls to become indispensable in policy.

I would say **Angela Merkel**, but she's not quite exciting enough for me. Europe – bleurgh.

I also love the businesswomen. Here are some who have gone to the top in businesses that are not primarily about clothes, diets or make-up:

Cheryl Sandberg, COO of Facebook

Irene Rosenfeld, CEO of Kraft Foods

Indra Nooyri, CEO of PepsiCo

Zoe Cruz, former co-CEO of Morgan Stanley, who was one of the highest paid woman on Wall Street

This is just my taste. These types of women may do nothing for you – you might prefer Oprah, or a really inspiring woman who works in your local sandwich shop. The important thing is to consider who you think of as inspiring, then to take it to your friends for discussion. Do they agree? If not, why not, and who would they choose? Chewing over role-model worthiness with your friends is also a great way to forget about guys and discover your abilities to talk about other stuff – bear it in mind when you're doing No Talking About Men.

How I followed this rule:

Pre-Man Diet

I dwelled occasionally, but not at the most helpful times.
Sometimes I reflected briefly on my qualities if I'd done
something particularly nice or showy and a family member
or friend gave me a pep talk/compliment session. But it was
soooo easy for me to channel all my sense of self-worth
into men – I reduced myself to the pinprick of their
approval on far too many occasions. As a result, my self-
esteem was rather volatile. I wasn't grounded and my vibe
oscillated wildly from the pumped up ('Yay! I'm awesome')
to the very low ('Nobody loves me').

How I did it

I implemented a regime. Whenever I did something even
vaguely good, I patted myself on the back. Sometimes,
literally. I took every boring moment when I'd ordinarily
think about something hypothetical relating to a man and
turned it into an opportunity to think shamelessly about the
positive facts of my existence. If this just sounds like
smugness, sometimes it was. And that's fine. You too have
a few things to be smug about. That's not what this rule is
about, of course, but sometimes it's just par for the course.
Whatever it takes to put things in perspective. For me, that
sometimes involves (or starts with) smuggery.

How it felt

Corny at times. But not too bad. OK, rather pleasant, actually.

What I let slip through the cracks

Every now and then you feel crap because a guy gets to you. I know I did/do. But I always tried (and continue to try) to offset it with some attempt to put it in perspective.

And now?

I've incorporated self-acknowledgement into my general mindset. It's a habit that was bizarrely easy to implement once I spotted how *little* I did it – and now, as soon as a guy rattles me or I see that I'm denying myself my dues as a full person because of him, I do a bit of positive, perspective-giving thinking and see whether it helps. It almost always does.

SOS!

Have you been feeling negative about your romantic situation despite your best intentions? Has constructive thinking about your standing as a person first and foremost been clouded by a rejection or a moment of 'I WANT A MAN, GODDAMNIT!'

We all go through that. It's natural. It's why we're emotionally intelligent. But don't let it linger.

- Do something fun as hell. Go on a rom-com marathon with your best friend. Go for a cycling weekend with a good mate. Throw a dinner party for your nearest and dearests and make it really lovely.

- Get grounded. I find a few minutes of focused breathing, eyes closed, can do wonders. The holy grail is to feel mindful when concentrating on your breathing – don't worry about it. Just try to enjoy the in and out of your breath, and listen to the sounds around you. It'll do wonders. That, or you'll get so bored and impatient that whatever you do next will be done with great vigour.

- If you're dealing with a romantic failure that's shadowing your status as Individual Extraordinaire, try to recognise that it wasn't

meant to be. That is, you're not a failure
regarding men – you're a success inasmuch as
you strive to be good or happy or successful as a
person. You will get to where you need to go in
due course. There. Buddhism out of the way.
(That said, taking up Buddhism wouldn't be a bad
way to go …)

Rule Number

10

Know Your Obstacles

You need this rule if ...
- Everyone needs this!

Goes well with ...
- Every other rule

Joanne, 28, had had an intense week. She'd been stood up by a guy she was going to see for the second time. She'd shagged another one to make up for it – a semi-friend – who had then told her he couldn't 'do this' any more because he worried she was going to develop strings. Then, to comfort her, a couple of hard-partying girlfriends had dragged her out, plied her with shots, and helped her onto the receiving end of some really rather awful lip-locking from a random cheese-meister at a club under a bridge from which, when she eventually got out, it took her 1.6 hours to get home.

Thing is, Joanne didn't particularly relish upheaval. The week had made her feel like she was going crazy. So she vowed to take a break from it all, removed herself to her older sister's house in the north, and signed herself up for a bank holiday of babysitting. She came back refreshed and vaguely recovered from her quite frankly traumatising, Man-Diet-needing week.

By Wednesday, she'd already managed to get smashed once. On Friday she slept with the 'friend' again.

Something had to give. She realised that she was saying yes to people who may have meant well (the

girl), but who were leading her up a garden path with
snakes at the end (the boy in particular).

She needed a period of recovery and contemplation,
so the fact that she seemed completely unable to have
one (unless she removed herself entirely) was ...
concerning. So she sat back and decided to get real.
She needed to spot the types of people who were going
to take her to unwanted places before they took her
there ...

... in other words

You know those people who, whenever you're on a food
diet, are always trying to get you to have a brownie they've
freshly baked? Or tell you to stop being boring, unhealthy,
or needlessly concerned about your weight? They can be
anyone from donut-bearing colleagues to mothers to
friends. It seems that, whether consciously or not, they're
hell bent on getting you off-track.

The same is true when following the Man Diet. Certain
types of men can be the slippery slope straight to junk-food
love, but so can certain types of women. The women you'll
go out with will generally be your friends, and will thus
either want the best for you or will be motivated by the
desire to have more fun. This makes them all the more
dangerous of course, as you don't expect them to be the
cause of you falling off the bandwagon.

Male types, on the other hand, can often be the direct
cause of a junk-food love bonanza. Of course, one woman's
junk-food love nightmare is another's instant best friend or
husband-to-be. But I think it's possible to outline a few of
the types you need to be aware of. If you can spot the

danger types, from your game player to your clear-conscience cheater, you're going to avoid at least some trouble and/or heartache along the way.

The women to watch

1. The party girl

We all have friends that seem immune to hangovers – or rather, can still get up after three weeknights staying out until 3am. They're great fun; just the people you want to head out into the night with when you're strong and ready for trouble. But when you're on the Man Diet, you might want to steer clear.

Who she is: When you're out with her, not getting wasted isn't an option. You turn your back and there's another round on the table. You may start off saying: 'I'm just having one', then suddenly it's 4am and you're somewhere you had no intention of being. Now, when you and the party girl have a top night out, it usually involved serious physical overhaul, from smooching on dance floors, to bedding waiters, to arriving home knowing you won't be able to lift your head the next day.

Why she's dangerous: If you go out with her, you're very likely to break several Man Diet rules:

- Pursuit, whether out of drunkenness or late-night impulsiveness.
- Drunk texting and other booze-related behaviour destined to add horror to your hangover.

- Getting into a horny rampage and jumping on the first man who seems up for it.
- Allowing some less-than-quality gentleman to take up your time, and waking up the next day feeling anything but mentally robust and able to focus on your lofty endeavour (see rule five).
- It'll also inevitably spawn lots of man talk, gossip exchange from the night, and so on (rule four). I love that stuff and I am the first person to do it – as my friends will attest – but it's not helpful while on the Man Diet.

So: If she wants to meet, suggest dinner. After food, it's harder to get into the cocktail-downing mentality. Or just postpone seeing her – the party girl always has plenty of people to call on.

2. The devil-may-care

Who she is: She has a very strong character and people tend to follow her. And unlike the party girl, who may well have a boyfriend and just genuinely loves wild living, this girl is probably single and has an attitude towards sex that makes you forget the existence of junk-food love. Her skill is in making it *seem* like everything is just water off a duck's back – she can bed men, have threesomes, spend the night in a club toilet or do something outrageous at a house party – and none of it bears any emotional imprint or leaves any marks beyond a good laugh. Who knows if she's repressing things or secretly damaged? She may or may not be. But whatever it is, she makes lots of casual sex, or mega drinking or mad japes, seem cool and easy. For example, you'll often find her being violently sick at some point in the evening when she's gone flat out. But up she gets and heads back into the party.

Why she's dangerous: It's very easy to fall into a 'monkey see, monkey do' pattern with such ladies (although not the puking, hopefully). Because they're force-of-nature types, you see their influence in lots of friend groups. You see her living the wild single dream, scar free, and you feel like you can do the same. So you throw boundaries to the wind – unsure as to why you have them anyway – and next thing you know, you've gained a stone of junk-food love weight through a dozen outrageous hook-ups – of which a large proportion will inevitably be far from ideal.

You may not have a friend like this, or you may have one in the making – one minute she's settled with her boyfriend, the next she's free and single and it's devil-may-care central. This girl's USP is that her influence can extend beyond the actual night out – she lingers, more like an idea, in your consciousness. But it's OK – once you've clocked her as a type to be enjoyed with care that is.

3. The man-hunter
This could have been you before you became aware of the Man Diet – perhaps you were habitually finding yourself in hot, drunken pursuit of any XY chromosomes floating about after 11pm.

Who she is: The man hunter is the aggressively single woman, who feels her singleness intensely, either as a sexual opportunity she must exploit at all times or as a quest for The One that she can never fully lay to rest. Every man is an option, and no attractive male goes unnoticed and without comment. She sees things in terms of possible set-ups or connections. So if you let it known you have a brother, you'll be able to spot her a mile off when she asks: 'Is he single?'

Why she's dangerous: When you're out with her, she goes into overdrive. Alcohol is the springboard she uses for approaching large groups of men, chatting to them, and if possible, exchanging a number or bodily fluids. With her, going out is flagrantly all about meeting guys.

So: She can be a bit stressful to be around, since your intended dinner will inevitably be turned into a man-meeting bonanza. And somehow, whether you're at a restaurant or a lounge bar, she'll always manage to find a man to hunt down. This is great fun – and a brilliant service – if you've been off junk-food love for a while and are craving something bad for you, or you're just desperately horny and need some male company, action, whatever. But while you're actually Man Dieting, she's going to make it impossible for you to stick to the rules. Try to put her off for a bit, or see her for brunch. Anything but drinks.

4. The married/loved-up friend

I think between them, *Bridget Jones* and *Sex and the City* pretty much covered this category. Smug marrieds, pitying mums-to-be – I don't think most of us encounter such extremes often. But there are versions of them everywhere. So beware.

Who she is: She's your best friend from school, your friend from work, a friend of a friend. She comes in all forms. As you head towards your thirties and beyond, lots of your friends will be married or breeding. She's merely one of them who has taken your singleness to heart and made it her job (very sweetly) to fix. She can get on a girl's nerves, even though more often than not, she's amongst her closest friends.

Why she's dangerous: She never lets you forget you're single. If you're not meeting people, why aren't you? If you are, who are they? What happened? Now, I ask: is all this interest altruistic? Maybe. It might also be that for safely coupled folk, it's *fun* talking about romantic prospects and also how sucky it is to be single (in their view) since they've crossed to the other side.

For those big couply dinner parties, if you can sense unwanted focus on your love life, feel free to decline, or excuse yourself early. Also, never forget the power of the short but sweet reply. If she insists on trying to break your No Talking About Men rule, keep putting her off with: 'Oh you know! Nothing to report.' And move on …

The men to avoid

This book is primarily about *you*. But of course, you're reading it because of your encounters with men. Knowing what types of men are out there who are most likely to get you off track is an essential part of the Man Diet toolkit. Because learning to recognise the kind of man you're dealing with can save you a lot of junk-food-love-related weight gain. I promise.

Here are some male types. When you see them, beware ladies. They're derailers.

1. Married ... and happy to cheat

'MBA'. No, it's not a business degree. It means 'married but available' and is exactly what a 40-something man said to a friend of mine at a birthday dinner recently.

It's odd. You can meet an attractive, intelligent man. His interest feels like a sunburst. But it turns out that after all that, he's married. Or maybe you spy a wedding ring, and next thing you know, the man is telling you you're beautiful. What's weird about it is that these guys are often young and seem to have good marriages. It's not that in reality they are miserable on the home front; it's that they honestly want both wife and external sex. To them, it's perfectly fine to hit on you. Their brains obstinately refuse to admit that there's anything wrong with having both the Madonna by the hearth and whore-figure outside. It may sound harsh, but there's a reason that this is the most famous dichotomy in sexual psychology. They feel entitled to it, and that's that.

Maybe there isn't anything wrong with it, but it strikes me that being a married man's sometime shag or fling – the topping on the cake of his life, so to speak – isn't going to make *you* happy after a while, even though it's rather fun for him. And that's before we even address the issues of conscience regarding wifey and kids.

How to spot one: Next time a weirdly attractive, charming man tries romancing you out of the blue, ask yourself: 'Is this too good to be true?' Because the answer may well be yes. If he's not wearing a wedding ring, ask outright if he's single. If he is married and you proceed, you're entering a dark, dark zone of junk-food love.

Why they're dangerous: Charm, confidence, flattery. You might think you'd never give in to a cheater. But you'd be surprised. First of all, the number of taken men who think nothing of a shag or dalliance with another woman shocks me. Second, the thing about many of these young cheaters is that they are very attractive, very sly about their status, and flatter you just when you're feeling low. Not every, or even most men are cheaters, but there are lots around.

2. All charm, no intention

There are few things more attractive in the first instance than charm. By this I mean a good smile, great eye contact, flirty wit, and apparent consideration for your needs – helping you with bags, remembering what drink you like, adjusting the room temperature if you're too cold or hot, and so on.

But some guys are just like this. They have a special interest in *you*, they are single and clearly up for it.

What it often really means is this: they are charming guys, they are used to making women flutter with their charm, they enjoy doing so, you are just another one – and they may or may not be single.

How to spot one: From the second you meet one of these guys, you're knocked off your socks. When he shakes your hand, or before and after kisses, he holds your eyes. He's poured you a drink before you've even sat down. This could be because he's a friend of a friend and is hosting a dinner party – or perhaps he is trying to charm you for professional or social reasons. For example, he could also be an hotelier, actor, barman or other person used to customer service or performance. Your mistake is to confuse body language and good manners with real interest. Hey, some women are a sucker for a man in a uniform, or the idea of one – this is where we fall foul of flirty waiters etc.

Why they're dangerous: You fall for the charm, and they give you just enough to make you feel special. But they have no intention of going out with you. The tantalising bits of flirtation combined with the devilish good looks are a seductive combo, but you eventually realise you've been banging your head against a wall in trying to get a concrete show of interest out of him. This realisation is a real break-through in the battle against junk-food love. If you can spot them immediately, you're really doing well. Hoorah!

3. The 'keeping options open' guy

This guy is hard to spot until you're actually seeing him. He's the one who drives you crazy with mixed signals – something that usually starts just when you're beginning to think you might like him. Why? He's keeping his options open, and because he has lacklustre feelings for you. Is he a player? Possibly. But not necessarily.

For my last book, I talked to dozens of guys about why they'd string a girl along – and one of the biggies was that a reasonable, nice woman is better than no woman at all. But a woman that a man thinks is just OK from the outset is not a woman he's going to commit to. As harsh as it sounds, you're a stop-gap. These are the guys that may well drive you to the Man Diet in the first place. They're probably dating other people. They might see themselves as Adonis bachelors. Just make sure you *leave* him as a bachelor.

How to spot one: He's just keen enough to keep you interested, but within a few meetings, you begin to sense a distinct lack of progression. He's very protective of his evenings without you, sadly, because he doesn't want to limit his chances of meeting someone else.

Why he's dangerous: During the course of many conversations with male friends, I have been shocked to learn how many men are averse to conflict and awkward conversations. So rather than step into conflict territory by telling you he's not keen enough to commit, many men would much rather conceal the truth, and usually with a certain degree of charm. The result is that it looks like they're keen when you're together but when you're apart, he's cold and aloof. Nothing ever feels easy. His texts say one thing, their frequency another. The mixed signals will send you mad if you let them.

4. Great looking, but ultimately boring guys

These men are so good looking – and unfortunately, know it – that they've wielded excess power socially and romantically their lives through. When you give them the compliment of your attention and your attraction, they won't repay it in a particularly rewarding way. The main thing is that when you stop and listen to them critically – through the purr of your admiration – you'll notice that, yup, they really don't have much to say. And what they do say tends to revolve around themselves. Urgh, one-sided conversations? What a turn-off. *Don't waste your time.*

How to spot one: Good body, pretty face, aversion to asking questions. Except when he can answer them himself.

Why they're dangerous: OK, in an ideal world, you'd walk away the second you noticed how self-absorbed he is. In reality, it's easy to end up falling for their looks, hook, line and sinker. The one upside to this type is that girls like *you* will tend to lose interest in *them* first. But that's if you actually date them. Spot them right away and you'll bypass that rocky initial period of hoping and praying he'll show an interest, of worrying that he's too much of a dreamboat for you, and so on.

5. Douchebags
I have a soft spot for most types of the guys in this list. Just because they're like this to you or me doesn't mean they don't have their upsides to other women. But there are certain men that I could never even be friends with after seeing their 'romantic' behaviour.

I call them douchebags. Plain and simple.

How to spot them: They come on very strong sexually, give away early that they assume you'll be putty in their hands, and call every shot according to their own comfort – such as bars near their house, letting you get rounds, and long phone calls to their friends while you're just sitting there. The absolute worst, though, is the refusal to wear condoms because it doesn't feel quite to their taste – never mind your sexual health and comfort. I hope you don't get to the sex stage with these types, because selfish sex follows tosser-like behaviour.

Why they're dangerous: You'd think you'd spot a douche-bag a mile off and any communication would end before the third sentence. Not always so: they can look rather good and they can seem flattering when you're feeling vulnerable. Also, sometimes one is confused into thinking tossers are attractive simply because they're a challenge.

6. Asexual

These are those guys who seem willing and/or keen to go on dates but never make a move. They are almost always gorgeous and good company.

How to spot them: Like the married man, they can seem too good to be true. Intelligent and arty, friendly and witty, but the last thing on earth you can imagine them doing is staring at your chest. You might meet them at parties and talk for hours, before exchanging contact details at the end … but no kiss. Your friends all ask what's going on, but you can already sense the answer is 'nothing', as there just ain't no sexual energy there.

There's another version of this guy: the buff metrosexual with a perfect bod. For him, women are a potential source of distraction from the gym and the protein shakes. Most mortals won't have bodies good enough for this guy – but he still likes to have a good time out and about. This guy will date you, but purely for his own amusement so don't expect any hot sex from him.

Why he's dangerous: He lures you out on pseudo dates, where you spend the evening wondering if he's even slightly interested in you. When the time comes to kiss goodbye and he pecks you on the cheek, you can feel anything from desolate to disappointed. I've certainly kicked myself for wasting Saturday nights in this way.

7. Ex issues

This guy is completely useless for any girl with a regular ego. He uses his ex as an excuse to keep things slow, keeping you at arm's length where he can call on you when it suits him or when he really does have issues with the past. Either way, he's going to be:

a) conversationally boring
b) emotionally cut-off
c) a romantic dead end

Wow, what a combination.

How to spot him: Rather than openly tell you early on that he needs to take things slow due to a recent break-up, he'll drop it in there after sex when you're cuddling, or when you want to make plans to see him again. He'll find a way to bring it up just when you're showing signs of being keen. It's emotional blackmail because no girl wants to 'take things fast' after they've heard that, and he knows it.

More obvious ways to spot ex issues men are if he's on the phone to her all the time, they post flirtatious things on each other's Facebook walls for all to see, and they're texting. Although, I'm not sure how you find out about the contents of his phone. I'm against that kind of snooping, on principle.

Why he's dangerous: He seems available at first and he's very good at raising your hopes. Then the guillotine blade falls. The only way to find out if a guy has ex issues is to ask around as subtly as possible. And then run a mile the second he mentions her in a manipulative way.

8. The networker

Is it you or your network he likes? This guy is after you for what you can do for him, rather than who you are. If you're loaded and successful, there's a brand of man who has no pride and may be after your money, plain and simple. But more common is the guy who thinks you know people that could be useful to him – a senior colleague, family friend, agent, cousin.

How to spot him: He makes himself obvious pretty quickly, which is good. Until that time, be on the lookout if you're set up with him or meet him online and you turn out to work in the same or complementary industries. If it's the same industry and you're at a better company or you're more senior, this calls for high alert. If it's a complementary industry – you're a journalist and he's a PR, for example; he's a screenwriter; you work for the BBC – turn up the alert to an orange. Keep your ears pricked for any probing questions that are obviously related to career-advancing information-gathering. There's a chance he's also interested in you, but you'll never be able to tell. Also, it shows heinous social skills and astonishing egotism to confuse dating with networking. You don't want either of those traits in a partner.

Why he's dangerous: He's not interested in you – just your contacts. Falling for him would be the worst kind of mistake. Finding out down the line what he was really after could be as painful as finding out he's been cheating.

9. The mysterious godlike creature

This one is a killer. He's gorgeous, quiet, considerate, distant and incredibly good in bed (on the few times you happen to end up there). He's so mysterious and quiet, in fact, that you fill in all that missing information with wild projections of your own about how amazing he is. His incredible hidden depths. His godly form a mere reflection of his godly soul. And so on and so forth.

But there are a couple of things about this superbly attractive guy. He's not really putting himself forward for a relationship. He's not as preoccupied or mesmerised by you as you are by him. But you fancy him so much, and you're so convinced there's far more to him than meets the eye that you're willing to break all rules of decorum to keep seeing him. When he lets you that is.

How to spot him: Instant, violent physical attraction on your part. But it's his gentle, interesting aura that draws you to him. He's graceful. You throw caution to the wind and make your interest known. This is how things start, so you never know if he'd have approached you of his own accord (he probably wouldn't). He's never readable. You never know when you'll see him again. In fact, you never know what he'll do next. He gives off a powerful sense of mysteriousness to you – even when your friends find him banal. This often means he comes from a different background to you, or moves in a totally different sphere.

This exact thing happened to a friend of mine with a Croatian bouncer in Camden. When she turned up at his house that night, he turned out to be Buddhist – not to mention gorgeous. She was enthralled. But he refused to see her again. Game over.

Why he's dangerous: He seems distant and unavailable because he *is* distant and unavailable. He has no intention of worshipping your madly sexy mysterious awesomeness the way you worship his. He is not up for a relationship with you – or possibly with anyone. But drawn in by him anyway, you refuse to acknowledge this and will spend valuable time throwing away vast amounts of emotional energy on a lost cause. You'll also get hurt when, in the end, he goes out with someone else, reveals the existence of a wife and child in Lithuania, or abruptly moves to the Solomon Islands. The other big thing with this guy is that he is almost certainly not as fascinating or intriguing as you think he is. Remember this when you feel yourself wavering.

10. The ex

Nothing feels like home. And – for many women – nothing feels quite like sex with someone both familiar and verboten. Exes can know their place, and you can know their place, which is: romantic dead end, friends only. But that doesn't stop them leading you into a thicket of frustrated, sometimes damaging energies. You're not off the hook, of course – it takes two to tango in matters of ex-sex. But if you want to avoid just slipping into junk-food love territory with an ex, here are some pointers:

How to spot him: He's not just some guy you had a thing with. He'll be the result of a meaningful, somewhat serious relationship. And right now he'll be asking you for last-minute drinks, or being very available when you ask him. There are no boundaries with him – you know that if you meet him, you can and probably will sleep with him.

Sure, you can waste time with casual exes. But with a big, or biggish ex, you will be led by instinctive reactions, you'll feel wildly irrational, and will feel four million times more pleasure, significance, guilt and frustration. The second sign of danger is that you're still in touch – i.e. you've allowed yourselves to act like the door is only lightly closed but not sealed shut. Now, call me draconian, but I think if you've broken up for good reasons, such as constant rowing, madly different values and ideas about how life should be lived, plus massive incompatibility, then there's nothing to be gained by trying again. And so, again sounding draconian, you should really try to get over that person, and the best way to do that is by going cold turkey. Being all friendly and in touch with the person you loved and shagged is not going to make your life easier. Do you really want them as a friend? Exactly. You hate their girlfriends-that-aren't-you's guts.

So: Those biggish exes that you're still in touch with are toxic to the Man Dieter. It's hardly rocket science, I know, but these guys can destabilise you, big style – and not for any good reason at all. They're big fat ice cream cartons of junk-food love and I urge you to stick your spoon in something else. Like Phish Food.

What about smallish or medium exes, you ask. They create the same problems, perhaps with less damage due to a lower intensity of connection, is what I say. We're trying to avoid pointless expenditure of sexual and emotional energy – and pouring it into someone who is a done deal and belongs to the past, or who is not offering you anything more than a complicated orgasm served at 2am midweek, is not part of our Diet.

Why he's dangerous: It's probably clearish from the above, but to be extra clear: exes are dangerous because you are intensely, automatically linked to them and so they hold a lot of power over your heart and happiness. What they do can hurt you, arouse you, or melt you almost as much as when you were together. The only difference – I believe – between a boyfriend and an ex that you're sleeping with is that whereas before he offered you commitment, now he doesn't have to. And vice versa, of course – but I can only speak for the experience of having a male ex. And keeping ex-sex no-strings is either impossible or a path to madness. Probably it's both. Because sooner or later, he'll go out with someone else. If you've slept with him recently, that's going to suck very, very hard. (The same could be true of you to him. But again, we're troubleshooting here.)

Everything I'm saying, of course, assumes that the ex is not a viable option for the future. If you want to get back together with him, then that's a different story (though having sex with him might not be the best way to achieve it). Remember, with the Man Diet we're trying to cut down the amount of energy we donate to non-future candidates. Few are more non-future than a man you've already been out with – and broke up with.

11. The box-ticker: nice but dull (to you, anyway)

When you've been single for a while, the pressure builds. People accuse you of being too picky. Your mother just wants to see you settled with a nice man – good salary, kind heart. Chemistry – well, you can't have everything! Perhaps not, but no amount of 'I should like this guy' will make up for a numbness when you kiss, or a secret eye-rolling when he talks. Which is why the widespread practice among single women afraid they're 'too picky' or destined to 'end up alone' is to hang on in there with guys who don't float their boat. Don't do it ladies! It's not damaging like sleeping with a heart-breaker, but it's still crappy for you, and unnecessary.

How to spot him: He's the guy who is probably fairly keen, who obeys all the rules of politeness and buys you drinks, but with whom you can't help spending the last hour of your date thinking up ingenious ways to avoid having to kiss him. He's also the guy you agree to see 'one more time' if only because you have no one else on the scene.

Why he's dangerous: You feel literally guilty about not liking him and will probably have an inner monologue along the lines of 'I always choose the bad guys. Why is it that as soon as a nice guy comes along I'm not interested?' And so on. So you keep seeing him in your conscientious effort to 'give him a chance', but you aren't enjoying it. So it's pointless and unpleasant at the same time. We want nice guys, and – despite what your friends say – you *can* have both nice and sexy. So hold out.

A Little Checklist

If you don't know your type, here are some benchmarks to point you in the right direction.

See him again if:

- At the end of the first date, you feel like there's a pleasant question mark. You may have kissed or you may not have, but either way, you feel positive and low-key happy. Basically, you'll be pleased to hear from him again, even if you're not dreaming of him that night or doodling his name in your diary.
- From the second you saw him, you couldn't wait to kiss him – *and* you enjoyed the conversation. The close-of-night snog has sent you wild with hope and you've air punched. Although just be careful not to have too many expectations yet.
- There's something attractive about him, though you're not sure how attractive, or what it is. It's probably worth finding out what it is – so long as it's not his arrogance.
- He is amazing, even if you're not attracted to him. Someone with a megawatt brain, true humour or

some other wonderful trait – or potential trait – is worth your time, even if it doesn't become romantic.

Don't see him again if:

- His chat left you cold – for example, you could predict everything that came out of his mouth, three sentences off – i.e., he's a big fat cliché monster.
- You were dismayed at his lack of questions – i.e., it was a one-way street.
- He talked about things that could only make you feel bad, like other women, his exes, or political views you find abhorrent.
- You could see he was a nice guy, but that chin was never going to be the chin on the man for you.
- You found kissing unenjoyable.

Zoe on the rule:

I use this rule all the time, mostly where it concerns men. It may sound cynical to categorise people you don't necessarily know, but trust me, having a broad sense of 'types' can be damned useful.

When it comes to dating behaviour, most people fall into certain camps. One person can occupy several camps throughout their lives, but a guy who operates through charm for power-gain is a type, plain and simple. He may not always be like that, but I find it's helpful to look at guys who appear to be charmers (for example) with caution, then let him convince you otherwise.

One pointer for the road. It's so simple but rather interesting: if you find a guy really attractive, you can bank on the fact that throughout his life, many, many other women will also have found him so. No always, but mostly. I'll leave it to you to determine the impact this has on his dealings with women.

SOS!

Have you been allowing danger-zone people – men or women – through the net? All you need to do is look at why or how: man-crazy girlfriends who forcefully insist on you going out and getting wasted with them? Guys who you know are trouble but kid yourself might really be great? See if you can prepare yourself better for their persuasions by thinking out in advance what you want to happen (i.e. you don't want to fall for a clear player; or start sleeping with a guy just because he's there; or get absolutely trounced with a friend just because she wanted you to).

Remember, we all do it. Friends' pressure, the promise of crazy fun, cute guys who use charm to win you over: all these things are real and worth paying attention to – and sometimes indulging. But right now they're at cross-purposes with us: so just reread the list of types and think again. Trust your instincts: you'll know who's who already; it just takes a little skilful thought to realise. And remember that saying no politely is always just fine.

To Wrap Up…

It's funny. The word 'diet' conjures up such strong feelings in women. For many of us, it signifies deprivation, discipline, discomfort and unpleasantness in the name of virtue and, ultimately, results. Because when it comes to physical weight loss, the more you restrict, the better the results.

But I hope you've found, or will find, the Man Diet to be a positive experience. Rather than being about deprivation, each rule was designed to be refreshing and interesting to fulfil. As you go forward, I want you to remember that this diet is not about punishment; it's about exploring what new boundaries can do for you. I guarantee that if you have followed the rules, not only will you have a healthier approach to men, you will have discovered some useful things about who you are.

Crucially, the goal of this book is not to make you a better woman for its own sake, or to make you suffer for virtue (God forbid!), but to make you a happier woman. Happier women are better women.

This book and going forward
This is a bespoke diet. One woman's Man Diet will mean following three rules for one month; another's will lead her

to follow all ten for ten months; some women will just read the book and – I hope – think about some of the ideas raised. In short, the book will mean different things to different people.

Crucially, what I didn't want to prescribe is the death of fun, or an inconvenient, scary overhaul of your life. I've been on enough food diets to know that that won't work in the long term: saying no when everyone else is saying yes has to come from a genuine desire to say no, not the rules of a regime.

And I know what it's like because not only have I been there, I am there now. My friends and I all drink far too much and wouldn't be seen dead on a weekend night without a glass or five. We all love a good man-gossip and we turn to each other when something goes wrong. We get miserable. We get horny. And so, we occasionally do things – drunkenly or otherwise – that we shouldn't. Asking you (or me) to stop all this for good would just take the air out of our social lives and put a cloud over our mental landscape.

BUT. Intelligent change is good and it's possible. There *are* valuable adjustments to be made for most of us. And challenges are not inherently bad – particularly those posed by the Man Diet.

One of the points of this book, if you haven't already discerned it, is that following the Man Diet can lead to making the odd, very liveable, permanent change. For example, since doing the Man Diet, I make better choices regarding the men I say yes to, about who and when I pursue, and the expectations I carry with those pursuits. I genuinely enjoy drinking a bit (just a bit) less since I hate monster hangovers laced with regret – and the itch of a man-related incident whose importance, or lack thereof, I can't quite grasp in my stupor. I still try to check Facebook less and when I do, to limit my snooping. I try to limit my availability for instant chat. I get a lot wrong, too – just after writing this book, I went mad and asked three men out. Two three-hour dates ensued, none ending with a follow-up call. I exhaled, let it go, and reread my own chapter.

The Man Diet goes to the core of your life: after all, what are the decisions we make about men and ourselves if not that? In dealing with men, we deal with ourselves – our insecurities, desires, hopes, dreams, fears, anger, irrationality, our pasts. And there is no failure when you're talking about life itself. There are only challenges and moments of self-knowledge.

So, give it a go if you haven't already. Because during and after the Man Diet, you'll feel better. Sort of less scared of what may happen, and more content with who you are. That's where I am now: the man may – or may not – follow.

Although I encourage you to think of the Man Diet as a set of rules of thumb to follow indefinitely, that might not be your path. Even if you follow the diet for a month, you'll come out a happier woman.

The maintenance stage: life beyond the Man Diet

Losing weight is the exciting part – it's quick, challenging and novel. But as any dieter will tell you, after a while it loses all excitement and is just a bland old 'way of life'. A slog, in other words. That's why so few diets are successful in the long term.

Unlike food diets, the Man Diet isn't a slog in the long term, after those initial pounds of dead emotional weight have been shed. But it does require a bit of vigilance in order to last as a positive 'way of life' (to use dieter's terminology). Because although you can relax when you've finished the diet – if you choose to 'go off' it at all – I don't want you to let loose and forget about it.

Here's how it'll go. After a while – whenever you feel you've sufficiently explored what each rule can do for you – you can downgrade vigilance from orange to green. At this stage, you'll have thought enough about each rule to sense when you're partaking in junk-food love, and when you should pat yourself on the back and show yourself some affection. Simply being aware of the reality of your actions, or a situation, will serve as a check to emotional weight-gain behaviour.

Crucially, what the diet does is naturally reduce your appetite for the things that are worst for you. That is its brilliance: whereas chocolate cake never stops being good, feeling empty or crappy about some guy or guys in general does. I am now wholly not tempted to go home with someone with whom I have zero connection *or* who spells trouble – for example, who might not be single, or for whom any girl will do. Call it self-protection, call it prudery; but I can see so much more clearly now (just like the song!) when something is going to be bad for me *on balance* than I did before the Man Diet. I have consciously recognised that I don't like the feeling I have after sleeping with someone I know doesn't really fancy me. It's even more intolerable when a killer hangover goes with it.

Although rational knowledge of consequences doesn't always stop people doing things – smoking, eating loads of chocolate cake – in this case it seems to play a big part in controlling appetites. Because if you've followed the Man Diet, you'll be familiar with that really good feeling of, say, waking up without the horror of regret; of having had conversations with friends that leave you feeling stimulated rather than more obsessed than ever with someone or something; of having achieved something else with your time than a dossier on an ex's female friends. That good feeling is a powerful motivator and it really helps to change your habits.

That's all very well, you say. But it's a Friday night. I'm out, getting pissed, craving late-night kebabs of junk-food love. It's business as usual: weekend nights packed with parties, pub sessions, dancing. I can't very well go off booze and men! I'd have no fun or life left! To which I say: the Man Diet isn't about ruining all your fun. Live your life – go out, get pissed, but all you have to do to be a lifelong Man Dieter is ask: 'Am I sure I want the hangover that's coming to me? Is it worth getting wasted here and now? Would it be hard, or actually fairly easy, to stop now?' It might be easy. Ditto going home with someone for a big platter of junk-food love. It might be quite easy to simply ask yourself: 'If they won't take my number and arrange to see me in less drunken circumstances, is it really worth shagging them now?' It's just a matter of having the thought. That's the Man Diet in its maintenance phase.

Perhaps you've slipped back into talking about guys all the time with your friends. Or you've allowed nightly Facebook stalking sessions to recommence. All you do, when you spot one of these junky patterns, is tweak. You reread the relevant chapters, and you rein things in for a week or two. Then, with the Man Diet back in your mind as a living, breathing, relevant defence against self-poisoning behaviour, you can go back to your life as usual. It's not nearly as hard, or dull, as staying off the chocolate cake. And as months and years pass, the self-affirming tenets of the diet should help keep your head high and guide you through the ups and downs of a relationship.

Singleness and the future

Unlike pretty much every other book out there speaking to single women, this one is not that interested in whether you find a man or don't. I'm not saying being single is the best way forward like some of the shriller American books you can find on Amazon. Nor am I saying that the holy grail is finding a man, and that if you follow the Man Diet, you will.

This is about you, being happy in your own skin, and doing yourself justice so that you can thrive. I think the rest follows – whether that's a husband and kids or not. And if you stay single into your thirties and beyond, ignore the social messages saying it's shameful and that you're somehow a freak. As I've shown in Do Something Lofty, some of our noblest foremothers felt that they couldn't achieve their life's work in the shackle of wifehood and motherhood. Common sense – and statistics – show us that there is a strong link between single women, or those without families, and professional success. One possible reason for the connection is that men are afraid of ambition and intelligence. Well, it's never worth tamping those things down to try and get a man. Wait for one that loves those parts of you and until then, you have the luxury of fulfilling your dreams single-mindedly.

It's also worth remembering that to an older, married eye, being single even in your forties and fifties seems a land of marvellous opportunity. An older friend of mine, Harriet, 50, had a dinner party recently, to which she invited one couple, three single women (and her husband). She observed: 'It was quite plain that Mary's husband Richard was a burden and that she could have had a much better time if she hadn't been married. That wouldn't have been the case if everyone else had been in couples. But they weren't: they were all single. And all my husband's friends are single women. There are tons of single women. When you're single you have so many more degrees of freedom to have fun. Mary is hampered by Richard.'

Lifestyle freedom aside, what of fertility? The baby thing troubles me as it does many of my friends – how will I have kids if there's no man on the scene? How, between now and age 35, will I magic one up who I rate enough to breed with? But believe me when I say that the media works hard to scare women into reproducing in a smaller window of time than is strictly necessary. Society still wants us to be young breeders, to pop them out in the midst of our careers. But more and more women are having babies later – you can do it at 40. If that's what your life requires, that's what you can do. And you can find alternatives to finding a partner – you can get a gay friend to artificially inseminate you, you can freeze your eggs, you can go to a sperm bank. You can adopt, you can try to get pregnant at 41, you can decide not to have kids. There's no shame in any of this: it's working with the options. I believe our options are more open than we are led to believe.

Don't panic. Sit back, relax, and enjoy the ride, and – so long as you've got a copy of *The Man Diet* by your bed – all will be well. You have so many tools at your disposal, from your brain to your spirit to your freedom to your emotional intuition to your willpower, and now's the time to put them to work for you. For real.

Feminism and Further Reading

What women do, sexually and romantically, is still a political hot potato. So you can't investigate the sexual relationships between men and women without raising the F-word. Put more crudely, women's bodies (who they have sex with, who has sex with them, when they want to have sex, and how) are still a battleground in what remains of the war of the sexes.

Less and less are women and men of the West at odds with each other. But women are definitely at odds with something – their obsession with thinness, being hot, having sex like a porn star, alongside a failure to achieve a critical mass in top-level jobs in politics and business, is not indicative of calm waters on the sexual playing field.

So as I researched and wrote *The Man Diet*, I felt increasingly interested in the feminist implications of such a book. In advising women to think more carefully about sex; in assuming that in general women experience sex differently than men; in encouraging them to think about and do things that have nothing to do with looking pretty or being enticing or meeting a man, I was coming up against something sniffing awfully like feminism. And I wanted to bring you some of that, since I think giving a feminist context to your choices illuminates their importance and gives them a meaning that makes the rules more natural to follow.

But what does feminism mean?

It's a confusing term, feminism. In part this is because its meaning has necessarily changed over time. Long ago we achieved the objectives of Emmeline Pankhurst and the suffragettes. Not only can we vote, nobody would dare raise a public objection to any path in life we chose to follow, from rock-climbing to barge-driving to running political parties (that's not to say such paths are easy). Betty Friedan, were she still alive, might still see women being kept down by some notion of *The Feminine Mystique* (1963), but she can hardly argue that most of us are housewives, bored out of our skulls.

Incredible feminist firebrands took over in the 1970s (Germaine Greer's heyday) – and the 80s and 90s saw some pretty powerful polemics. But then things appeared to languish. Feminism became confused with Spice Girls-style Girl Power and, over time, with simply taking off your clothes. Now, to strip is to be empowered. To be hot is to be the ultimate woman. Mothers take their daughters pole-dancing because it's 'really liberating'.

Some attempts have been made recently to get feminism back on the rigorous path it requires in order to force change – is this the third or fourth or fifth wave now?

Interestingly, feminism has once again become a big selling point. Caitlin Moran's *How to Be a Woman*, which is a non-serious survey of the trials, tribulations and fun bits of being female, created a storm, rose to the top on Amazon, and commanded posters in the Tube. Although it's not feminism in the way that academics like Simone de Beauvoir, Germaine Greer, Susie Orbach, Naomi Wolf and Susan Faludi write about it (who are so passionately making a point and so busy backing it up with examples, references, history, studies, literature and so on that they don't have time to add much humour), it bills itself as feminist. Feminism by detail rather than by idea: first periods and the horrors of childbirth rather than the 'eternal feminine' and 'the beauty myth'. This kind of literature has been tremendously successful.

Me, you and the big F

To me 'feminism' is the attempt to resolve the realities of being female – being the object of male attention; necessary motherhood if you want biological children – with true liberty. I don't think the realities mentioned above need impinge on women rocketing to success in whatever way they choose, but, unfortunately, the world often has different ideas.

But I leave motherhood and plastic surgery and the horrors and statistics of rape to other feminists. My slice of the pie – and one that I hope you consider yours – is the pre-marital relations between you and men. Dating. Singleness. And my impression, as I've tried to survey the state of British women today, is that we are doing wonderfully, but that we're also shooting ourselves in the foot. We sell ourselves a little bit short – sometimes a lot short. One of the big ways we do this is by ingesting junk-food love by the boatload. To be invigorated and free to be a feminist, we need our self-worth intact. Where possible, we need to not feel shitty. And in one way, that's what the Man Diet is: a pre-feminist programme whose calling card is high self-respect. And, of course, feeling a little less rubbish.

Reading

OK, so, I love reading, but until recently, only fiction. Novels are my bag. But in reading up for *The Man Diet*, I found that when it comes to feminism, non-fiction can be riveting. And so I urge you, if you have any desire to understand your own struggles, from the question of motherhood and work right down to the pain you feel when wearing skyscraper heels, to try a few classic texts. They're brilliant, and they'll speak to you whether you're an academic type or not. (Warning: they may make you a bit angry too. Sorry. But it's worth it.)

The ultimate Man Dieter's feminist reading list

Mary Wollstonecraft:
A Vindication of the Rights of Woman

It's not necessarily easy reading, but the passion and extraordinary turns of phrases employed by the mother of feminism – and *Frankenstein* author Mary Shelley – make it an absolute firecracker. Her comments and rage regarding uncomfortable female clothing, ill usage by good-for-nothing males and the crap, frippery-filled education given to girls will rankle with any modern woman. Added interest lies in Wollstonecraft's own deeply messy personal life: romantic woe and depression, not to mention untimely death. Politically she belonged to the English 'Enlightenment' crew, a progress-seeking bunch that also included William Godwin and Francis Bacon.

Harriet Martineau:
Autobiography

When an academic friend of mine turned up at the pub wielding a funny-looking book with a Victorian lady etched on the front, I thought: 'What's this?' And, while he was in the loo, I began reading it out of boredom. It is not only hilariously frank – Martineau's earnest descriptions of her childhood sickliness and poor looks can't fail to steal the heart – but it's admirable. Martineau decided that her lot was spinsterhood: that to achieve the life and output of the mind she wanted, singleness was necessary. And, since she was one of the first people to stick their oar in the field of 'political economy', she managed to make her dreams – her conscious ones anyway – come true. She's a great inspiration for rule five, Do Something Lofty (though I'm not proposing you spend a life denying yourself male love).

Rosalind Miles:
The Women's History of the World

The central question here is: why are women never
in history books? With this well-written, even
amusing, book, Miles makes a valiant effort to make
up for a whole lost history, a sea of lost voices and
deeds. This is one of the ones that might make you
angry – for Miles doesn't stint on outlining the
amazing things women have done in return for
absolutely no recognition. But it's our duty to read
about our squashed-down past, and with her
instantly gripping style and nice short sentences,
Miles's book is also a pleasure.

Simone de Beauvoir:
The Second Sex

You've almost certainly heard of this classic, but –
written in 1949 – might consider it out of your
normal interest area. I hadn't picked it up either. But
I was glad when I did: it's one of those books where
every sentence carries some idea or point that makes
you think: 'That's SO true!!!' It's remarkable how
early de Beauvoir wrote the book – before the
second wave feminists – and how relevant all her
arguments are. 'One is not born, but rather becomes,
a woman' – surely no truer statement has been
made, at least if you believe culture and society
impact gender roles. De Beauvoir's point – and this
might also make you angry because it is so true – is

that 'normal' and the 'default' settings of humans have always been male. Woman is treated as a deviation. This still holds to a degree: language formulations like 'men and women', 'sons and daughters', 'his and hers' prove the point.

Betty Friedan:
The Feminine Mystique

This book created a frenzy in the US when it came out in 1963 because it set out to explode the idea that women are naturally happy as housewives – a belief stemming from what she called the (false) feminine mystique. It's a classic and really quite fun to read, even if it hasn't dated well. After all, housewifery – while still around – isn't widely considered the only alternative to a life of neurotic careerism any more. We've moved on to 'wanting it all' – but perhaps we wouldn't even be able to conceive those words if it weren't for Friedan. Her look at the advertising industry – and the woman-ensnaring economic motives of its chiefs – is worth a read alone.

Germaine Greer:
The Female Eunuch

You'll have heard about it and possibly rolled your eyes. Yes, Greer advocates tasting your own menstrual blood and dispensing with bras, 'a ludicrous invention'. But the book is amazingly passionate, articulate and interesting. Twenty years after *The Second Sex* was published, Greer shows how far women still had (and still have) to go. The enigmatic title refers to her conviction that society – with its economic and social norms, preferences and systems – drives women apart from their true, vital selves, i.e., that they can't experience their own libidos, bodies, minds and souls properly and freely. I think some kind of *Female Eunuch*-style separation from yourself might just be happening when you have that numb feeling during sex … (just saying).

Susie Orbach:
Fat is a Feminist Issue
Here, Orbach skewers a different type of diet: the food diet, and asserts that women get fat as a reaction against notions of sexiness and femininity. It's also a self-help book for people with eating disorders. Next time you swear to start a diet, take a look at this book – there may be other forces (gender ones) at play in your relationship with food. A classic and gripping book.

Susan Faludi:
Backlash: The Undeclared War Against American Women
OK – you may not be American. But once again, this is iconic, and compulsive reading. You may recognise its title from *Bridget Jones's Diary* – Bridget's

mates are all reading it (it came out in 1991). Anyway, Faludi says consumerism is selling women down the river and – in her preface to the 15th-anniversary edition – she maintains it still is.

Naomi Wolf:
The Beauty Myth

Warning: this book will enrage you. Or rather, it will enthrall – Wolf's ridiculous intelligence, her rhetorical might insist you keep reading. But as soon as you put it down, you'll see sneaky female oppression in everything. Certainly in magazines and media representation of bodies and female plights. The central point here is that once society stopped being able to keep women down with laws, it had to think of something else and that something is the beauty myth. Wolf hammers home the point through sex, religion and a variety of other angles, that the way things have been set up, women never feel beautiful enough. And therefore, they never feel good enough.

Ariel Levy:
Female Chauvinist Pigs: Women and the Rise of Raunch Culture

If you read nothing else on this list, read this 2005 polemic. It is a blistering, madly readable argument that says: just because you look hot, as defined by *FHM*, or thin, as defined by *Vogue*, or strip or pole dance out of choice, does not mean you wield 'feminist' power. Quite the opposite. Levy's a young, hip 30-something whose writing style is absolute nectar for any young woman even vaguely interested in her surrounding culture.

Natasha Walter:
Living Dolls: The Return of Sexism
OK, OK, if you read just one book, read half of this and half of *Female Chauvinist Pigs*. Walter is serious, clever, learned and rigorous in her exploration of where things are going wrong with feminism today. We're too busy, she argues, dressing like strippers and buying our little girls giant-breasted Bratz dolls to ask whether we're *really* empowered – or still enslaved to nothing more substantial than our looks.

Michel Foucault:
The History of Sexuality
A three-volume series that is perhaps the most influential piece of writing ever published about modern sexuality. Man Diet readers may be particularly interested in the idea of the sexual secret, whereby we're constantly talking about sex in a misguided attempt to understand it.

Gail Dines:
Pornland: How Porn Has Hijacked Our Sexuality
The title should tip you off: this is an excoriating look at the ways in which porn is destroying intimacy. Great if you're interested in the effect of porn in your own relationship or life, since this is definitely a hot topic. Keep in mind the book received plenty of criticism, too.

Bibliography

Adshade, Marina, 'Online Dating Sites Creating "Beauty Inflation"', *Big Think*, 10 May 2011

Akass, Kim and Janet McCabe, *Reading Sex and the City*, I.B.Tauris (2004)

Angel, Katherine, 'That's Amora', *Prospect Magazine*, 1 August 2007

Argov, Sherry, *Why Men Marry Bitches: A Woman's Guide to Winning Her Man's Heart*, Adams Media Corp (2010)

Argov, Sherry, *Why Men Love Bitches: From Doormat to Dreamgirl – A Woman's Guide to Holding Her Own in a Relationship*, Adams Media Corp (2002)

Bandura, Albert, *Social Learning Theory*, General Learning Press (1977)

Behrendt, Greg & Liz Tuccillo, *He's Just Not That Into You: The No-Excuses Truth to Understanding Guys*, Harper Element (2005)

Bernstein, Elizabeth, 'Scary New Dating Site: The Real World', *Wall Street Journal*, 19 March 2011

Bialik, Carl, 'How Many Marriages Started Online?' *Wall Street Journal*, 28 July 2009

Bloom, Lisa, *Think: How to Stay Smart in a Dumbed Down World*, Vanguard (2011)

Brown, Helen Gurley, *Sex and the Single Girl*, Barricade Books (2004)

Carver, Raymond, *What We Talk About When We Talk About Love*, Vintage (1989)

CBS News, '"Sex and the City" linked to DUIs?' *CBS News*, 24 April 2009

Chandra, K., et al., 'High-risk sexual behaviour & sensation seeking among heavy alcohol users', *Indian J Med Res* 117, 88–92 (2003)

Collins, Marcus, *Modern Love*, Atlantic Books (2004)

Copeland, Libby, 'The Anti-Social Network', *Slate*, 26 January 2011

Daly, Meg, 'The Allure of the One Night Stand' in Damsky, Lee (ed.) *Sex and Single Girls: Straight and Queer Women on Sexuality*, Seal Press (2000), 194–204

Damsky, Lee (ed.) *Sex and Single Girls: Straight and Queer Women on Sexuality*, Seal Press (2000)

de Jour, Belle, *Intimate Adventures of a London Call Girl*, Phoenix (2005)

d'Felice, Cecilia, *Dare to be You: Eight Steps to Transforming Your Life*, Orion (2009)

Donath, J., & Boyd, D., 'Public Displays of Connection', *BT Technology Journal*, 22 (4), 71–82 (2004)

Eisenberger, N., et al., 'Does rejection hurt? An fMRI study of social exclusion', *Science* 302, 290–292 (2003)

Fine, Cordelia, *Delusions of Gender: The Real Science Behind Sex Differences*, Icon (2011)

Friedan, Betty, *The Feminine Mystique*, Penguin Classics (2010)

Gaddam, Sai & Ogas Ogi, *A Billion Wicked Thoughts*, Dutton Books (2011)

Graham, M., et al., 'Does the association between alcohol consumption and depression depend on how they are measured?' *Alcoholism: Clinical and Experimental Research* 31 (1), 78–88 (2007)

Gray, John, *Men are From Mars, Women Are From Venus*, Harper Element (2002)

Greer, Germaine, *The Female Eunuch*, Harper Perennial (2006)

Griffin, C., et al., '"Every time I do it I absolutely annihilate myself": Loss of (self-)consciousness and loss of memory in young people's drinking narratives', *Sociology* 43 (3), 457–476 (2009)

Goldman, Emma, *Living My Life*, Vols. 1 & 2, Dover Books (1970)

Gurstein, Rochelle, *The Repeal of Reticence: A History of America's Cultural and Legal Struggles Over Free Speech, Obscenity, Sexual Liberation, and Modern Art*, Hill and Wang (1996)

Heminsley, Alex, *Ex and the City: You're Nobody 'Til Somebody Dumps You*, Pan (2007)

Henderson, Lauren, *Jane Austen's Guide to Dating*, Headline (2005)

Hensley, W.E., 'The effect of a ludus love style on sexual experience', *Social Behavior and Personality* 24 (3), 205–212 (1996)

Flanagan, Caitlin, 'The Hazards of Duke', *The Atlantic*, January 2011

Foucault, Michel, *History of Sexuality* Vols. 1, 2 & 3, Penguin (1998)

Joinson, A. N., '"Looking at", "looking up" or "keeping up with people?" Motives and use of Facebook,'

Proceedings of ACM CHI 2008 Conference on Human Factors in Computing Systems, 1027–1036, (2008)

Jordan, A., et al., 'Misery has more company than people think: Underestimating the prevalence of others' negative emotions', *Personality and Social Psychology Bulletin* 37, 120–135 (2011)

Lang, A., 'The social psychology of drinking and human sexuality', *Journal of Drug Issues* 15, 273–289 (1985)

Lanier, Jaron, *You Are Not a Gadget*, Allen Lane (2010)

Lee, Abby, *Girl with a One Track Mind: Confessions of the Seductress Next Door*, Ebury Press (2006)

Lee, Aileen, 'Why women rule the internet', *TechCrunch*, 20 March 2011

Levy, Ariel, *Female Chauvinist Pigs: Woman and the Rise of Raunch Culture*, Pocket Books (2006)

Lohmann, Raychelle Cassada, 'Teen Angst', *Psychology Today*, 13 April 2011

Lyvers, M., et al., 'Beer goggles: Blood alcohol concentration in relation to attractiveness ratings for unfamiliar opposite sex faces in naturalistic settings', *Journal of Social Psychology* 151 (1), 105–12 (2009)

McDonnell-Parry, Amelia, 'Once Again Ladies, Drunk Dialing Is Strictly Forbidden', *The Frisky*, 31 March 2011

Millar, Abi, 'Daytime Dating', *itsnotokcupid*, 17 Jan 2011

Mootee, Idris, 'Are You Suffering from Facebook Addiction Disorder (FAD)?' *Futurelab*, 1 June 2008

Moran, Caitlin, *How To Be a Woman*, Ebury Press (2011)

Norwood, Robin, *Women Who Love Too Much*, Arrow (2009)

O'Shea, Samara, 'The Grass is Rarely (Almost Never) Greener', *Huffington Post*, 16 April 2008

Oswald, D.L. & Russell, B.L., 'Perceptions of sexual coercion and heterosexual dating relationships: The role of aggressor gender and tactics', *The Journal of Sex Research* 43, 87–95 (2006)

Owen, J., Fincham F.D. & Moore J., 'Short-term prospective study of hooking up among college students', *Archives of Sexual Behavior*, 40 (2), 331–341 (2011)

Petersen, Trudie & Andrew McBride, *Working with Substance Misusers: A guide to theory and practice*, Routledge (2002)

Plummer, Ken, *Telling Sexual Stories: Power, Change and Social Worlds*, Routledge (1994)

Prause, N., et al., 'The effects of acute ethanol consumption on sexual response and sexual risk-taking intent', *Archives of Sexual Behaviour* 40 (2), 373–84 (2011)

Quilliam, Susan, 'A problem shared is a problem doubled', *Mail Online*, 19 July 2007

Richtel, Matt, 'Attached to Technology and Paying a Price', *The New York Times*, 6 June 2010

Rowan, David, 'How Badoo built a billion-pound social network … on sex', *Wired*, 25 April 2011

Rudder, Christian, 'The Big Lies People Tell In Online Dating', *OkTrends*, 7 July 2010

Savage, Dan, 'The Dating Game', *Forbes*, 14 December 2006

Sax, Leonard, *Girls on the Edge: The Four Factors Driving the New Crisis for Girls*, Basic Books (2010)

Schneider, Sherrie & Ellen Fein, *The Rules: Time-Tested Secrets for Capturing the Heart of Mr. Right*, Warner Books (1995)

Sloshspot, 'A Man's Guide to Drunk Texting', *Sloshspot*, 21 April 2010

Stefanone, M., 'Contingencies of self-worth and social-networking-site behavior', *Cyberpsychology, Behavior and Social Networking*, 14 (2), 41–49 (2010)

Storr, Antony, *Solitude*, Flamingo (1988)

Strauss, Neil, *The Game: Undercover in the Secret Society of Pickup Artists*, Canongate (2007)

Strimpel, Zoe, *What the Hell is He Thinking? All the Questions You Ever Asked About Men Answered*, Fig Tree (2010)

Stroud, Clover, 'Why Women Drink Too Much', *The Sunday Times*, 9 November 2009

The Economist, 'Love at First Byte', *The Economist*, 29 December 2010

The Sun, 'David Cameron: Why £7.5m a year will help give every child a chance', *The Sun*, 10 December 2010

Townsend, Catherine, *Sleeping Around: Secrets of a Sexual Adventuress*, John Murray (2007)

Turkle, Sherry, *Alone Together: Why We Expect More from Technology and Less from Each Other*, Basic Books (2011)

Vargas-Cooper, Natasha, 'Hard Core', *The Atlantic Monthly*, January 2011

Walter, Natasha, *Living Dolls: The Return of Sexism*, Virago (2010)

Womack, Sarah, 'Female drink rate is worst in Europe', *The Telegraph*, 22 April 2005

Wolf, Naomi, *The Beauty Myth: How Images of Beauty are Used Against Women*, Vintage (2007)

Wollstonecraft, Mary, *A Vindication of the Rights of Woman*, Dover Publications (1996)

Wright, M.O., Norton, D.L. & Matusek, J.A., 'Predicting verbal coercion following sexual refusal during a hookup: diverging gender patterns', *Sex Roles* 62, 647–660 (2010)

Wu, P. L. & Chiou, W. B., 'More options lead to more searching and worse choices in finding partners for romantic relationships online: an experimental study', *CyberPsychology & Behavior* 12 (2), 1–4 (2009)

Zeldin, Theodore, *Conversation: How Talk Can Change Our Lives*, Hidden Spring (2000)